Rise of the Dead

Jeremy Dyson

ISBN: 0990398412

ISBN-13: 978-0-9903984-1-7

DEDICATION

For Camille

CHAPTER ONE

My phone says it's three minutes after eight on a dewy spring morning. Beneath the cloudless sky, I squint at the glare on my screen. I'm sitting at a crowded train station, but I might as well be alone. Commuters around me listen to their headphones, read their magazines, or tap mindlessly at their phones. We spend our whole lives learning ways to block each other out. It's safe to stay locked away in the dark bunkers of our minds.

To kill a few minutes, I read a news story on my phone about a plane that went down in the Hudson River. I follow a link to another story about protesters rioting on Wall Street. Reporters witnessed explosions, looting, and civil unrest. Another story covers a similar incident in the capital. I notice another article about a CDC quarantine on a hospital in Atlanta. Another report speculates the events are all related though the circumstances don't suggest a coordinated attack. All that means is they really don't have a clue why so many incidents are happening at the same time.

I almost feel like asking the guy next to me if he has seen the news, but I don't. I figured out a long time ago that the quickest way to make a stranger dislike you is to interrupt them while they are checking their social media feed. Everyone would probably be happy as hell if the only way we ever interacted with each other were through an electronic device. I know that's how I feel. Ask me for the time, and I'll tell you, just so that you will hopefully shut up and let me get back to texting someone that isn't here. Everyone feels the same way, whether they want to admit it or not. If you think I'm lying, just look around sometime.

This is the last train I will ever ride in my life. I swear. I'm never taking the train again. It's not just that I don't like riding the train and that I like waiting for it even less, it's the crowded, dreary feeling of everyone on it that makes me crazy. I'm only here because I forgot to change the clocks an hour ahead last night. I don't even notice stuff like that unless someone nags me about it. So I had to hurry to catch the express this morning to get down to the city on time. I'd rather be in my car, even if that means sitting in gridlock, watching the minutes pass as I slowly die. But if I did that today, I'd be late for sure.

A bell rings, signaling the approaching train. Since I only have two hands, I have to put my phone away before I finish reading the last article. I grab up my cup of coffee and portfolio full of papers. We shuffle aboard the passenger cars like a horde of mindless zombies. I find my seat among the mix of office workers in their buttoned-down shirts with collars and ties and students with backpacks heading into downtown Chicago.

I decide I had better review the notes for my lecture though it will likely put me to sleep again. This hour of the morning is way too early for me, especially since it's an hour earlier than it should be. I sip my coffee and wait for it to kick in, so things make sense again. For a couple of minutes, I rifle through my papers and look them over. My eyelids start to close. I yawn, which draws a yawn from the guy in a flannel shirt across from me. He pulls some headphones out of a backpack and puts them over his ears. He stares out the window, listening to some depressing song. I shove my stack of papers back in the folder. I know what the notes say anyway. It's the same talk I've done for years.

When the train pulls to a stop at the Arlington station, the doors slide open, but no one at the station boards the train. From my seat, I stare absentmindedly at the racetrack where we had watched Independence Day fireworks last year. The horse racing facility is deserted this early in the morning. The parking lot it shares with the train station is the size of several football fields, and is already filling with cars from the morning rush hour. By noon, the lot will be packed for the afternoon races, with thousands of people cheering in the grandstands. Whenever I pass this stop, I am tempted to cancel my plans and spend the day at the track. I never do it anymore, though. Even though I know life is too short, I never do anything about it. Besides, I made promises. When my daughter was born, I quit placing bets. Amanda insisted on it. Said she wouldn't have our child growing up around degenerate gamblers.

"I have never gambled in my life," I swore.

She just rolled her eyes at me. Women. They can kill you with the smallest of gestures when they want to. Especially if you really love them.

The doors of the train remain open for several minutes too long. I look out the windows on the other side of the train and see the frustrated people in a line of cars on the four-lane highway. A bald guy with a long goatee has his finger up his nose. I watch him, amused because he doesn't know I'm watching him. We all live in our own little world, or so we think when we think we're alone. After a few minutes of staring at him, I realize I have yet to see a single car heading in the other direction on the street, and the doors of the train are still open.

At that moment, the conductor clicks on the intercom and informs us that a traffic accident ahead is the cause of the delay. Service is suspended until the tracks can be cleared. He goes on to explain that passengers can either wait until the train is ready to resume service, or take one of the buses Metra has provided to pick us up. Judging by the growing traffic jam on the roads, a bus is not likely to get me anywhere, so I decide to get off the train and make a phone call while I look around to see if I can discern the cause of the accident. From the station platform, I see a handful of squad cars, a firetruck, and an ambulance. Several smashed vehicles block the tracks, and there's a line of gridlocked cars piling up around the nearby intersection.

Maybe, I think, being stranded at the track this morning is a sign that today is my lucky day. Maybe it's fate that brought me here. I entertain these ideas even though I don't believe in signs or fate. I leave nothing to chance. Like I said, I won't even gamble. I used to spend a lot of time at the track, but what I did here could hardly be called gambling. Using a system of comprehensive statistical analysis, I evaluated probable outcomes for each race. It's the same methods statisticians use to put together baseball teams and predict elections. I created formulas to bet on the most probable horses. I wrote a book about the whole "experiment." You might have heard about it. It's called The Horse Experiment. That was almost ten years ago, so it's old news by now. Nobody remembers it anymore, except the college students that have to hear me talk about it every year.

I check the time on my phone. It's now eight-twenty, and I am supposed to be downtown in forty minutes. I call the college to let someone know about the delay, but I can't get through. I call a professor I know on her cell phone, but I only get an automated message about high call volume. I hang up and see other train riders around me all on their phones as well. So that explains the problems with the phone.

I feel the briefest flicker of unexplainable fear. Nothing more than a vague sense that something terrible is about to happen. Not like a premonition or any bullshit like that. Just this weird feeling, like I'm imagining a spider crawling over my skin. It freaks me out because the last time I felt that way was about two minutes before I lost control of my car on the highway and hit a truck. I look around. In the midst of all these other people, the feeling goes away. The idea of safety in numbers is a powerful illusion.

I try the mathematics office at the college again, get the same result, then call my wife. At this time in the morning, Amanda has probably just dropped off our daughter at elementary school and is driving to the high school where she teaches. If it weren't for this lecture today, I would be driving Abby to school. After several failed calls, I finally hear a ring.

"Blake?" Amanda says. "I was just trying to call you."

"I'm stuck in Arlington Heights," I tell her. "There's a car accident at the railroad crossing or something."

"I just heard about that on the radio during the traffic report."

"Yeah," I sigh. "I don't think I am going anywhere very soon. I can't get a hold of anyone at the office. The phone lines are messed up."

"I know. I tried to call you, like ten times, but it wouldn't go through."

It is pretty clear to me that something is not right. The news reports I read earlier have me paranoid, maybe. But, there's no sense in taking any chances.

"I think I am just going to head back to the house as soon as I can figure out a way back there," I say. "You should too. Call out today. Pick up Abby and meet me back at the house."

"I'm sitting in a ton of traffic right now. I can see the light is out up at the intersection. Maybe it'll clear up after that."

"No," I say. "Go home." Her slow response makes me think she is probably rolling her eyes.

"I have to get to the school," she says. "Especially if something goes wrong today while all the kids are there."

I want to tell her to turn around anyway, but I know she won't ignore the obligation she feels. Amanda always feels responsible for everyone and everything. We couldn't be more different that way. I typically don't give a damn about anyone but my family. Amanda tells me all the time that I don't act like I even care about them. I really do, even if I get distracted and don't notice when she gets her hair done. Instead of debating with her more, I tell her I will head towards Abby as soon as I can.

"What?" she interrupts me. "Blake, I'm losing you, the phone —"

The rest of her sentence sounds like it has been transmitted through a paper shredder, and then the call drops. I hit redial, but the call won't go through. I want to smash my phone on the ground in frustration, but I don't. I'm not typically a violent person, even when all I want to do is hit someone in the face.

Hundreds of passengers have left the train and are milling around the station platform. Most of the people are trying to get through to someone on their phones. Others just gape at the flashing lights of the emergency vehicles in the distance. We stand there, hundreds of us packed together on a train station platform, but we all might as well be alone. Sure, we are all sending text messages, or trying to call someone, but for the most part, we just want to block out the background noise of everyone around us.

Then the sound of gunfire explodes through the morning air. The crowd on the platform goes silent. It's like someone paused the movie we're all pretending to live in. Every head turns to follow the sound, which seems to originate from the smashed vehicles. It's too far for any of us at the station to see what is happening.

After several seconds of frozen silence, the sound of more rounds of gunfire slash through the air. I hear screams in the distance, the blaring of car horns and the squeal of tires against the pavement. Near the intersection, several motorists are trying to turn around. Drivers are pulling off the road, tearing through the grass embankment, or attempting to jump their vehicles over the concrete median and into the empty lanes going the other direction. Even though I can't see them, I hear the revving engines and skidding tires from the cars on the other side of the train now, too.

A red pickup veers off the highway and tries to jump the tracks at the front of the train. It lands at high speed, hits the easement sidelong, then rolls towards the platform. People scatter as the empty pickup bounds onward through the grass, bounces alongside the train and careens towards the crowded platform. The driver is flung from the vehicle. His limp body seems to swim through the air until it clips the side of the train engine, leaving a smear of blood across the windows on its way towards the gravel.

A few people are able to scramble through the closing doors of the train. I get caught in a rush of people heading for the parking lot. Some people run along the platform towards the rear of the train. I have never heard so many people screaming. The sound is like the wailing gulls that flock to the beaches to kill each other over some measly crumbs. I keep moving for fear of being crushed by the hundreds of people behind me running in terror from the out-of-control truck which is still plummeting down the station platform, plastering the bodies of people to the brick surface.

A young woman beside me gets shoved and knocked to the ground. I grab her arm to keep her from getting trampled and pull her along with me. No one else is stopping to help anyone. I run along with the throngs of terrified people, just as clueless as to what ignited all this. There seems to be even more gunshots now, and not just from the intersection.

The crowd I'm in keeps moving forward through the parking lot. Some people are already getting in their cars. I glance at a thick, bearded guy who, from the steel blue jumpsuit he's wearing, looks like he's a mechanic. He shoves his elbow through the window of a Cadillac and gets in. Cars begin racing through the parking lot toward the exit to the street. A young kid in a green backpack running in front of us gets swept away by a Hummer that passes inches from my face. I flinch, and when I open my eyes again there is just an empty patch of pavement in front of me and one of his sneakers on the ground.

I want to stop running for half a fucking second and figure out what the hell is causing all this panic. I don't even have a clue as to where I'm running to. I keep hold of the girl, as much to hang on to something tangible in this confusion as to help her. We keep moving forward in the direction of the racetrack. I chance a look back over my shoulder towards the station. There is a trail of bodies left by the careening truck, which has smashed into the ticket window and caught fire.

The train engineer is trying to get the train headed back the way it came. Several people run alongside and struggle to grab hold of the train and get on. Some of them lose their grip and are ground under the wheels of the train as it moves along the tracks. As the train pulls away, I can see the highway behind it. Many motorists abandon their automobiles, but some drivers remain locked in their cars, staring at the terrified people running by them. Cars and trucks slam into each other while attempting to turn around. The drivers don't even bother to slow down or swerve to avoid the many pedestrians now fleeing on foot.

"We are dead if we don't get out of this parking lot," I say to the girl. She keeps moving beside me but seems to struggle to keep it together. "We have to get to the racetrack."

We keep running, gasping for air for two hundred yards until we are at the turnstiles. On this side of the park, there are two entrance gates for the racetrack. There are four admissions kiosks and the gates connecting them together are closed and locked. Ten-foot high steel bar fences surround the entire park. They would not be impossible to climb over, but it would not be quick or easy. A bald guy in a gray business suit is trying to smash one of the kiosk windows with his leather briefcase.

Beyond the locked gates, the five-story grandstand is separated from the fences by a garden courtyard of cobblestone walkways that meander through flower beds and enormous bronze statues of legendary prize horses. Behind the garden, the grandstand stretches a couple hundred yards long with floor to ceiling windows that run the length of the ground floor. A security guard emerges from the doors of the grandstand, stuffing a donut into his mouth with one hand and cupping a holstered pistol with the other. He looks out at the parking lot and sees all of us crowding the locked gates and yelling to get his attention. He drops the donut and runs towards us, brushing the crumbs from his graying, stubbled beard. Keeping his hand wrapped around the handle of his holstered revolver, he fumbles with a set of keys hooked to his belt loop.

"What the fuck is going on?" he demands, as he unlocks the gate for us. About thirty people push through the turnstiles and charge into the entryway behind us. The guard holds the door for a half dozen more still running in our direction.

"Who is doing all that shooting?" he asks me.

"Police," I say. "At least some of it."

"Are they okay?" he asks.

"I don't know who is okay." I shake my head.

A few more people come through the gate; the last one is a cop who is limping badly.

"Shut the goddamn gate," the cop says, pointing his gun at the security guard.

There are still cars speeding through the parking lot. A man is standing on the roof of an SUV firing round after round at anything that moves. It's hard to tell how many people are lying dead in the vast parking lot or how many are injured and struggling to move. Some people are still trying to make their way to the racetrack. From the entrance, it looks like a few people are on their knees, trying to help save someone who is bleeding on the ground. One person is trying to crawl here.

"Wait a minute," I say to the cop. "There's still people alive out there. They need help. We need to let them in. Can't you call for backup or something?"

"Anyone still out there is as good as dead," the cop says. "There is no backup to call." He looks back at the security guard and says, "Shut the gates."

The guard slides the gate closed. I look out at the parking lot then, at the people trudging slowly towards us in their torn clothes, drenched in blood.

I see the shooter on the SUV, who is now surrounded by thirty or forty people reaching up to grab him. He runs out of bullets and they pull him off the car onto the ground. His body is swallowed up in a crowd of them.

I notice the kid with the backpack heading towards the entrance. I tell myself it can't possibly be the same kid that was hit by the car right in front of me, but it is. He is on his feet though one leg is severely fractured below the knee. He is still hobbling towards the racetrack, his head streaked with blood. He stumbles forward somehow, his face showing no indication of pain or fear.

That's when I figure out what is happening, but I still can't allow myself to believe it.

Through the gates, I see more of the dead bodies getting up and walking. The crowd that took down the shooter moves away from the spot where he fell, blood dripping from their chins, hunks of flesh clutched in their hands. What is left of the gunman is just some ravaged clothes and a red stain on the asphalt. The dead carry off and devour the rest of the remains.

"They're all dead."

Almost everyone is lined up at the gates now, looking out at the parking lot in horror and disbelief.

"I need everyone to move into the building," says the cop. "Now."

CHAPTER TWO

There is a landline phone on the information desk, and I rush over to try making a call. A dial tone hums in my ear, but after I punch in Amanda's number, nothing happens. All I want right now is to know my wife and daughter are alive. If only the damn phone would work, I could warn her before she gets caught up in something like this. Maybe there's still time. She can pick up Abby and get somewhere safe if there is such a place. I can be pretty damn persistent when I'm frustrated, so I hang up and dial again. Nothing but dead air. I'm tempted to smash the worthless piece of crap, but the security guard is staring at me as he ushers traumatized survivors to a row of benches along the windows.

I turn around to avoid his glare. After dialing the numbers one more time, I wait for the silence on the phone to end. I stare down a short hallway at the darkened windows of a trackside Irish pub. It was my favorite place to grab lunch while I waited for the races to start. The food was terrible, but I had a thing for the waitress. She had a thing for guys with lots of money. This was back before I met Amanda, so I don't feel bad talking about it. I'm not bragging or anything, and that kind of girl isn't the kind you brag about anyway. Back then, my life was just kind of crazy like that. Once, I bet half a million dollars on a ten-to-one horse called Preacher Man. That was as close as I've come to a religious experience in my life. Honestly, I knew I would win. Besides, I couldn't think of anything else to do with my money. If you knew all about the kind of cash I had in those days and where it all went, it would probably make you sick as hell. I was so young and stupid, and everyone around me wouldn't shut up about how brilliant I was. I even believed them at the time.

When I turn back around the security guard has lost interest in me. He is focused on trying to keep the man who was assaulting the admission kiosk with a briefcase outside from going further into the facility.

"The other entrance is locked," says the security guard. He has a thumb tucked into his belt and with his other hand, he wags a finger towards the group to urge the man to back off.

The grandstand is a sprawling corridor of glass and marble, consisting of numerous betting counters and television monitors, real classy. Flat screen televisions mounted on the walls near the betting counter play a closed circuit loop about trackside amenities, upcoming concerts, and the million dollar race next month that will probably never happen now. This place still feels so familiar to me after all these years. That feeling is the only thing that keeps me calm. Otherwise, I'd be going out of my mind.

The survivors gather at the floor to ceiling windows. Quiet and afraid, they stare at the walking dead collecting at the fence. Every cough, sob, or curse echoes hollowly across the white marble floors. A few people continue trying to reach someone on their cell phones, but the calls only result in anguished expressions on their faces.

A dark-haired kid with thick, black glasses and a gray hoodie starts messing with one of the televisions on the wall. He presses the buttons on the side of the casing before smacking the monitor in frustration.

"Don't mess with the televisions," barks the security guard. "There's no outside feed on these. You can try the ones in the pub." He points past me to the hallway. The kid with the glasses and a few other people start to flow in that direction.

"No," says the cop. The sudden sound of his voice at my back catches me off guard. He limps around the corner from the entryway. "Everyone stay together. Don't leave this area."

The security guard runs past me to assist the cop. The security guard favors his right leg, and only hobbles along at the same pace he would walk at anyway. The cop grunts and has to reach his arm above his head to drape it across the broad shoulders of the stooping security guard. The police officer shifts his weight off his wounded leg and the pair inch forward to the information desk. I get out of the way so the cop can sit down on the tall stool behind the counter. He really doesn't look so good. Sweat beads on his forehead and trickles down his golden-brown face. He still clutches his gun in his hand like it's part of his muscular arm now. The cop struggles to regain his breath. He grimaces as he watches his blood soak the left leg of his pants.

"Is that phone working?" the cop gasps.

I am surprised to discover the handset is still next to my ear. I've been listening to nothing for several minutes. I shake my head and put the receiver back on the base station.

"Is anyone a doctor here?" the cop calls out. No one by the windows seems to hear him. They can't take their eyes off the scene outside. The cop mutters some angry Spanish at the wound. He clutches his leg with the hand that isn't holding a weapon and growls in pain. The sound turns the head of the young woman that I dragged here from the parking lot. She leaves the group at the windows and heads toward the cop. When her shadow eclipses the cop's face, he lifts his gaze to meet hers. His agonized grimace slips away. I notice her comforting brown eyes for the first time, and I actually start to feel a little better, too.

"I'm not a doctor," she says. "But, I'm in med school."

"Better than nothing," says the cop.

The med student pushes up the long sleeves of her white henley and ties back her auburn hair. She bends down and removes the cops hand from his thigh to find a gunshot wound. Her sinewy hand slides beneath his leg and feels around the back of his thigh. Looking for an exit wound, I guess.

"The bullet went through," she tells him. "It's not as bad as it could be." She manages an easy smile. When most people smile, it makes me sick. Anybody who knows me will tell you; I don't smile all that often. This girl smiles genuinely, though. There is nothing but warmth and sincerity behind it. It's nice, but I don't look her in the eyes because I'm not used to such honesty. When you finally meet someone nice in this world, all it usually does is make you feel like more of a phony.

"It sure feels bad," the cop grunts. He releases a deep breath, and his shoulders relax.

"Keep pressure on it." The med student stands up and glances around before wiping off her hands on her fitted denim jeans.

She turns to the security guard and says, "Can you find me some medical supplies? A first-aid kit, or anything you got."

It takes a moment for the security guard to realize she is addressing him. He was busy counting the number of buttons left undone on her top. His face flushes when she dips slightly to meet his gaze. The security guard nods and turns to leave, but the cop calls him back.

"Bring anyone else in the building back with you. Round up any weapons and ammo you keep on the premises," the cop urges.

"Roger that," the security guard nods. He turns again and rushes off towards the other end of the building, tugging at a radio lodged between his belt and his protruding gut. Exhausted, he pauses at the first betting counter. I wish he would just walk instead of giving himself a heart attack. He leans a hand against the wall of the betting cage and has to inhale deeply to finally pull the radio free.

"Joey." His heavy breathing makes speaking difficult. When there is no answer, he clicks the button again. He inhales deeply and says louder, "Joey, wake up!"

"Alright, alright. Jesus, Frank! What the hell?" The radio volume is cranked up so loud the whole goddamn world can hear.

"Get the hell up here! Bring everyone in the building to the east entrance now." Frank resumes his labored jog towards the other end of the grandstand.

"What's going on?" Joey yawns.

"All hell broke loose. Get your lazy ass to the entrance," growls Frank. He grumbles a few more angry words to himself before disappearing behind the grand staircase.

"What's your name?" the cop asks the med student.

"Danielle," she says. She pulls open a drawer below the information desk and rummages through the contents.

"You have done this before, right Danielle?" he asks.

She closes the drawer and sighs. "That's next semester. I've studied it, though." Danielle turns and looks at me, "Give me your tie."

Without hesitation, I loosen my Italian silk tie and pull it off over my head. It was a Father's Day gift from my wife. How unoriginal. It was an expensive tie, and she thought I should try to look more professional. I pointed out I don't have a profession anymore, other than talking about myself. That really made her eyes roll.

The med student takes the tie with her calloused hands and undoes the knot. She fashions a tight tourniquet around the cop's wounded thigh. The cop lets out an agonized groan. He buries his face in his forearm to wipe away the moisture welling up around his eyelids. It's pretty unsettling to watch, so I move around to the front of the reception desk. I take my cellphone out of my pocket by instinct. When I don't know what else to do, I take out my phone as if it has all the answers. The phone displays the time above a picture of Amanda and Abby that I set as a background. The probability that either of them is still alive is not comforting to think about considering the survival rate of the people that were at the train station this morning. I send her a text message that just says, "Where are you?" I don't even want to think about the odds of me finding my way to them now, or ever seeing either one of them ever again.

Chatter from other police units squawks from the cop's radio as I wait for a response. I replay the phone call with Amanda in my head, trying to recall if she said anything to indicate where she might have been driving at that moment. I wonder if I will ever hear her voice again.

An idea comes to me, and I feel stupid for taking so long to think of it. There is an app to locate any device on our account using GPS.

I had this bad habit of leaving my phone everywhere. Amanda rolled her eyes every time I asked to borrow her phone to locate mine. I could make her completely nuts sometimes. I open the app and stare at the rotating bars as cell towers work to triangulate a signal from her phone.

"I guess I'm lucky you were around here," says the cop to Danielle. "Gracias." Then his face turns into a grimace of pain as she applies pressure back on the wound.

"Don't thank me. Thank that guy." She tilts her head in my direction. "I would have been trampled to death out there if he didn't stop to help."

"Lucky for me, he did," says the cop.

I look up from my phone, and he gives me a nod of gratitude.

"I wouldn't call any of us lucky," I say.

The GPS application shows Amanda's phone as offline. I check the box to have the app notify me when it locates the phone, and then I put the phone in sleep mode to conserve the battery. I don't have a charger, and it might be a long time before I get out of here. My head aches and I wish I had a chance to finish my coffee. I don't even recall dropping it. My hands still quiver from the adrenaline. I lean against the desk and pinch at the bridge of my nose. I want to close my eyes, but whenever I do, I just see the parking lot again. Torn apart bodies getting up to rip apart more people. I can't help but imagine what could be happening at Abby's school, or to my wife out there on the road.

Another transmission crackles from the radio on the cops shoulder and pulls me back from the thoughts of my family. "Requesting additional units," a voice yells. "Damn it, is anyone else still alive out there?" There are more clicks, gunshots, and static. The voice comes back briefly before screams and gunshots drown it out. The cop here hasn't bothered to transmit a response at all. It gives me another uneasy feeling.

"This thing is happening everywhere," I say. He doesn't answer but takes his stare off the wounded leg to look me in the eyes. "Isn't it?"

The cop turns the volume down on his radio. He glances around at the rest of the people. They are all gathered near the windows, watching the world go to hell outside. The more terrible something is, the more people feel the need to look at it. When the cop feels confident no one else is listening, he returns his attention to me.

"Hey," he says. "What's your name?"

"Blake," I tell him.

"Okay, Blake," he whispers. "My name is Marco. Now, Blake, these people don't need to hear that all right now. We are safe inside here for the moment, so I need you to help me make sure everyone stays that way by not panicking. You got me?"

I just watched hundreds of people die outside. It wasn't even those things that killed them. They killed each other. It was the panic. Instincts kicked in, and we stopped pretending to treat each other like human beings. I know the cop is right.

"Got it," I say.

Marco looks at Danielle too, and she nods as well.

"Between us, all I can tell you two is this shit is happening all over the city. At seven this morning, I was sitting in the cruiser half asleep, nothing was going on. Twenty minutes later there was a call about a homicide, followed by some assault at a hospital, and a nursing home on fire. We got a call to a car accident here. Calls were coming in from all over; it spread so fast. It may be all over the country. I don't know for sure. But right now, we need to keep these people from trying to leave here no matter what. It's not safe out there."

"So you think help will eventually arrive?" I ask him.

He looks me in the eye and says, "I think it will, eventually."

By the slight hesitation in his voice, I can tell this is not what he truly thinks. It's a lie he has chosen to believe in. I wish I could believe it too. My feet carry me away from the information desk, and I join the crowd near the windows. Pressed against the fence are hundreds of the walking dead. They smear blood on the bars until the paint no longer gleams white.

Only a few cars speed along the roads anymore. Several vehicles on the streets are surrounded by the dead. They pound their hands against the windows to get at the survivors inside. Someone in the street makes a run for it. She doesn't get wherever she is trying to go. The things outnumber and corner the long-haired blonde, and then the horde drags her to the ground. The bloody female crawls beneath a car, but they just keep coming. There is no way she could survive for long with the horrific amount of injuries she has suffered.

It's only a matter of time before she bleeds out. After several long minutes, the corpses lose interest. The dead woman struggles to her feet, then joins a throng of undead surrounding another nearby vehicle.

From a couple of office buildings across the road, smoke drifts up into a pristine and cloudless sky. In one of the many shattered windows, a figure appears, engulfed in flames. It drops silently toward the ground, crashing into the hood of an abandoned vehicle below.

At the racetrack gates, the dead continue to gather, moaning at the sight of us. The people inside stare back at them through the glass. I understand what transfixes them as I look upon the monsters that human beings are capable of becoming. We entertain ourselves with imagined nightmares like this, only to be overcome by them. Maybe we did more than envision them. Maybe somehow, we made them real. I can't make sense of the world I see outside. It defies all logic or reason. The only thing I can be certain about is that no one out there can help us now.

"Folks, I need you all to move away from the windows," says Marco. "We don't need to draw more attention to ourselves in here."

I pry my eyes from the faces of the dead and step away from the glass. Without the scene outside to occupy them, the survivors take a renewed interest in the injured cop.

"Hey, man," questions a guy with long golden hair. His flip-flops smack the ground as he approaches Marco. "How do we even know none of those things got in here?"

"We're fine," sighs Marco. "Everyone just keep calm. Grab a seat in the lobby here and stay together."

More people head over to question the cop then.

A woman with cropped blonde hair and a business suit leans on the desk and scowls at Marco. "What happened to everyone?" She glances at the wound on his leg. "Are they infected with something?"

"I don't know, lady." Marco hisses.

"Does anyone know if there is another way out of here?" asks a short guy wearing long sleeves of tattoos down the length of one arm.

"We can go out the exit on the other end of the building," says a kid with a pair of those enormous headphones wrapped around his neck.

"No one is going anywhere," Marco says firmly. For a few moments, the group of terrified survivors falls silent again.

The short man slams a tattooed fist on the desk. "You can't keep me here, man. I have a right to go defend my home and my family," he growls.

"My husband is still out there," cries a heavyset woman in an eggplant blouse.

The people crowd the desk, raising their voices. Marco tries to speak over the chorus of panicked questions rising like a tidal wave before him, but eventually he takes his gun out and holds it up until the mob falls quiet again. Initially, Marco used his badge to take charge of the situation. Now, he had to resort holding back the fears and panic of everyone at gunpoint. You don't need to be a genius to see things were getting out of control here. Marco winces from the pain in his leg but manages to stand up.

"All of you, back up." The cop holds the gun in his hand like a stop sign; the barrel pointed at the ceiling. A little reminder to everyone that he still has it. His eyes are like a couple of road flares that warn everyone away. "Just stay back. Sit down and stay calm. No one is going out there right now."

For the time being, Marco keeps everyone under control. The people back away from the desk. A few of them huddle near the betting counter, whispering quietly and glancing sidelong at the injured cop. A police uniform is something most people are conditioned to respect. Some people already need to be reminded at gunpoint. It can't last, I think. None of this will last very long at all.

The sound of running feet heading towards us echoes across the airy building. For a second, I worry the dead are inside. I stare down the long building and wait for the source of the sound to appear.

Frank, the security guard, emerges from behind a betting counter carrying a red bag with FIRST AID in thick white letters across the side. Another uniformed guard trails behind him that I presume to be Joey. He is just a kid, with shaggy black hair poking out from the rim of his navy blue security cap. He fumbles with a noisy, black duffel bag in one hand and a couple of flak jackets in the other. A couple of sunburnt groundskeepers in green jumpsuits and four aging cleaning women bring up the rear.

"Joey grabbed two spare Glock twenty-ones from the security office," says Frank, breathing hard. He pauses to gasp for air. Finally, he coughs out another sentence fragment. "About 2000 rounds of ammo."

"Any nine-millimeter rounds?" asked Marco.

Frank hands the first aid kit to Danielle, then takes the duffel bag from Joey, drops it on the desk and shakes his head, still panting. Frank seems to scrutinize Marco after the question about ammunition for his gun. Marco just avoids his gaze. Instead, he watches Danielle as she rifles through the contents of the medical kit.

"So," Frank asks Marco. "What's the plan?"

"We keep everyone in here alive, and we keep out anyone that's dead."

"Holy shit," blurts Joey. The kid has made his way over to the windows and his jaw drops when he glimpses the scene outside.

"Stay away from those windows, kid," calls Marco. He unzips the duffel bag and pulls out one of the guns. The cop swiftly loads a magazine and sets the gun on the desk. He draws the sidearm from his holster and tosses it in the bag. Marco glances around at the faces of the other survivors, finally settling his focus on me. He removes another gun from the bag.

"Blake," he says. He waves me over to the desk with the hand holding the gun. "You ever fired a gun?"

I had never even heard a gunshot until this morning, and the sight of any firearm fills me with terror. Holding that kind of destructive force in my hands makes me afraid of what I might do. I realize from the manner that he asked the question that Marco doesn't trust anyone else here with it. I am not sure I would either. Besides, I calculate my odds of surviving the day are going to be better if I am armed.

"I used to hunt a lot," I lie. "Rifles mostly. I fired some handguns at the range once or twice."

Marco's eyes twitch for a second, and then he gives me the smallest smirk. He flips the gun around, so the handle is there for me to take. "It's you then," he says. "Don't let me down, Blake."

As soon as I take the gun from his hand, the televisions go black. The power has gone out. A concerned murmur rises among the group. Some of them begin to move back toward the doors. Marco vacates his seat again and tries to urge them to stay back. The crowd entirely ignores him and swarms past the desk toward the locked front doors.

"Quiet!" Marco screams and the crowd stops.

From the parking lot, the sound of squealing tires pierces the air, followed by the sound of metal smashing into metal. Gunfire erupts outside. I hurry over to the windows to see a rusty van has smashed through the fence about twenty yards from the doors and rolled into the courtyard. Two men in jeans and black leather vests move towards the doors as they fire at the hundreds of corpses pouring in through the hole in the fence.

"Get everyone out of here," Marco yells at Frank.

The crowd heading towards the door reverses now. They knock each other down and run straight at us. Without any idea where we're going, I start running again. The security guard, Joey, is in front of me, hauling the duffel bag. Danielle runs just behind him, and she pauses to look back. I put my hand on the small of her back to urge her to keep moving. Marco yells at the men outside the doors. His voice falters when gunshots ring out, followed by the sound of shattered glass hitting the floor.

Danielle keeps slowing down, looking back over her shoulder at the sounds behind us. "Go," I tell her. We run past the betting cages, a food counter, a set of elevators, and another betting counter.

"Hold on," yells Frank. I stop and look back. By now, I am more than fifty yards ahead of the struggling security guard. He waves us back with an arm. "Everyone in here."

Frank fumbles with a ring of keys and unlocks a door to one of the betting counters. The cleaning ladies and groundskeepers push through the entry. The line of other survivors forms behind them. The glass is bullet proof. It's practically a vault in there. There is not much chance of anything breaching the room. So, it isn't a bad idea. Except for the slim chance of anyone ever coming back out.

The dead are inside the building now. The crowd of people presses toward the betting cage door. People begin shoving each other aside, fighting to get inside. They can't all possibly make it into the room in time. A few people split off from the rest at the betting cages and run towards us. Joey runs back towards Frank, but I hold out my arm to stop him.

I look back, and I see Marco, rounding the corner near the information desk. He holds his abdomen and hobbles on one good leg. The dead are right behind him. He doesn't have a chance. A dozen bloodstained hands haul him to the ground, and he screams and unloads his gun into the mass of dead bodies that swarm around him.

"Forget it. We need to go somewhere else." I grab Joey by the sleeve of his shirt to ease him around. He shrugs my hand off but turns and heads away from the cages. A tall black guy in a navy tracksuit glides passed us. The short-haired blonde woman pulls off her heels and runs in her bare feet. The short guy with all the tattoos on his arms moves behind her, urging her on. I wait for Danielle, who stares at the spot where Marco vanished.

"Come on," I urge her. "There's nothing you can do."

The six of us are split off from the rest of the group now. It's too late to go back. So, we keep running. Behind us, the hall fills with the sound of people screaming and the moans of the dead. The sound echoes off the airy marble interior of the building. It keeps us moving as fast as we can.

Before rounding the grand staircase, I take one last look back. No one is coming behind us. The door to the betting counter is still open. The dead that aren't ripping apart people on the floor outside are pouring into the room. Most of the corpses seem not to notice us now, but a few pass the mayhem at the betting cage with their eyes fixed on us.

After we pass a row of slot machines, quiet and dead with the loss of power, we cut through a food court. Eventually, we reach the flights of motionless escalators. Joey scrambles up the unmoving stairs. I check back to be sure none of those things are getting too close.

"Hold up," I insist. "Where are we going, Joey?"

"Upstairs?" he says.

"We'll be trapped up there," I say.

"We need to get the fuck out of here," urges the black guy. "We need an exit."

"Where is the security office?" I ask Joey.

"Far," he says. "Outside. Past all the stables, by the other entrance. I had to drive the truck to get here from there."

"We go there then," I say. "We'll take the truck."

We follow Joey to the end of the apron level of the grandstand, and out the entrance on the opposite end of the building. Through the windows, I see a few dozen more dead people walking around in the courtyard. We file out the doors and head for the gate. The corpses don't notice us as we make a run for the security SUV parked at the curb. Joey turns the key, puts the truck in gear, and hits the gas before I get the passenger door closed. He takes a right turn into the rows of long white stables. The horses hang their heads out from the stall windows, chewing without interest as we speed past.

I tell Joey to pull right up to the door of the security office, in case we need to leave in a hurry. He parks just far enough from the security office that we can open the truck doors and slip inside. Here, on the opposite side of the park, it still seems quiet. The white entrance gates are closed, and the street beyond is empty except for a single car wrapped around a telephone pole across the road. I scan the area for signs of trouble as the group makes their way inside. Through the air comes the distant popping of an automatic weapon firing. I glance down at the gun in my shaking hand. I had forgotten it was there all this time. It wouldn't have mattered much back there anyway. There were just too many of them.

"Blake," Danielle says.

I raise my eyes to find her looking at me.

"I'm coming," I say. I turn away from her gaze and scan the area one more time. Once I am sure she has left the doorway, I turn around and head inside.

CHAPTER THREE

The heavy duffel bag thuds down on the office desk and Joey rifles through the contents desperately until he finds a two-way radio. "Frank, come in," Joey pleads. "Frank... Frank, Jesus, Frank."

"He's gone, Joey," I tell him. "They never got the door closed."

Through the thin walls of the security office, bleeds the muffled sounds of distant, sporadic gunfire, and the persistent siren of a squad car abandoned nearby. I flip the light switch on the wall, but there is no power. Subdued daylight filters through the window blinds above the desktop. The windows run the length of the building to provide a clear line of sight of the entrance. There are sliding glass panels along the sides of the building to allow the guards to check the vehicles coming and going. The place is hardly a fortress, but it's better than nothing.

In the back of the office sits an empty holding cell with a thin wooden bench mounted on the wall. Adjacent to the cell, the black guy searches through several gym lockers. There isn't much else. A bathroom. A mini fridge and microwave. A folding table and chairs in the middle of the room where the blonde woman sits down and digs through her purse. Danielle picks up the phone at the workstation and checks for a dial tone, and then she sighs and places the handset back on the base.

"This is bad," moans the guy with the tattoos. "This is real fucking bad. We're dead, man. What the fuck are we going to do now?"

The blonde woman lights a long, thin cigarette with a shaky hand and leers at the guy with the tattoos that is pacing anxiously around the table. He rubs his hand over his shaved scalp and rattles off an endless list of complaints about the situation. Just watching him makes me feel even more anxious.

I stare at the slow, steady movements of the second hand of the clock on the wall. Over an hour has passed since I heard from Amanda. Instead of thinking about what we have to do to stay alive, I just keep thinking about what could be happening to my wife and daughter at each passing moment.

The blonde woman sighs loudly as she exhales a plume of smoke.

"Will you sit down?" she snaps at the tattoo guy. "You're making me anxious."

The man stops pacing to shoot an annoyed look at the woman.

"Lot of good you are," he grumbles. He waves the cigarette smoke away from his face and resumes his pacing. "Why don't you put that damn thing out and help think of a way out of this?"

Danielle leans over the desk and lifts a blind to get a look at the road.

"It seems like it might not be as bad over here," she notes. "Maybe we should get back in the truck and get out of here while we still can."

"The chick has a point," says the guy with tattoos. He finally stops pacing and looks around the room. "What are we waiting around for anyway? We should get the hell out of here."

"And go where?" I sigh. "The roads are a mess. We don't even know if anywhere is safe."

"He's right," agrees the black guy. I look up to see him leaning against the lockers with his arms folded across his chest.

"Look, I only live a few miles from here. Just drop me off at my house," the tattoo guy pleads with Joey. "Then you can all go wherever the hell you want."

"No one is taking the truck," I say. "Not right now."

"It's not your goddamn truck, is it?" the tattooed guy spits back at me. He steps toward Joey and reaches for the keys, but the young security guard puts them back in his pocket. The tattooed guy continues to hold his hand out expectantly. "You want to give me the keys or what, kid?"

"Don't give him the keys," I insist.

The tattooed guy lets his hand drop and turns away from Joey. He moves slowly toward me and jabs a menacing finger at my chest. "No one is talking to you, man," he growls.

On a good day, when things were normal, this guy would still be an asshole. Somehow you can just tell. It seems like he is trying to decide whether or not to throw a punch at me. Instead of waiting around to find out I shove him back and level the gun at his chest.

"No one is taking that truck." I form each word slowly and steadily as if I were communicating with someone who speaks a different language. For several long seconds, he looks at the barrel of the gun and says nothing. Then he smirks and locks his scornful eyes with mine. Maybe he's trying to decide whether to take me seriously or if he should just try to grab the gun out of my hand. I have never pointed a gun at anyone before. I don't know how to hold it to seem threatening. I am not even sure if I would really shoot him.

The black guy unfolds his arms and clears his throat. He casually approaches, and he positions himself in the middle of us. "How about we all just calm down and talk about this shit reasonably?"

The tattooed guy rolls his eyes and scoffs in disbelief. He turns and shakes his head and moves himself to the other side of the room. A long moment passes before I lower the gun. Even though I avoid making eye contact, I can feel the nervous stares from everyone in the room as I walk over to the desk. I really don't want anything to do with these people. The only thing I want to do is keep them from doing something stupid that gets me killed.

"I know we all have people out there that we want to get to. I do too," I admit. "This is the last place on earth I want to be right now. But Marco, the cop, he told me this is happening all over the city. We don't have a chance if we go running around out there right now. We have to be smart. We have to have a plan."

"So, what, are you going to hold us here at gunpoint?" the blonde woman gripes. She stamps out her cigarette in the ashtray, squishing the filter like an accordion, then drops the butt on the floor and flattens it with her foot.

"No," I sigh. "I am not holding anyone hostage. If anyone wants to leave now, go ahead. Otherwise, we wait until it's safe. The gates are electric, and the power is out so the only way to get the truck out is to crash through somewhere and then those things are going to be all over here, and there'll be no going back."

For a long minute, everyone looks around at each other, saying nothing.

"This is bullshit!" the tattooed guy yells. "If you all want to wait to die here, fine. I'm getting the fuck out, though." He heads toward the door, muttering as he passes me. He reaches for the handle, then turns to see if anyone is going with him. When he realizes no one is following he says, "I'm not going to wait all day for you idiots to make up your minds." His voice quavers slightly. It seems pretty obvious he is afraid to go out alone, but the man is too arrogant to turn back now. He shakes his head and leaves without closing the door behind him.

When it's clear he won't be coming back, the black guy walks over and closes the door and slides the deadbolt. I am relieved not to be dealing with the tattooed guy anymore, even though I am certain he has no real chance out there.

From the windows, we can see the tattooed guy running over to the gate and watch as he struggles to climb. He drops down into the street and twists an ankle as he lands. He collapses on his back, gritting his teeth and clutching his leg.

"Oh no," cries Danielle. She turns toward the door, but the black guy latches onto her arm and shakes his head. Joey and the blonde woman hurry over to the window now to see what is happening too.

While the tattoo guy struggles to get to his feet, several corpses stumble into view from the edges of the pavement. He notices the dead body in a slate gray suit and tie coming at him from his right. The tattooed guy punches it in the face, then grabs it by the tie and pulls his fist back to hit it again. He doesn't see the corpse approaching from behind him until the zombie grabs his arm and bites down on his bicep.

"We can't leave him out there," says Danielle. She shrugs her arm free, but the black guy moves in between her and the door.

"You can't help him now," he says.

"Yes, I can," Danielle insists. She steps around the tall black man, but he puts a hand against the door to keep her from opening it.

"If you go out there," he says. "They'll know we're in here."

Danielle looks back at me, her eyes pleading with me to do the right thing. I don't know what that means right now. As horrible as it is, we watch the tattooed guy screaming for help, and we do nothing as they fall on him less than fifty feet away. The corpses rip out pieces of his face with their teeth. His eyes open wide with terror, as he kicks and swats at them with his limbs. He twists his body away from their grasp and nearly makes it to his feet before they bring him to the ground again. A dark-haired corpse in a blood-stained flower-print dress claws a chunk out of his calf. The others find his abdomen, they bury their hands in his stomach, oblivious to his weakening fists pounding their heads. The hands of the corpses emerge entangled in his intestines, which they gnaw at as the man finally passes out.

I can't stand to watch anymore, but I can't turn away either. My mouth hangs open in shock, and I get the nasty metallic taste that comes just before I throw up. I swallow and bury my mouth in the crook of my elbow when I start to gag.

"Look," the blonde woman blurts out and points at the street. Incredibly, a screaming obese woman in a bathrobe runs right passed the guy being eaten alive. She doesn't even glance at the gruesome scene. The zombies get back to their feet, soaked in blood, and begin their slow pursuit of the woman.

Blood spreads in a pool around the tattooed man lying in the street. I stare at the ugly tattoos that cover his unmoving arm, the faded images destroyed by numerous bite wounds. I wonder how long it will take before he gets back up. A hand clasps my shoulder and startles me.

"It's okay, man," says a deep voice. It's the black guy in the track suit. "You tried to tell him."

I look down at the gun in my hand, thinking how strange it looks to see my hand holding it. I put it down on the desk and turn away from the window. Though it must look like it, I don't feel guilty at all. I am just feeling sick from the horrors of this day. I don't know how to handle this insane world that didn't exist a few hours ago. Mostly, I'm afraid. Afraid of what I might have to do to stay alive.

"That fool made his own choice," he says. "Quentin," he says. He holds up a hand. It seems like such a meaningless gesture right now, but for some reason, I feel immediately reassured by the small, familiar civility.

I reach to clasp his hand briefly and introduce myself, and then I think about it and add, "Thanks." I nearly apologize when I notice how damp with perspiration my hand is in contrast to his.

"Don't sweat it, man," Quentin says. He wipes his palm against the fabric of his pants, then uses it to open a drawer of the desk and starts digging through the contents. Even when we were sprinting through the grandstand for our lives, this guy didn't break a sweat. Somehow he seems to be handling everything with a calmness I have trouble comprehending.

The blonde woman returns to the table and removes her blazer and drapes it over the back of a chair. She retrieves another skinny cigarette from her purse. "That's great you all are friends now, but can we get back to figuring a way out of here before we all end up like that guy?"

Danielle whirls around from the window and opens her mouth to say something back at the blonde woman. They lock eyes for a moment, but Danielle bites her lip instead. She rolls her eyes as she turns back to look out at the street again. "He's getting up," Danielle reports softly.

I'm surprised at how quickly that happened. It's only been a couple of minutes since he stopped moving. None of us can resist taking another look outside. Maybe it's curiosity or disbelief that makes us need to see the man return from the dead. The corpses ate much of the muscle tissue from one side of his neck, so his head tilts in that direction. He lingers at the gate and stares at the security building, his pale face jawing at the air. It's like somehow he still remembers we're inside. I have a strong urge to go out and put a bullet in his head, so I don't have to see him standing there anymore. After a few moments, guilt forces most of us to turn away again. Danielle remains watching him at the window for a moment longer than the rest of us, and then she steps back and seats herself at the table next to the blonde woman.

"That poor man," Danielle mourns.

The blonde woman scoffs and turns away in her chair. I can't say I blame her for not wanting anything to do with the rest of us. When people are dying all around you, it seems pointless to bother getting to know anyone. If any of us thought we could make it on our own, we would probably try. But going alone won't get you very far. We already saw that for ourselves.

I pull out a chair and sit down next to the blonde woman. Though she looks only a few years older than Danielle, she seems to regard the younger woman as a child. The gray designer business suit and pixie hairstyle match her dour demeanor. She emits an exasperated sigh and avoids making eye contact with anyone. "Miss… whatever your name is," I begin to say.

"Dom," she snaps.

"Dom," I say. I lower my voice to a whisper and try to sound cordial. "I'm just as thrilled as you are to be locked in here. So, let's just all try to get along for awhile."

"Sure," Dom answers. "Whatever."

Quentin finally stops searching the drawers when he locates a couple of flashlights. He removes the batteries and installs them in a little radio sitting on the desk. Quentin has to turn up the volume to hear over the police siren that is still blaring somewhere nearby. The room fills with the white noise of static. He scans through the stations and stops at an emergency alert.

"…avoid all contact with affected persons," a robotic voice states. "Seek shelter immediately. Martial law will remain in effect until further notice. Stay in your homes and await further updates. This is not a test. A national state of emergency has been declared by FEMA and the CDC. An unexplained occurrence is causing bodies of the recently deceased to reanimate and attack the living. Citizens are advised to…" The same message repeats again and again, but it doesn't provide any information as to what is causing this or how they plan to stop it.

Joey opens a refrigerator in the kitchenette and starts poking around the meager contents. "I would have brought something for lunch if I knew I'd be fucking trapped in here all day," he says. He removes a brown bag from a shelf and reaches inside. "Frank just brought a little microwave burrito and a fuzzy avocado or something." He holds up a kiwi then tosses it back into the brown paper sack.

I realize by his disappointed expression the security guard isn't trying to be funny. Quentin glances up from messing with the tuner on the radio to look at Joey. He shakes his head and goes back to twisting the dial.

"Poor Frank," Joey laments. The kid stares at the items left behind by his deceased partner with a sorrowful expression. It took a while, but the loss of his buddy Frank is hitting home. That's what it seems like until he says, "He never had anything good to eat for lunch."

I stare at the kid in amazement as he closes the fridge and slumps down in a chair at the desk. It's hard to believe someone can be so oblivious. He swivels from side to side in the rotating seat of the chair and spins his pistol around his finger by the trigger guard as we look on in fear. The kid looks around and realizes everyone is staring at him and stops spinning the pistol.

"What?" he asks.

"Are you really that stupid?" asks Dom. "Seriously. I can't believe someone actually gave you a gun." She smashes another thin cigarette filter into a nub, then drops it on the floor and flattens it with her foot.

Joey calmly slides the weapon back into the holster on his hip and watches until Dom turns her head away. Then he mutters to her back, "Lesbian." Her face tightens with anger, but she refuses to acknowledge the comment. She just reaches for another long, skinny cigarette from the pack on the table.

Quentin gives up finding a different station, and so we listen to the radio repeat the same message again. The radio tells us to stay off the streets. I guess it makes as much sense as anything for now. We can't stay here forever, though. There's essentially no food or water. Eventually, we have to come up with some sort of plan. Instead of putting my fear and anxiety aside long enough to think rationally, I fidget and twist the platinum wedding band around and around on my finger. When I sit back in the chair and put my hands in my pocket, I feel my phone and check it again. It still has no signal. My eyes gaze at the background photo of my wife and daughter once more and then set the phone down on the table. I force my eyes closed and try to put all of that out of my mind. I need to focus.

"Why do you keep looking at your phone?" Danielle asks. Her eyes glance down at the screen of my phone.

"Just seeing if I have a signal," I lie. I immediately realize that she isn't buying it.

"Are they okay?" she asks. "Your family. I just happened to see the picture," she adds by way of explanation.

"I don't know," I admit. I hand my phone to her so she can see the picture if she wants to. She looks at it for a long moment as if she is studying their faces.

"They look sweet," she smiles.

"Yeah," I sigh. I realize I sound a little annoyed. I notice creases forming above her brow, and realize her genuine concern and my voice softens. "Sorry. I'm just trying to figure out what to do next."

"No, it's fine," she says. "It's not my business anyway."

"Shhh," I say. Over her shoulder, I notice a shadow passing across the outside of the window.

Quentin flips the radio off and for the next hour, we hardly make a sound. At first, it seems like just a couple of them have managed to find their way through the racetrack to the security office. As more time passes, more and more shadows fall on the windows. I can't understand what is drawing them close to the building.

Without air conditioning, the temperature climbs inside the cramped security office. It's getting pretty uncomfortable, but we don't dare open a window. Maybe they can smell us in here. Maybe that is what draws them. Who knows.

Morning drags into the afternoon, and when I peer through the blinds again, I see about twenty corpses walking around. I realize they are probably wandering towards the sound of the police siren, heading towards the noise until they reach the closed gates and have nowhere to go. Occasionally, one stumbles into the building, and then we wait in horror for more sounds that indicate they are trying to get inside. I wonder how much longer we should stay here now. If they keep coming there will be more than we can handle soon. It's just a matter of time before they discover we are inside this building.

"We need to come up with a plan before they figure out we're in here," I whisper.

"The radio said to stay off the streets," Dom reminds me.

"Yeah, I know," I concede. "It's a risk we have to take. There's no food or water here, and if we so much as sneeze those things will be all over us."

"Alright then," Quentin agrees. "You got someplace in mind?"

"No," I admit. "We're just going to have to see what we find out there. Let's think one move at a time," I say. "The most important things are water and food. Two blocks from here over the expressway, there's a gas station."

"We don't need gas for the truck," says Joey. "It's full."

"Damn, boy," says Quentin. He shakes his head in frustration.

"They have food and water there," I repeat. "At least, enough to last us a few days."

"Might be people there too," Quentin says. His tone indicates that people could be more trouble than anything else.

"It won't be any safer there," Danielle points out. "I'm really not sure about this."

"I'm not going to say it isn't risky," I concede. "If anyone has another idea, I'm listening."

I wait to hear out any other opinions, but no one has a better option.

"If we do this, we're going to need more guns," adds Quentin. "We won't be getting very far with what we got."

I can't think of any store nearby that would have guns, but I remember the courthouse is a block in the other direction. There are always county sheriff patrol cars parked in the garage there.

"I have an idea for that," I whisper. "The courthouse. There's lots of vehicles. We can probably find some guns there too. We'll go there first."

"That's in the opposite direction. How many stops are we planning on making here? What about waiting for help?" Dom asks. "I thought that was the plan?"

"The gates are closed on this side of the park. They're collecting outside like fish in the bottom of a net," I say. I peer out the edge of the window and count about forty corpses outside now. "There's already twice as many as there was an hour ago. The longer we wait, the more there will be outside when we try to leave."

"Unless we give them something to chase away from here," Quentin rubs at the goatee on his chin as he thinks. He stands up and takes a look at the truck outside. "I think I have an idea."

CHAPTER FOUR

The door to the security building flings open and Quentin steps out, firing off three rounds to the left. He whirls around to the right and fires three more quick shots, then moves to cover the back of the truck. I take a deep breath and charge out behind him, expecting the dead to be right on top of us. I glance around and realize Quentin has already dropped any corpse near the doorway. There are half a dozen bodies sprawled on the ground. The guy didn't even waste a single bullet.

"Damn," I gasp. For a moment, I lose focus and just watch him put down several more of the undead. The guy makes it look so easy.

"Watch my six," Quentin barks between shots.

"What?" I scream.

Quentin stops shooting. "My back! Watch my back."

I move to the front of the security vehicle and can feel the eyes of the approaching dead fix on me. Joey dashes between us and fumbles with the keys to open the door of the truck. I raise the gun and aim at a chubby Hispanic guy dressed in a uniform from a fast food burger joint. A greasy white apron smeared with wet blood hangs from his neck. My first shot misses the guy completely, but somehow takes out a corpse ten feet behind him. I aim for the stupid, pointy paper hat on his head and shoot again. The next shot tears a hole in his shoulder. As bad as I am shooting, I feel like I am getting the hang of handling a gun. I fire again and hit him right where his heart should be. Then I shoot him in the leg. The corpse collapses from the last shot, but it keeps crawling towards me. I finally put a round through the paper hat and it explodes like a packet of ketchup. The damn thing finally collapses on the pavement and stops moving.

I glance around at the other undead, realizing they are getting too close. My eyes keep returning to the body on the ground. With my aim, I don't have time to waste. There are still dozens of corpses shuffling around the body of the cook. I point the gun at the closest of the dead, a redhead in a floral dress, but can't pull the trigger for some reason. Now, I know damn well that cook was dead before I shot him, but putting a bullet in someone still feels so wrong. I never killed anything before, except a few houseflies or a spider. Maybe this isn't any different, but it sure does bother me a whole lot more than squashing a bug. I try to steady my hand and take the shot, but before I do the head of the woman snaps back, and she collapses to the ground.

"What the fuck you doing?" Quentin roars. He stands next to me, loading a full magazine into his handgun, his eyes darting from left to right.

"My gun jammed," I stammer. I can be such a liar sometimes. Especially when I don't want to seem weak.

Quentin looks down at the gun in my hands and scowls. He pulls back the slide of his pistol and fires off several more rounds into the approaching dead. The truck engine roars to life as the mob of corpses close around us. I tap Quentin on the shoulder, then retreat inside the security office. He keeps firing as he backs through the doorway, then slams the door shut as the first corpse lunges at him. Quentin leans back against the door as the dead moan and pound away at the steel. The banging sounds cease after several seconds. The moans of the dead fade to a distant murmur.

After a few moments of silence, I peer through the blinds. Joey eases the truck away even though several corpses claw at the vehicle. A few stragglers remain in the vicinity of the security office until Joey honks the horn. The sound helps draw the rest of them away. Then I notice the dead body of the cook again. He might have been a bastard for all I know, but nobody deserves to go out like that. I don't know why, but I imagine what his life was like. I always beat myself up with stupid thoughts like that when someone dies. Even someone I never met. It's like I feel guilty for not giving a damn about anyone until it's too late.

"What the hell was that all about?" Quentin asks me. His voice startles me, and I pull my hand away from the blinds. He scrutinizes me through narrowed eyes for a moment, then drops his gaze to the floor and shakes his head. "I thought you knew how to handle a gun."

"Just want to figure out what it takes to stop those things," I lie. "Now we know we have to go for the head."

Quentin sighs and massages at the muscles on the back of his neck. "Next time do me a favor and let me know before you go and do something stupid like that," he pleads. "You feel me?"

"Sure," I agree. After his shooting display outside, this is not a guy I want to piss off.

Several long minutes pass. We wait and listen for the sound of the truck approaching.

"What's taking him so long?" Dom complains.

"Something must have gone wrong," Quentin whispers. "We should move while it's still clear."

"Shhh," urges Danielle. She cocks her head to one side and listens.

I hear the distant squeal of tires, followed by the roar of the engine. The tires squeal again when Joey slams on the brakes and the truck skids to a stop outside the security office. I push through the door and move to cover the front of the truck. The plan worked better than I hoped. The area surrounding the office is entirely clear of the dead. Quentin slides around to cover the rear of the truck. Dom and Danielle heave a couple of duffel bags of supplies into the trunk. As soon as they close the hatch, Quentin hops in the passenger seat, and the rest of us crowd into the back. Joey floors the gas pedal, veers right and accelerates towards the fence. I clench the front seats and brace for the impact.

The security truck plows through the metal, tearing fence posts out of the ground. Once we clear the fence, Joey wheels the truck hard to the left to make for the road. The uneven ground of the field is full of holes and mounds of dirt. The truck bottoms out several times and I feel the undercarriage scrape against the ground. The violent movements toss us out of our seats. I grip the armrest on the door and hang on for dear life.

The truck hops over the curb and onto the street, and then Joey swerves left towards the courthouse. The rims start to grind against the pavement. At least one of the tires is flat, and we are half a mile to the courthouse. I think the truck can make it, but I wouldn't bet on it. Somehow when we get to the parking garage, we have to find another car, or we're screwed.

The undead alongside the road notice the noise of our vehicle approaching. They lurch into the street, reaching for the truck as we pass. Dead bodies lie strewn across the road like speed bumps. Some have tread marks on their clothes from vehicles crushing them once or twice. They drag their mangled bodies through the streets. Joey weaves between them when possible, but rolls over them when necessary. I cringe at the sound of their bones cracking beneath the vehicle.

Joey swerves to avoid an abandoned blue Volvo station wagon parked sideways in the middle of the road. As we pass, I notice someone sit up in the drivers seat. I turn and look back to see the window roll down enough for a hand to stick out and wave at us. Whoever that was in there, they were alive. I think about telling Joey to stop and go back, but I don't. Our car is full, and one of our tires is flat. We can't risk stopping, not for anything.

The courthouse is a few hundred yards ahead, but a long line of abandoned cars blocks the entrance. There are only a few wrecks in the opposite lane, so Joey cuts across, driving over broken glass and blood stains. Joey takes a hard right back through the cars and clips the front end of a cherry red Porsche to squeeze into the entrance.

Dead bodies in orange jumpsuits with their hands cuffed together wander around outside the courthouse. Maybe this won't be so difficult after all. Joey cuts a right turn into the first floor of the parking garage. There are plenty of parked cars up and down the aisles. Most of the owners never made it out to them.

"What now?" asks Quentin. "Should we just start checking doors?"

"Keep driving around," I tell Joey. "Find a dead cop to run over."

"Oh man," Joey says. He turns the truck, following the signs on the ceiling toward the next level of parking. "Do you even realize how crazy that sounds?"

As we turn up the incline to the second level, the running lights of the truck shine on a corpse wearing a police uniform. The cop crouches over the body of a man in, what used to be, a nice suit. Joey puts his foot on the brake and stops the truck.

"Do it," I urge him.

Joey punches the gas and I shut my eyes and wait for the inevitable sound of metal crushing bone. When I open my eyes, I see blood splattered across the windshield. Joey slams his foot on the brake. Quentin is the first one to jump out of the car. He walks over to a female corpse crawling between two parked cars alongside us and fires off two rounds. The sound is like explosives in the confines of the concrete parking structure. It won't take long before we have a lot of company in here.

I get out and head back to the body of the cop. Danielle, Dom, and Joey start to get out of the truck, but I tell Joey to keep it running and stay behind the wheel. I don't want to abandon the truck until I know we have another vehicle.

"Hurry up," urges Quentin. He looks up and down the aisle of the parking garage, then reaches down and retrieves a purse from the ground and dumps the contents out on the cement.

I kneel down next to the uniformed body. The knees of my pants quickly soak in the puddle of blood. I try to ignore the bloody mess that used to be the head of a human being while I slide the gun from the holster. Then I start digging through his pockets. My hands close around a clump of hard plastic and ridged metal.

"Got them," I say.

Bright yellow lights flash in my peripheral vision. I look up and see Quentin clicking the remote key that unlocks a silver Mercedes-Benz M-Class SUV parked a few feet away. I punch the buttons on the keys I took off the cop, and a squad car back down on the first level chirps in response. When I turn my head to look at Quentin, I notice half a dozen corpses are at the bottom of the ramp, making their way up towards us.

"We'll take the Benz," I tell Quentin. "We can get the squad car on the way out."

Quentin gets behind the wheel, and I wave the others over from the security truck. Quentin steers the SUV up the incline, loops around the second level, then follows the signs back down to the first floor. The walking dead that pursued us are halfway up the adjacent incline. They turn when they see our car heading down the next row and follow us back down to the first level. I hit the remote start on the car keys I took from the cop.

"I see it," Quentin points to a handful of squad cars parked in a row. Only one of the police units has illuminated taillights. He brings the SUV to a rolling stop. I hop out the door and dash the four or five steps to the cruiser. I reach for the handle but stop to duck when I hear a gunshot. I look back to see Quentin leaning out the SUV window and pointing the gun at a corpse that collapses in front of the Mercedes.

The dead are swarming toward the parking garage now. As soon as I open the door of the police cruiser, Quentin hits the gas again. The SUV barrels through a pair of dead cops that flail at the windows.

I throw the squad car in reverse and back it out of the garage. The crowd of walking dead proves too dense to weave the vehicle through, especially backward. I can only watch as several corpses vanish under the trunk. The wheels rumble over the bodies and jostle me in the seat. Once I am out in the entry drive, I throw the car in gear and press the gas pedal down to the floor. The powerful engine pushes me back in the seat. I catch up to the Mercedes as they reach the main street and hook a left.

We speed passed the gridlock of abandoned cars. My hands are slick with sweat and shaking as they hold the steering wheel. I try to take a deep breath to calm my nerves, but the adrenaline rush still has my heart pounding. When I pass by the blue Volvo, I remember the figure in the car. I glance at the rearview mirror, and I see the hand waving from a crack in the window. I take my foot off the gas and watch the Mercedes pulling farther away from me.

"Damn it," I curse myself for deciding to do something stupid that could get me killed. I hit the brake and wheel the cruiser around and roll up beside the Volvo. There is a young girl, maybe thirteen or fourteen, alone in the car. She ducks down beneath the window as I pull alongside the vehicle, but I can still see the dark brown on top of her head. There are not any walking dead close by, but I still don't like the idea of getting out of the car here alone. I press the button to lower the passenger side window.

"Quick," I tell her. "Get in."

The girl peers over the frame of the door and scans the street with her frightened brown eyes. Then she looks at the letters on the side of the squad car. Without a word, she opens the door and steps out of the car. She pauses before touching the handle of the passenger door of the cruiser.

"Come on, kid," I urge her.

The girl looks at my blood-soaked clothes and realizes I am definitely not a cop. She whirls away and darts back through the door of the Volvo. Damn it.

A couple of corpses in the middle of the road are starting to get a little too close. There is no time to try and reason with her. I fling open the door and run around the cruiser. Just before she slaps her hand on the lock, I rip open the door of the Volvo. The girl screams when I reach into the car and drag her out.

"Easy," I sooth, but the girl howls at the top of her lungs.

I pull her by the arms until I can get her out of the car enough to put her over my shoulder. Her elbow smacks the back of my head as she flails. I know I am scaring the hell out of her right now, but it is either this or leaving her here to die.

I dump her in the back seat of the squad car and slam the door. She wails and pounds her fists against the window. Thank God the rear doors of the cruiser don't open from the inside. I turn to go around the back of the car and bump into a guy in a maintenance jumpsuit with half the skin peeled off his face. His dislodged eyeball dangles by a thread of optic nerves. I stumble backward at the sight of him and struggle to stay on my feet when he lunges at me. His mouth opens, and his hands grab at my shirt. I reach for the gun tucked in the back waist of my pants, but the dead man lunges at me again. I instinctively raise my arm to fend him off while I fumble with the handle of the gun, but I lose my grip, and the gun falls to the ground. His massive hands seize upon my wrist and elbow, and he pulls my arm toward him and opens his mouth.

A hole suddenly appears in the forehead of the corpse. I look down to see dark flecks of coagulated blood spangle my shirt. The massive body falls to the ground. I look down at the corpse in shock and try to process what just happened. I hear Danielle's voice, telling me to get in the car. I take my eyes off the body on the ground and spot the Mercedes driving away. Then I notice Danielle getting behind the wheel of the squad car.

"Hurry," Danielle pleads.

My hand finds the handle on the passenger door of the cruiser, and I collapse into the seat. Danielle hits the gas, and I watch her eyes darting from the SUV in front of us to the young girl in the rear view mirror as we race down the road.

"You're going to be okay now," Danielle says to console the distraught girl in the back of the car.

"I want to go home," she begs. "Please. Just take me home." The girl pulls her knees up to her chest and lowers her face and cries.

"Blake?" Danielle calls to me trying to bring me out of my shocked silence. "Are you okay?"

I glance down at my arms, still unsure that none of the blood on me is mine. That was too close. I think about how I raised my arm to try to fend that corpse off. This reaction is an instinct developed by humans through millions of years of evolution to protect our vital organs. But now, even our instincts just make us more vulnerable. No matter how much we prepped for disasters, the human species is not equipped to deal with this. This is the end of the line for us. The human race won't survive this.

The chirp of an electronic device in the car snaps me back to reality. It sounds like it could be my phone. My heart races. I dig it out of my pocket and look at the display. No alerts. One of the many devices in the cruiser must have made the noise. I glance around the console and spot the police radio and snatch up the handset.

"Can anyone hear me?" I plead. I am not even sure I am using the damn thing right. I jab at a couple of buttons and twist a dial then try again. "Is there anyone alive out there?" There is no answer. Nothing but dead air. I transmit again, "Please, we need help. If you can hear me, please respond."

"They can't all be dead," says Danielle. "That's not possible. Right?"

I don't want to believe that, but the way things are going, it seems likely. After a few long moments with no response to our transmissions, I put the radio back on the hook. "I think from here on out we have to assume the worst," I admit.

The gas station comes into view with the SUV parked out front of the convenience mart doors. The vehicle is empty. Then I see Dom and Joey haul out armloads of snacks and water and dump the crinkling plastic bags into the back of the Mercedes. Quentin peers up from behind the hood of the vehicle, picks off a corpse on the road then ducks back down.

Danielle pulls up behind them, and as soon as the car comes to a stop the girl in the back starts yanking on the door handle.

"Let me go!" she screams. "Let me go!"

"I'll go see if they need help," I tell Danielle. "Keep the car running."

"Blake," she places a hand on my arm as I open the car door. She glances at the girl in the back seat of the cruiser. "I'm going to try and calm her down. She's terrified."

Although I doubt anything Danielle can say will get through to the girl right now, I nod and tell her that's a good idea. I leave the cruiser and hurry over to the SUV.

"There's a police radio in the cruiser," I inform Quentin. "I tried, but I can't get anyone on it."

Quentin grunts and glances around me to where Danielle squats to talk to the girl in the back of the Crown Vic. His scowl tells me he isn't too happy about something. I wait for a minute, but he just turns and focuses on the corpses coming up the road.

"What is it?" Better to just get it out there and over with now. I can't afford to have him pissed off at me.

"What did I say, man?" Quentin hisses. He pulls the trigger and drops another corpse near the compressed air pump.

"What are you talking about?" I wonder what I did to piss him off so bad.

"Tell me before you decide to do something stupid," he gripes. "Remember that conversation?"

"I had to help her," I insist. "I couldn't leave her there. For god's sake, she's just a kid."

"Don't we got enough problems already?" he growls. "Now we got this damn kid to worry about." Quentin leans his head to the side, and we both glance at the cruiser again. When I look back at Quentin, his expression has softened. He grabs the handle and pulls open the door of the truck and shoves a two-way radio in my chest. "Next time you get a stupid idea," he warns.

"I know, I know," I interrupt him. "I got it."

The bell on the gas station door jingles as Dom and Joey come out again with their arms loaded with jerky, chips and candy bars. They dump it all into the back of the Mercedes.

"Last trip," says Dom.

"Move it," Quentin urges her. "We ain't got all day, sweetheart."

Dom pauses with her hand on the door handle and starts to open her mouth, but one look at the tall black man with the serious expression is enough to silence her. She whirls and vanishes into the darkness of the store.

"So where to now, boss?" Quentin asks.

I'm not sure what to make of his question. Nobody ever called me boss before for one thing. Maybe he's being sarcastic, or pissed off, or maybe he's just the kind of person that feels the need to give everyone a nickname to feel comfortable around them. For a long moment, I just look at him. "We should keep going west," I say. "We have to get farther away from the city. Maybe we can get to the highway."

"Less people out that way," Quentin agrees. He scratches at the goatee on his chin. "Sounds like a solid plan, I guess," he shrugs. "We'll follow you, boss."

This time, I can tell he isn't being sarcastic at all. It's just his way of easing the tension I suppose. But still, anyone calling me boss just makes me cringe. "Do me a favor?" I ask. "Don't call me that."

I turn to go back to the squad car and notice a corpse wearing a bicycle helmet stumbling around the trunk. Danielle is so preoccupied with the girl she doesn't see it coming.

I raise the gun and fire off a round that puts a hole in his bright yellow shirt. The corpse wobbles and bumps against the trunk of the car. The girl in the police car lets out a scream and tries to run, but Danielle blocks the door, putting herself between the girl and the dead cyclist. My second shot cracks the bicycle helmet right off his head, but the corpse still stumbles towards Danielle.

"Stay in the car," Danielle pleads with the terrified girl. Danielle scrambles to get herself inside the cruiser and slam the rear door closed, but it's too late. The door strikes the shoulder of the dead man as he lunges toward her. Danielle clings to the door handle and leans back as the thing waves an arm around inside the car.

I let out a deep breath and pull the trigger again. The bullet punches a hole in the forehead of the corpse. Danielle releases her grip on the door handle, and the body slumps to the ground at her feet. I almost lower the gun, but then I notice the dead waitress ten steps back, and a couple of steps behind her there is a long-haired teenage corpse wearing a black trench coat.

"We got more coming," I tell Danielle.

"Time to go," Quentin yells as Dom and Joey push through the gas station doors. I glance over to see him reloading the handgun, and then he takes aim at the corpse of a postal carrier and fires.

Danielle closes the rear door to the police car, apologizing as she locks the screaming girl in the backseat again. I walk around the cruiser to the passenger side, shooting at the dead as I move. Firing the gun on the go proves too difficult for me, and I waste several rounds trying to hit the waitress in the head.

Joey and Dom hurry back out to the Mercedes, having heard the gunfire pick up. They dump the supplies in the back and climb in while Quentin runs around the front of the SUV and enters on the driver side.

"We're going west," I tell Danielle.

"West?" she squawks as she throws the car in reverse. She backs the cruiser up, knocking down the waitress. "Sorry," she says. I'm not sure if she is apologizing to the dead waitress, or to me for damaging the car. She shifts the car into drive and looks around the road again. "Which way is it?" she wonders.

"West!" I repeat.

"Just say right or left!" she yells in frustration.

I point to the right, and she peels out of the gas station onto the road. I glance back to make sure the Mercedes made it out behind us. The four-lane road provides enough room to weave through the shambling dead and abandoned vehicles. Clouds of smoke billow from fires burning unopposed in the surrounding townhouses. Through the haze, I catch glimpses of the chaos down the side streets as we pass. A stroller lies mangled beneath the wheels of a car, a few feet away from the half-eaten remains of an infant in the street. A charred body lies smoking on the lawn of a burning home.

A few survivors hail us from a second story window. I almost tell Danielle to stop the car when I see them waving their arms, but then I spot the dead below. There must be fifty or sixty of them pounding their way through the flimsy glass windows to get inside. We will just get ourselves killed if we stop to help them. So I force myself to look away from their faces and don't say a word as Danielle continues down the road.

We approach a sign for a grocery store at the entrance to a strip mall. The closer we get, the louder we hear a blaring alarm. The sound is coming from a bank with a Ford Escape overturned in the lobby. Hundreds of walking corpses crowd the vast parking lot between the bank and the grocery store. They must have been drawn there by the sound. The giant storefront windows of the grocery store are all smashed in. Shopping carts are piled high by the automatic doors like someone tried to make a stand there. By the look of it, it didn't end well. Everything here belongs to the dead now.

We cross the intersection and follow the road over a hill. I stop breathing when I see the community college campus on the left.

"Oh my God," gasps Danielle. "The school." She slows the car to a stop in the middle of the road and stares at the college in disbelief. At the entrance, an ambulance and a couple of squad cars sit with their lights flashing in the intersection. A long line of abandoned cars stretches back to the parking lot, their doors flung open, some with the running lights still on. Hundreds of undead students spill across the road below from the campus lawn. There is no way in hell we can make it through so many of those things.

"Damn it!" I pound a fist against the dashboard of the car. We have to go back now and figure out some way around this nightmare.

"I have a friend that goes to that school," Danielle says. She squints her eyes at the crowd in the road.

"Turn the car around," I urge her. "Go back to the last street."

She stares at the shambling students. They shuffle towards us in their sneakers. She doesn't even seem to hear me. It's like I'm talking to a wall.

"Danielle!" The sound of my voice yelling her name startles her, and she whirls to face me. Her eyes are filled with real terror now. She blinks at me a few times then looks back at the road and wheels the car around.

"Where do we go now?" she asks.

"Take a right at the light. We can try the next block over."

Danielle swerves to avoid a dead crossing guard holding a stop sign in the middle of the intersection. The maneuver causes us to clip an abandoned shopping cart that careens off the hood and cracks the windshield. The girl in the back seat lets out a scream as the police cruiser fishtails. I clench the door handle in case Danielle loses control, but she recovers and keeps the car on the road.

"I want to go home," the young girl pleads. She bangs her fists against the fiberglass partition between the back seat and the front. "Please, stop the car."

"Everything is fine," Danielle assures her, but the girl just begins to sob.

"She's okay," I tell Danielle. "Just worry about the road." We don't have time to deal with the girl right now. Not until we get someplace safe.

At the next intersection, the road comes to an end at an abandoned pizza factory. A police barricade blocks the left side of the intersection, so Danielle hooks a right. Unfortunately, this route takes us past the north entrance to the college. I just hope there are less of those things this way.

I feel my stomach tighten as the cruiser climbs the hill again. As the car approaches the college, Danielle has to weave through a graveyard of smoldering automobiles. Dead bodies drift through the clouds of smoke that seem to keep getting thicker. She brings the vehicle to a stop.

"I can't get through," says Danielle. She scans the road ahead but with all the smoke we can't see more than a hundred feet in any direction.

"There's a cemetery on the left." I point to the wrought iron sign above the entryway. "We'll cut through there."

Danielle steers the cruiser through the open cemetery gates. I hop out and scan the area while Quentin drives the Mercedes through the entrance. He hurries over to help me pull the gates closed. I kick down an iron post on the fence that locks into a recess in the ground, then step back as the first corpse lunges at us from the other side of the barricade. It reaches through the bars, clawing at the air in front of my face. More of the dead converge on the entrance from the street. Even the ones that are burnt to a crisp just keep coming. They press their smoking bodies against the gates, filleting their charred flesh off on the iron bars. The smell of singed human hair and skin wafts through the air. I cover my mouth and nose with my hand and retreat from the smell.

"I don't know how much farther we can get," I tell Quentin. "It's even worse out here than I was afraid it would be."

"Maybe we should check out the office," suggests Quentin. "See if we can lay low here a while."

I look around a minute, thinking it over. For a second, I wonder about the dead people in the ground, but I decide it doesn't matter. Dead or not, they aren't going anywhere.

"These fences will keep them out, and all this open space makes it easy to see anything coming," Quentin adds.

I shade my eyes and look towards the office. It sits at the far side of the grounds halfway up the hill. I spot a single corpse, his body swaying in the shadow of a tree.

"We might as well have a look around," I agree.

CHAPTER FIVE

"I hate cemeteries," Dom shudders. She peers over her shoulder at the countless rows of tombstones. "I hated them even before all this. They freak me out."

Quentin cups a hand to the glass door to try and see inside the lobby of the office. "Looks clear," he reports as his hand closes around the handle. He holds open the door and waits while we pass inside.

Afternoon sunlight slants across the room from elongated windows that span the top of the two-story entry. Even though there isn't much more than a few wooden platform benches, the quiet, empty lobby is a welcome sight. I cross the tile floor to a pair of service windows and peer into the darkened office beyond.

"Oh thank God," Danielle exults. "Bathrooms." She ushers the young girl over to the bench where Dom is fishing a pack of cigarettes out of her purse. Dom flashes a sardonic smile to express her displeasure at having to keep an eye on the kid.

"Hang on," Quentin whispers. "Everyone keep quiet until we make sure it's clear." He moves over to the restroom door and listens for a moment. Quentin leans his shoulder against the door to nudge it open and slips inside. A moment later Quentin returns and gives Danielle the nod and holds the door to the restroom for her, and then he eases the door closed.

"Blake," he points a finger at a door on the adjacent wall of the lobby. I nod and then he proceeds to check the other restroom.

The door across the lobby sits below an EMPLOYEES ONLY sign. I check the handle, and I'm relieved to discover it's locked. The long hallway on the other side appears dark and empty when I peer through the glass.

I return to a stack of brochures about the cemetery on the service counter. I open one up and examine the map of the cemetery grounds inside. The office building is much larger than I expected, connecting to a chapel and a number of other administrative rooms. There are several other entrances we'll have to secure, too.

Quentin returns from checking the bathroom and I wave him over to the service counter and hand him the map. He studies it a moment and grazes his hand over the stubble of the trim goatee on his chin.

"This place is pretty big," I point out.

"I can see that." He throws me a sidelong glance to let me know he doesn't need me to point out the obvious.

The problem with hearing how smart I am all the time is that it makes it hard to remember everyone else isn't a complete moron. It's not like I try to be condescending, but I guess I come off that way, sometimes.

"Of all the places we could possibly go, you guys take us to a cemetery," Dom complains. "A cemetery... When dead people are attacking everyone."

"At least, all the ones around here are in the ground," says Joey. He rummages through a plastic bag of provisions taken from the gas station.

"We can't be so sure about that yet," Quentin reminds him. "If we are going to be here awhile, we better check out the rest of the building," he says.

"If we bust open that door and those damn things are back there, we won't be able to keep them out," Dom counters.

Quentin sighs in frustration and looks to me to back him up.

"She has a point," I concede. "But I still think we need to check it out. We don't want any surprises."

"Why don't you break one of those teller windows and climb through that way?" Dom says. She points a lit cigarette at the service counter. "That way those things won't be able to walk right in here."

"Not a bad idea," admits Quentin. He casually picks up the metal garbage can and hurls it through the glass. Pieces of shattered glass plink against the tile floor of the lobby. Quentin snatches up the duffel bag, drops it on the counter and unzips it. After a minute of digging through the duffel, he locates a flashlight and uses it to clear away the shards that remain in the window frame. Quentin climbs through the opening and waits on the other side. "I ain't doing this by myself," he gripes.

I wait a moment, hoping someone else will volunteer. With a grunt of exhaustion, I pull out the gun and hand it to Joey. I grab another flashlight and one of the two-way radios from the duffel bag on the counter, then toss the other to Joey.

Quentin clicks on his flashlight and scans the back office while I lift myself over the counter. I drop down on the other side and follow him to a door at the back of the room. The office door opens to a dark hallway with several closed doors on each side. Through the doorway at the end of the hall, faint sunlight reflects off the tile floor in the corridor that runs along the back of the chapel.

"Hello?" I call out. Quentin swivels back around and puts a finger to his mouth. I am not sure if announcing our arrival is a good idea or not. It's a crapshoot, just like everything now.

We work our way down the hall and find nothing behind the closed doors except a couple of offices and a closet full of cleaning supplies. The corridor behind the chapel is empty and silent. I cross to the door and shine the beam of the flashlight into the chapel through the small rectangular panes of glass. Rows of empty pews sit before an altar in darkness.

Quentin points the beam of his flashlight at a nondescript black double door at one end of the hall. In the opposite direction, a smidgen of sunlight infiltrates the darkness through the slim glass panels of the exit doors. Checking the outer doors is a priority, so I head toward that end of the hallway first. The handle doesn't budge when I try to pull it open. So I head back to the opposite end of the hall.

"Any idea what's in there?" I ask Quentin.

"You can do the honors," he says. He steps back from the black metal doors. "I'll cover you."

I put my ear to the surface of the black metal door. The only sound I hear is the hard pumping of my heart. I press the handle down and push it open. The inside of the room is coffin-dark. The beam of my flashlight passes over the tiled walls, several rolling tables, then lands on a casket lying on its side on the floor. The sight of the open coffin causes me to panic immediately. I sweep the flashlight quickly across the room. The light sweeps over a corpse with blood dribbled down the front of his suit and necktie coming toward us. Before I can fix the light back on him, Quentin fires a couple of shots into the darkness. I adjust the light back on the corpse and Quentin fires off a round that snaps the head of the thing back and sends it crashing into a steel table.

A second later the radio squawks. "Everything alright?" Joey asks.

"We're fine," I respond. I use the flashlight to scan the darkness again to be sure there aren't anymore. Quentin lowers his gun and steps out of the room. I almost head out behind him, but then a thought occurs to me. Training the flashlight on the body, I stare at the blood-soaked hands.

"Wait," I whisper to Quentin.

"What?" he says.

"That guy had blood on him. He wasn't alone in here."

We look again around the empty room. "Where did the other one get to then?" says Quentin. "I haven't seen one open any doors yet."

"We must have missed it somehow. We better check out the chapel," I suggest.

The light inside the small chapel comes in through a giant mosaic window near the rafters. When we open the door, I hear a quiet groan. We crouch down and take cover behind the back row of pews.

"Shit," sighs Quentin.

"Did you see where it is?" I ask.

Quentin shakes his head. We listen to the silence for a few moments. I elevate myself enough to see over the tops of the seats. At first glance, nothing seems out of place. We duck along the center aisle towards the altar. As we approach the front row, I spot a bloody handprint on the edge of the pew to our left. A pool of slick blood seeps out into the aisle. Quentin raises the gun, and I realize I am holding the flashlight still, but gripping it more like a weapon now. On the floor, an elderly man lies unmoving in a black suit. Bloodstains cover his white collared shirt. There is a bite on his right hand and another bite on his other forearm that appears much worse. Out of the corner of my eye I see Quentin raise the gun.

"Wait," I blurt. I push Quentin's arm, so the gun isn't pointing at the body. The chest of the unconscious man appears to rise slightly. "I think he's breathing."

Quentin nudges the leg of the man on the ground a couple of times. The man remains unresponsive. Quentin notices me watching him expectantly. "Well, I ain't checking him for a pulse," he says.

"Damn it," I mutter.

We leave the man on the floor and walk out of the chapel. We take the dark hallway and unlock the door to the lobby.

"It's clear," I announce. "But we found a guy in the chapel who has a bite on his arm. He's unconscious, I think."

"Did you shoot him?" Joey wonders.

"He's not dead," I say.

Danielle leaves the girl on the bench and retrieves the first aid kit from the duffel on the counter.

"Don't be stupid. He's probably sick," Dom asserts. She pauses to take a long drag off her cigarette. "We can't take any chances."

I try to remain calm, but my skin feels hot. Dom scrutinizes my expression, and then rolls her eyes smugly and taps the ash from her cigarette.

"We don't even know if this is some kind of virus or what," I insist. "What do you think?" I ask Danielle.

"It might be a virus, but it could be something else," Danielle says.

"Like what?" Dom questions her.

"Like, something else," snaps Danielle. She opens the first aid kit and examines the supplies inside. "We don't know anything about what is causing this yet."

"What do you think it is?" Quentin asks Danielle.

She looks at him, then me, and with a faint voice, she says, "I really don't know." She snaps the medical kit shut. "All I know for sure is that if I don't get in there and help him, and he dies, then he will become one of those things."

"Shhh." Quentin raises a hand. "Listen."

There is a dull thud, a rattle of something shaking, another heavy thud. It sounds like a fist pounding on solid wood. The sounds of broken glass hitting the floor and a faint moan echo down the hall.

"I told you," Dom gloats. She smashes her skinny cigarette butt out on the armrest of a bench. She drops the filter on the floor and toes the embers before making her way to the restroom.

"It does sound like our friend is up," sighs Quentin. He picks the gun up off the counter and heads towards the rear of the building. A minute later, we hear a gunshot. The sound startles the young girl seated mutely on the bench. Without saying a word, Quentin comes back into the room and lays his gun down on the counter.

The young girl doesn't look up as I approach the bench and settle beside her. She stares at her pink sneakers on the floor and shivers though it is somewhat warm inside the building. I try to think of the right thing to say, something consoling, but I just watch her fingers tugging at the frayed holes the designer made in her jeans. She isn't just some kid. This girl had parents that cared about her. They even drove an ugly Volvo, probably just because the safety ratings assured them their little girl would be safe. At least, that's how I imagine it. I feel compelled to comfort her somehow.

My mouth suddenly feels too dry to speak, though. There are several plastic bags between the bench and the door, and I reach over and pick one up and set it down beside me. I remove a bottle of soda, and it hisses when I twist the cap off. The girl turns her head toward the familiar sound. Her tongue grazes over her lower lip and she swallows dryly. I hold out the bottle to offer it to her. She wraps her fingers around the plastic without making eye contact. She takes several anxious swallows then exhales and hands the bottle back to me.

"What's your name?" I ask the girl.

She covers her mouth with the sleeve of her varsity style jacket. "Melanie," she utters softly.

"I'm Blake," I tell her. "You hungry, Mel?" I reach into the bag and pull out a Twinkie and offer it to the girl. She still won't look at me, but she shakes her head. I pull the seam of the wrapper open and take one of the yellow sponge cakes out. With one bite, I eat half of the thing. It might just be because I haven't had any food all day, but this thing tastes more delicious than anything I can ever remember eating right now. Melanie arches her eyebrow as I eat the other half of the Twinkie and murmur ravenously.

"I haven't had one of these since I was a kid," I tell her.

"They're gross," she insists.

"You don't know what you're talking about, Mel," I taunt her.

"They're all like, thirty years old too," she adds.

"That's okay," I tell her. "So am I." She doesn't laugh, but it almost gets her to smile. The moment passes she seems to remember everything horrible that happened today and slumps back against the wall sullenly. It isn't much, but, at least, she doesn't look terrified anymore. In some ways, talking to her made me feel a little better too.

"You're okay, Mel," I reassure her. "Hang in there."

According to my phone, it is almost five in the evening. The battery is also halfway dead. I return the phone to my pocket and get up to look outside. In a couple of hours, the sun will go down. With each minute that passes, I feel even further away from my old life, and it seems harder to imagine things will ever go back to the way they were before this morning. Quentin flips on the radio again and scans the stations for anything that isn't static.

"That was really nice of you," Danielle says. I hadn't noticed her standing next to me until she spoke. She leans her back against the door and looks at Melanie.

"It doesn't seem like much," I shrug.

"You okay?" she asks.

"Yeah. Well, no," I stammer. "I mean, all things considered, I'm fine. Just thinking about my family out there."

"We'll find them," Danielle assures me. "I'll help you. I owe you that much for saving my life."

"Do you have people you want to find too?" I wonder.

"Sure," she nods. "My dad and my brother. They are in Pittsburgh so it might be awhile before that is possible."

"You think they're okay?" I ask.

Danielle looks away, at the memory of her home six inches away from her eyes. "I hope they are okay. That's all I can do. I don't think about it, though. It sounds weird, but I know they wouldn't want me to die in a failed attempt to get to them. They would want me to take care of myself."

"I know that should make me feel better about being here instead of with my family," I say. "But it doesn't."

"There's no one out there anymore," sighs Quentin. He spins the dial back and forth. "I'm not even getting the emergency broadcast now."

"The radio could be broken," says Dom. "It looks pretty cheap."

"That's ridiculous," says Danielle. "There has to be something to tell us what's going on and what to do."

The widespread power outages might have something to do with the silence on the radio, but it could also be that there isn't anyone alive to broadcast.

"Maybe no one out there knows what to do," I say. "We all saw how the police fared at the train station. I doubt there was enough time to activate the National Guard. We have to assume the government can't help us, and the media isn't able to tell us anything, and that we might never have power or running water again." I pause, and I glance up at their faces. My words are stirring up their worst fears. "If we are going to survive out there, I think we have to assume this is the end of all those things. The end of civilization."

"This has been one fucked up day," Joey sighs. He collapses on the bench and removes the security cap from his head and pushes the black strands of hair from his brow.

"Tell me about it," agrees Dom.

"Well," Joey says. "First thing this morning, Frank woke me up and—"

"God, I didn't actually mean tell me about it." Dom rolls her eyes, blowing a plume of smoke into the air. She squishes the filter like an accordion, then drops the butt on the floor and grinds it flat. She takes another one from the pack, lights it and exhales with a sigh.

It could just be all the smoke from Dom, but it suddenly feels hard to breathe in the lobby. I push through the door and step outside. The air outside is thick with the smoke of nearby fires. Visibility is, at best, a mile, and getting worse by the minute. The gunfire coming from the streets has been steadily decreasing all day. The sound of gunshots seems farther away, and further in between.

For a few moments at a time, you can still hear the birds chirping in the trees as the blowing wind rustles the leaves. It almost sounds like any other day. Then the distant rattling of machine gun fire returns, and when you listen closely, you realize it isn't the wind you hear at all, but the droning moans of thousands of undead.

A gas tank ignites in one of the cars burning on the road and unleashes an enormous fireball into the sky. Separate blazes engulf different wings of the college across the road. There is an odd scent in the air from all the things burning that shouldn't be. The sky grows darker, even though the sun is not yet setting. The spreading smoke from fires casts a ruddy glow over everything. The sight is not too far from what I imagined hell might look like. Maybe that's exactly what this is.

If this were any other day, any normal day, I'd be sitting down to dinner with my family right now, eating a boneless, skinless chicken breast with microwaved vegetables, probably. That's what Amanda cooks, most of the time. Abby would toss her green beans to the dog when Amanda wasn't looking, and I would pretend I didn't see it either. Instead, I'm watching the burning suburbs before me, and the line of dead people pressed against the fence. What I see makes it hard to believe I will ever have another ordinary day.

I'm not an idiot. I know what their chances are of surviving. That doesn't make it easier to accept that my family might be gone, or that I may never even know what became of them no matter how long I search. Something Danielle said earlier about her family keeps running through my head; how they wouldn't want her to risk dying to get to them when she could be somewhere safe. It makes sense. I wouldn't want my wife or daughter leaving any relatively safe location to try to find me right now either. It's that thought alone that keeps me focused on my survival.

Gunshots down by the cemetery gate draw my attention, and I spot a figure with long hair running through the gridlocked cars and smoke. Something about the hunched way the figure moves gives me the impression it's a man with long hair. He pauses to look around, then fires a gun twice at a couple of corpses trailing behind him. The undead at the cemetery fence turn away from the bars and toward the road.

I hustle down the slope toward the gate, whistling loudly to get his attention. I wave to him emphatically. For a second, he only gawks at me, as though he can't trust his own eyes. "Hurry," I yell.

The dead are already closing in on him. He scampers maybe twenty feet before he is surrounded. The man raises the gun again firing a couple of rounds to his left. Then he stops firing and looks down at the gun. He must be out of bullets, but it hardly matters. The living dead close the last few feet. I'm still about a hundred yards from the fence when he screams as the horde swallows him. I lower my arms and come to a stop. Even though I'm gasping loudly for breath in the smoke, I hear the last screams from the street. I bend over with my hands on my knees and stare at the lush, green grass. Once I catch my breath, I trudge back up the hill toward the office.

"Nothing you could do, man," says Quentin. I look up a little surprised to see him and wonder how long he's been standing outside. He takes a drag off a cigarette he's holding, coughs, and shakes his head.

"I know," I say.

"Might be better anyway," he says. "If we're as fucked as you think we are, we might have to worry about the kind of people we're going to come across. The kind of people that can survive something like this."

"What?" I ask, shaking my head. "Like roving gangs and post-apocalyptic warlords? That sort of thing? It's a little too early for all that."

"No," he says. "I'm just talking about scared and desperate people. Like those guys in the truck this morning. The ones that ran through the fence at the track."

"They needed help," I insist. I gaze back to the spot in the road where the guy with long hair had perished. "And so do we. We need all the help we can get."

"They shot a cop," he reminds me.

"I don't know," I admit. "But we can't just look out for ourselves. We can't turn our back on people. Not now."

"Maybe," he says, doubtfully. "Or maybe that will just be what gets us killed."

"You know I'm right," I tell him. "And I know you know it because you're still here with us instead of going it alone."

Quentin stares through the smoke to the street and takes a long drag off the cigarette. He hacks out a cloud.

"Do you even smoke?" I ask.

"Just started," he coughs, then tosses the rest of the cigarette away.

"We wouldn't have made it here without you," I say and pat him lightly on the back. "Thanks," I add.

He drops his gaze a moment as if he isn't used to much genuine appreciation thrown his way. When he looks back up, he shrugs his shoulders and with a smile says coolly, "Yeah, you all are pretty damn lucky I stuck around."

I take a few steps toward the office, but notice he lingers in the grass, contemplating the road. "You coming back in?" I ask him.

"I was just thinking it might be a good idea for us to keep someone on watch out here," he suggests. "In case those things get in, or someone else comes along."

"Not a bad idea," I agree.

He settles himself down on the grass, facing the road. "You go on in. I'll take first watch."

Before I open the door to the office, I take a look back at Quentin sitting in the grass. Our conversation was a bit unnerving. I'm afraid to turn my back and find he isn't there when I look again. I don't really know the first thing about him, but I know we need him. He knows how to handle a gun better than any of us.

"It's going to be dark soon," I announce. "We should try to get settled in before nightfall."

"Settled in?" blurts Dom. "You can't be serious."

"Going anywhere in the dark is a bad idea," I tell her. "We'll be safe here for the night."

"We are in a cemetery," Dom states. "I'm not spending the night in a goddamn cemetery."

"This is as good as any place we managed to find today," says Danielle.

"That doesn't mean we can't do better," complains Dom. "Those things will trap us in here."

"It's just for the night," I say. "We will reassess the situation outside in the morning. Maybe we will get some news on the radio, or those things might wander off in the night. For all we know, whatever is causing this might stop tomorrow, and those things out there will just be dead bodies again."

"Alright," agrees Dom finally. "But I doubt I'll be able to sleep in this place. Especially with all those things right outside the door."

"I doubt any of us will be able to sleep much tonight, but we are going to have to try," I say. "I saw some couches in the lobby of the chapel. It's not much, but they'll be better than these wooden benches. Dom, can you keep Melanie company while we move them here?"

Dom gives me a slight nod to confirm she is on board with the plan.

In the fading light, I walk down the hallway to the chapel lobby with Joey and Danielle.

"She's kind of bitchy," whispers Danielle when we're out of earshot. "It's hard not to smack her sometimes."

"Lesbians," explains Joey, as if this conveyed everything there was to know about the woman.

Danielle scowls at him, but when she sees his guileless face, she merely rolls her eyes and says nothing.

"Dom is just as scared and uncertain as any of us and dealing with it in her way," I explain. "Give her time. She'll get over it soon enough."

"She better," mutters Danielle.

There are three long couches spread around the lobby area. After a quick scan of the room with the flashlight, I head over to the closest sofa.

"Why don't we just sleep here instead of hauling this thing across the building?" asks Joey.

"I think it's best if we stay closer to the exit," I say. "If we need to block the doors, these will come in handy."

"This guy thinks of everything," Joey says to Danielle without any hint of sarcasm.

There is something very likable about Joey. Nothing seems to get to him. Maybe it's because he doesn't bother trying to comprehend everything going on around him that none of it ever bothers him. Ignorance is bliss, I guess. Perhaps reality just hasn't set in for him yet. I wonder what will happen when it finally does.

We lift the first sofa and haul it to the lobby. One by one we maneuver them down the hallway. By the time we set the last one down in front of the service desk, my muscles ache from the exhausting day. I happen to glance at my reflection in the glass above the counter and realize I still have blood splattered all over my clothes and on my face. There is nothing I can do about my clothes, but I head to the bathroom to splash some soapy water on my face. The cold water revives me momentarily, but when I lift my head up, I almost don't recognize myself in the mirror. My face seems so weary and somehow older. It's been one hell of a day.

I remove my phone from my pocket and notice the battery indicator is now red. In the privacy of the dim restroom, I spend a few minutes staring at photos on my phone. There's an image of Abby smiling and holding an ice cream cone. I can't remember where or when we took it. I skip to another photo of Amanda and Abby standing by a fountain. That was at the zoo or the park, or maybe it was the arboretum. All I want is to trigger a pleasant memory of them, but I'm struggling to remember the context from any of the images. It's like I wasn't even there with them even though I took the picture. The battery is about to die, so I give up and turn it off. To hell with it.

When I return to the darkening lobby, I find Melanie has already fallen asleep on one of the couches. Her head rests on top of her folded arms, and she had to use her jacket as a makeshift blanket. I crouch down beside her and adjust the jacket, so it covers her shoulders. I wish I could do more for her, but, at least, she is safe and sleeping now.

The door opens and Quentin enters the lobby and approaches me. I leave Melanie to sleep and step a few feet away, so we don't wake her.

"It seems pretty quiet out there now." Quentin yawns. His eyes are bloodshot.

"You look beat," I tell him. "I'm still too wired to sleep. Get some rest. I'll get you in a few hours."

"Alright," Quentin sighs. He almost seems disappointed in himself for needing a break. Quentin spots Joey searching through drawers in the office beyond the service counters. He waves Joey over and hands him the gun. "Find anything useful?" he asks.

"Just some breath mints," says Joey. "And a walkman from like, 1988. It even has a Guns N' Roses tape in there."

"Yeah, that'll come in handy," Quentin cracks. "Good work." He settles down on the couch with a groan. Then he removes his hi-tops before he stretches out with a tired sigh.

Sitting beside Dom on the bench, Danielle yawns as she watches Quentin nod off.

"I guess I'll try to sleep now, too," Dom sighs and smashes another cigarette before she rises from the bench. She drops her cigarette at Danielle's feet and taps it flat with her high heel. She avoids Danielle's stare and makes her way to the last open couch. With a tentative hand, she wipes the fabric of the sofa and scrunches her nose, before she slips off her heels and lays down.

"Guess I'll take this comfy bench then," Danielle says with obvious irritation.

Dom ignores the comment and makes a show of tossing and turning as she finds a comfortable position on the sofa. Danielle rolls her eyes and then reclines on the wooden bench.

On my way outside, I stop to grab a bottle of water to bring with me.

"Need some company?" Danielle offers.

"It's fine," I decline. "You're tired."

"There's no way I'll be able to sleep on this thing." Danielle sits up and pats the top of the wooden bench. "The grass outside will probably be more comfortable."

"Up to you," I say.

She follows me out the entrance and across the parking lot to the lawn. I pick out a spot that affords an unobstructed view of the lobby. For a few minutes, we sit there without speaking. I become distracted watching the corpses lined up along the fence. Even though it is nearly pitch black, the shapes of the undead are silhouetted against a backdrop of cars burning in the street. If there were no light, I would still know they were out there by the haunting sound of their collective rasps and moans.

Danielle nudges my elbow and jerks her head back at Joey in the lobby. With a pair of headphones in his ears, Joey rolls around in a chair from the office. He glides past the doorway going one way, then glides back from the other direction. He spins around on the swivel seat in the middle of the lobby floor, then takes breaks to twirl the gun around his index finger.

"It's like he doesn't have a clue what's going on," she says.

"I kind of envy that," I admit.

"Not me," Danielle says. "He told me earlier that I have a nice rack. In the middle of all this. Can you believe that?"

"Actually, that doesn't surprise me at all." For the first time today, I laugh a little.

"Oh," she says. "So, are you agreeing with him now?"

"No, no," I stammer. "I'm just not surprised he would say something like that."

Danielle stares at the wedding band I am aimlessly twisting around my finger. I try to casually put my hands in my pockets. She realizes the conversation is making me a little uncomfortable and instead of carrying on, she says, "I'm sorry. I shouldn't be like that."

"No," I start, but she cuts me off.

"I'm just trying to talk about something else," she says. "Something ordinary. So, I don't have to keep thinking about everything else."

"You seem to be holding up okay," I say.

"I guess," she says, "but inside it feels like each breath is more difficult than the last one."

"Yeah," I agree. "I don't really know how I am keeping it together at all. Just compartmentalizing, I guess."

"Come what?" she asks.

"Compartmentalizing," I say. "Focusing on the first step of solving a big problem instead of the entire thing. So things don't seem overwhelming. Most of us do it automatically to an extent, especially when dealing with something of this magnitude."

"Never heard of that," she admits.

"They don't teach you that in med school?" I ask cynically.

"I guess not," she rolls her eyes.

"It works as long as I have something to do," I tell her. "Sitting around and doing nothing is the hard part. That's when I start to feel like I'm going crazy."

She follows my gaze back down to the road. For a long while we just stare at the smoke, and fires, and the dead bodies that walk the streets. We listen to distant gun shots and the sorrowful moans of the undead and try not to be overwhelmed by all of it. Danielle lays back in the grass, and the next time I look over she has fallen asleep. I take out my phone and notice a few hours have passed while I watched the fires in the street burn out. The spring night has brought a damp chill.

I nudge Danielle awake, and we head inside. I wake Quentin up and hand over the gun. Danielle arranges herself on the couch, pulling her feet up to leave some room for me on the other end. Her lips appear bluish, and she shivers while she tries to fall asleep. I look around for something to serve as a blanket, but there is nothing.

"Just lay down already," she mumbles. She squirms forward toward the edge of the couch to make room for me to lay down beside her.

It feels too intimate at first, but I'm too damn tired and cold and troubled for the awkwardness to last. Within a matter of minutes, I can't even keep my eyes from closing.

CHAPTER SIX

"I got a signal," Quentin shouts. "Wake up!"

It takes a moment to get my bearings after I open my eyes. I notice my arm draped over a brunette woman that I barely know. I squint my tired eyes to focus on my surroundings and realize I'm sleeping on a couch in the lobby of a cemetery. There was a time when waking up like this would not have surprised me, but that was ten years ago. Everything comes back to me, and I realize the events that transpired yesterday were not from some awful dream.

Danielle mumbles something unintelligible as she wakes, and I move my arm away before she notices it was there. She opens her eyes, then glances quickly around the room. She feels my body behind her and cranes her neck to see me, then lets her head fall back on the couch.

I push myself upright and remove my phone from my pocket to check the time. The battery is dead.

"Damn," Quentin curses. He whips the antenna from one angle to another. "I had it a minute ago."

For a split-second, a voice cuts through the static. The sound snaps me right awake, and I awkwardly climb over Danielle and get to my feet. We gather around the radio, waiting while Quentin scans back to the frequency again. The radio crackles static, then finally, we get a clear signal.

"There are maybe sixty or seventy right outside the door," the broadcaster reports.

"Here we go," says Quentin eagerly.

"It seems like it's just a matter of time before they bust their way inside. If anyone can hear me, this is Roger Wolf broadcasting from just outside Rockford," the voice of the broadcaster falters. "My engineer and I are in the WKQZ building at 3718 Kennison Avenue, and we are surrounded by a large crowd of zombies. It sounds crazy, but I don't know what else to fucking call them. We have no food or water. We have power for now, but we have no idea how long the fuel in the generator will last."

"We haven't heard anything from the outside world for almost eighteen hours now. Neither of us here have any idea if our families are okay," the radio broadcaster continues. "If you can hear this honey, do not try to come to the station. If you are home, lock the doors and stay inside the house. Don't open the door for anyone. Tell Becca, daddy loves her."

The voice of Roger Wolf cuts out suddenly and for a moment it seems like the signal has faded, but then his voice comes back again. He clears his throat.

"Lot of help this is," groans Dom. "He doesn't know any more than we do." She moves away first and flops down on a couch and pulls a cigarette from her pack.

"If you can hear this, please send help. Yesterday, around nine in the morning, our show was interrupted by the emergency broadcast station. The message was that an immediate national state of emergency was being declared and that people were to return to their homes and await further instructions. Ten minutes later, we lost power at the station. We have not heard a damn thing from any government officials or police authorities since then. There has been no signal from any networks on the television since yesterday morning. It's like somebody just flipped the switch and shut everything down."

The announcer pauses. He takes a deep breath and sighs.

"Our producer, Simon Davis, hung himself in his office during the night. We woke up to find his dead body hanging from the ceiling, but somehow he was still moving around. He was dead as can be, but he was trying to attack us. I had to bash his skull in with a goddamn hammer to stop him. The only way to kill them permanently is to destroy the brain. For all we know, we could be the last people alive. We haven't seen anyone alive on the streets for hours now. Just more and more of these bastards surrounding the building and pounding on the door nonstop."

"I'm going back to sleep," grumbles Joey.

The radio broadcaster goes on, but I can't bear to listen anymore. It isn't the news, just a couple of desperate guys that are as helpless as the rest of us. There's no sense in waiting around for someone on a radio or television to tell us what we need to know and what to do. If we do, we'll be trapped just like them. The thought makes me wonder how many more undead might have gathered outside during the night.

"I better check the gate," I sigh and push open the door, then notice Dom, Quentin, and Danielle following me out.

The first thing that strikes me is the utter lack of human noise outside. There are none of the typical sounds of traffic or blaring car stereos from the street. Even the sound of gunfire that we had become too familiar with over the course of the previous day is alarmingly absent now. In its place now are the sounds of the dead. In the bruise-tinged light of impending dawn, the walking dead line the street and reach for us through the bars of the cemetery fence.

"There's more of them now," Quentin notes. "Maybe twice as many as yesterday."

"I knew it," snaps Dom. "Staying here was a really stupid idea."

"The fences seem to be holding up," I assure her. "It still looks like we should be able to get out okay, too."

"For now," Quentin interjects. "We have no idea how many more of those things might show up. It's only getting worse."

"But where do we go?" I ask. The question just hangs in the air unanswered.

A frightened voice behind us pleads, "I want to go home." We turn around to see Melanie stands at the door, staring down at the corpses along the fence in terror. Danielle hurries over and puts an arm around her shoulders and turns her around. She says something quietly to her that I can't quite hear as she maneuvers her back inside the building.

"No sense drawing more attention to ourselves out here," Quentin suggests, then follows Danielle inside. I head for the door as well, but I stop to take one more look back at the entrance. The gate was only designed to block the drive when the cemetery was closed, not to serve as a fortification. I am also not sure how much longer it will be before getting out becomes a real problem for us. Either way, we are running out of time here.

When I get back inside, I say, "We should all get something to eat, then load the supplies up, so we are ready to go once we figure out just exactly what the plan is."

Danielle, Dom, and Joey start going through the rest of the supplies we had procured from the gas station. Perhaps looted is a more accurate description of how we got supplies, but I don't feel guilty about taking anything to survive for as long as I can.

"I got dibs on the Skittles," says Joey. He grabs up a bag from the pile on the floor and tears off a corner with his teeth.

"It's only enough food for maybe five or six days," says Danielle. "Maybe a week."

"It's all junk, though," says Dom. "Jerky and trail mix. We can't live off that. I don't even eat junk food."

I am not surprised by the lack of real food we were able to gather. More urgently, we need the water, and we did okay there. We have maybe two hundred bottles of water and several dozen assorted sports drinks. Sure, our situation could be better, but we could be a lot worse off right now.

Quentin returns from the office and flips open a phone book on his lap. He flips through the yellow pages. "Food's a priority, for sure," he says. "But there's lots of places to find that. Only a few places to find guns and you can bet there are a lot of people out there looking for a gun or ammunition."

"The phones are down," says Joey. "That thing won't do us any good." He looks at me and shakes his head while gesturing his thumb at what he perceives as Quentin's mistake.

"Nearest place that sells guns is about ten miles from here." He flips the yellow pages shut and tosses it down on the floor. "Goddamn suburbs," he laments.

"We'll have to make due with what we've got then," I say. "That's too far."

"We should go to that big castle down the road," says Joey. He snaps his fingers a few times trying to think of the name. "The restaurant."

"Are you serious?" Dom sneers.

"Yeah," he says. "I went there when I was a kid. It could be like a fortress."

"Not bad," admits Quentin. "There will be a lot of food in a place that size."

"We could get swords there too," says Joey. "And armor suits."

"They don't have real swords," says Dom. "It's just a show."

"A show with real swords," insists Joey.

As ridiculous as it sounds, the idea doesn't strike me as a bad option right now. I have driven by the castle-themed restaurant numerous times. From my memory of it, I don't recall seeing many exterior windows and doors. There are also very few buildings in the area as it is divided off from the more populated shopping district by the Kennedy, a major eight-lane expressway. Unfortunately, there is nothing to keep the corpses from walking right up to the building from the parking lot.

"We might be able to get a good view of the expressway," Danielle says.

"If it's no good, we just stock up on food and keep heading away from the city," says Quentin. "Makes as much sense as anything I guess."

"We'll probably have to break in," I note. I doubt that is something we are even capable of doing. "I don't want to get there and be stuck outside."

"Leave that part to me," says Quentin. "I'll get us inside."

Again I wonder what exactly this guy did before all this. For the next five minutes, we eat mini powdered donuts and single serving loaves of banana bread and try to come up with some kind of plan to get us out of the cemetery gates. The best we can come up with is to draw the dead as far as possible from the gate to give us an opening to head out while they are distracted. Once we finish eating, we pile everything into the trunk of the police cruiser and the back of the Mercedes.

"Who gets to be the bait?" asks Quentin as I pick up the last packages of bottled water.

"I'll take the squad car," I offer when no one volunteers.

"I'll go along with you," says Danielle.

Quentin hands the gun back to me that I'd turned over to him last night and gives me one of the walkie talkies too. I wait for him to remind me not to do anything stupid, but he only gives me an appreciative nod. I haul the water over to the open trunk of the cruiser and set it down.

"I want to go with you guys," Melanie pleads. She dashes around the cruiser and wraps her arms around Danielle.

"There's more room in the other car." Danielle looks at me as she hugs the girl. She frees herself by taking hold of Mel's hands. "Listen," she soothes. "There's no seat belts in the back. It's not safe. We're just going down the road. It won't be more than a few minutes."

"No," Melanie latches on to her again. "I want to be with you guys." The young girl turns her face to show me a sulky look that my daughter has used on me a thousand times before to get what she wants. It always works. Amanda called me a pushover because I could never be the firm parent. I'd see that look and cave. I close the trunk and stare at Melanie's pouting expression.

"Hop in, kid," I relent.

Danielle stares at me doubtfully as Melanie releases her and hops in the backseat.

"It'll be fine," I assure Danielle. "Like you said, it's just a few minutes."

I settle in the seat behind the steering wheel, but I hesitate to turn the key in the ignition. Danielle sits beside me and takes a last look back up at the cemetery office.

"Are you sure we're doing the right thing?" asks Danielle.

"We have to move," I say. "I know that much." I don't seem very confident because I still have a hard time with this decision. It's not that I think we are better off in the cemetery, but we are moving in the opposite direction from where my family was when this all started. I am giving up hope of finding them alive to give myself a better chance of survival. I just saw them yesterday morning. As much as I had told myself they might be okay when I woke up and heard the radio broadcast, I realized that hope is fading. I'm also afraid of finding them. What if I manage to track down my wife or daughter, only to find they are walking corpses? I don't know if I could go on after that.

"Here we go," I say to Danielle, and start the car. I stick my arm out the window to wave to Quentin behind the wheel of the Mercedes. The circular single lane road takes us past the front gate and around to the perimeter of the graveyard. It takes me a while, but I figure out how to get the siren and lights going. That should be more than enough to draw the attention of every corpse in the area. At the far corner of the cemetery, I park the cruiser and leave the lights flashing and the siren blaring.

From where we parked, I don't have a clear view of the gate through the trees. I can see the SUV idling in front of the cemetery office. Now we wait. I open the car door and lift open the trunk. After a few moments of looking, I find some road flares at the bottom of the trunk.

I close the trunk and notice the dead are piling up along the fence near the cruiser. There must be close to a hundred undead already crowding along the barrier. The corpses in front get smashed into the iron bars from the press of bodies. Their moans grow louder now that we are so close to them; they drown out the wailing siren. They stretch their arms, their filthy hands covered in dirt and gore grasp at the air. The color of their dead eyes has started to turn milky, and their bodies give off a nauseating stench of rotten meat and excrement. I really don't enjoy being this close to such a large number of them.

Finally, the Mercedes accelerates toward the gate. Before I get back in the cruiser, I ignite a road flare and toss it near the fence. I don't know if that will hold their attention at all, but it is worth a shot if it buys us any extra time. I kill the sirens and gun the engine. The cruiser squeals around the curve near the main building and down the hill toward the front gate.

Several corpses are already limping around inside the cemetery. I jerk the wheel of the cruiser to veer around them as they launch their bodies at the sides of the car. The cruiser crunches over chunks of glass and metal strewn about the road from wrecks. Cars clog the four-lane road, but I get across it to drive on the campus lawn across the street. I follow the fresh ruts left in the turf by the tires of the Mercedes, then take a left at the light.

This road is relatively clear of cars, but the large crowd of undead that we lured to the fence are now up ahead to our left. They pour back into the street in pursuit of the first vehicle, and Quentin has to hug the far right lane to avoid them. I will have to plow through dozens of them to stay on the road. At the last second, I decide the best chance we have is to swerve the vehicle off the road to avoid them instead. The cruiser hops the curb and crashes down hard in a small drainage ditch. There is a heavy thud as Melanie smashes into the fiberglass partition between the back and front seats. For a terrifying second, the battered cruiser seems to be stuck in the soft earth, but I push the peddle as far down as it will go and the car continues up the slope into the middle of a golf course.

Not wanting to try my hand at crossing the ditch again, I accelerate down a fairway that runs alongside the road. The two-way radio crackles somewhere on the floor of the car and I hear the faint transmission of Quentin's voice. Fuck it. I don't have the time. He can lecture me all he wants later. Up ahead, sunlight glints off the aluminum roof of a large maintenance building between the fairway and the road. I speed towards it, thinking there must be an access road to the street. The gravel drive comes into view, and I breathe a sigh of relief when I see it goes clear to the road.

The cruiser fishtails after I take a hard right back onto the road. The flags atop the spires of the restaurant come into view over a copse of trees to the left. I steer around a fire truck laying on its side and blocking three lanes of the road. Then I spot the restaurant entrance up ahead. As we turn into the parking lot, I glimpse a large purple banner hanging from the roof with HELP painted across it in crude black letters. I hadn't thought of the possibility we would find anyone here, but now I had to wonder who or what might be inside.

"Mel." Danielle swivels around in her seat to peer into the rear compartment of the cruiser. "She's on the floor back there. I can't tell if she's okay," Danielle says.

The Mercedes idles in the middle of the parking lot along the south side of the building. I pull the cruiser alongside the SUV, and Danielle rolls down her window.

"Thought we might have lost you there," says Quentin. He glances at the backseat of the car and furrows his brow.

"Almost," I say. "Did you see the sign?"

"Yeah," he says. "That's why I hung back."

"We better knock first," I say. "How do we get in?"

"Service entrance," Quentin says. "Follow me."

He leads us around the back of the building and pulls up in front of some dumpsters by the service entrance. Instead of parking alongside him, I angle the cruiser the other way to create an area around the door that is blocked off by the vehicles and a pair of dumpsters. With any luck, this will keep those things off the doors awhile and maybe allow us to get back in the vehicles if we need to leave.

I get out of the car and open the back door to find Melanie on the floor of the backseat. She is out cold and has a blooming welt on her forehead. Danielle opens the rear door on the passenger side and looks her over quickly.

"Help me get her up," I ask.

"Wait," Danielle hesitates.

"What is it?" I wonder.

"Moving her might be a bad idea," Danielle explains. "It could injure her further."

"We don't have time," I sigh. "Those things aren't going to be far behind us."

Danielle bites her lip, then carefully helps me get the unconscious girl out of the car. I cradle her frail limp body, trying not to jostle her as I move toward the door.

"What happened?" Dom gasps when she sees me carrying Melanie.

"She's okay," I say calmly. "Just hit her head." I can't be sure if anything I said was true, but I hope it is. I just want to get Melanie inside and out of danger.

Quentin looks down at the girl with an expression like he tastes something bitter. He turns and is about to hammer on the door when it pops open from the inside. In the doorway, a gangly man with wiry hair and a grizzled mustache inspects us from beneath the brim of his tattered baseball cap. His gaze settles at last on the girl in my arms. A few feet behind him, a diminutive black kid with wide eyes and thick glasses shuffles his feet nervously.

A long silent moment passes before the guy with the mustache leans his back against the door to let us pass inside. "Better hurry," he urges. "A whole army of them are coming right behind you."

CHAPTER SEVEN

The heavy steel door slams shut behind us, then the room falls into total darkness for several seconds until the black kid clicks on a flashlight. The room looks like a loading bay with stacks of cardboard boxes piled high along the walls.

"This way," the guy with the mustache takes the flashlight from the kid and leads us out into a dark tunnel. An acrid scent hangs in the air. It takes a moment for me to identify what the smell is. They must keep the horses for the show inside. At least, I hope that is the cause.

"It smells like shit in here," gags Dom.

"That's just the horses," the guy with the mustache explains. "After a day or two you'll get used to the smell, and then you won't hardly notice it."

The unsteady beam of the flashlight stops and turns to illuminate a door on our right. The man with the mustache twists the handle and steps aside to let us in. A faint emergency light illuminates the room. It appears to be an employee lounge, with worn couches and half a dozen large round tables surrounded by metal folding chairs. My arms ache from carrying Mel, so I rush over to the nearest couch to set her down. Danielle kneels down beside Mel to examine her and caresses the girl's dark hair from her face. I glance around at the small kitchenette, refrigerator, and a pair of vending machines in the room. Then my gaze settles on the kid in the glasses.

"Is it just you two here?" I ask him. The question seems to startle him.

"Just us," says mustache. "I'm Chet, and that's Devin," he says jerking his head at the kid. Devin pushes his glasses up the bridge of his nose and then lowers his gaze to his black Chuck Taylor sneakers and shifts his weight from one foot to the other.

"Devin doesn't say much," Chet adds.

"Blake," I say. "You guys work here?" I probe, trying to figure out just what kind of people we are dealing with here. The two of them seem so different that I have to wonder how they wound up in this place together.

"We're the janitors," Chet explains. He glances around the room at the rest of us and his gaze pauses on Melanie. "What's wrong with the girl?" he asks.

"She just hit her head," I assure him. "It was a rough ride over here. What do you know about what's going on, Chet?"

"Not much," he sighs. "We were just working in here like usual when this all started. The manager told us he had to run home in the middle of our shift. Never heard from him again. First thing that told us something was wrong was when the power went out. I tried calling the managers and couldn't get any of them on the line. So me and Devin just waited around awhile for someone to show up. We didn't have a clue that anything was happening until we heard an explosion outside. We couldn't see shit out the front doors, so we went up top and found all hell broke loose out there."

"Up top?" I ask.

"The roof," Chet clarifies. "You can see for miles up there."

"How long has it been since you have seen anyone alive out there?" I ask.

"Not since last night," he said. "You should have seen the highway."

"What do you mean?" I ask.

Chet opens his mouth to speak, but then stops himself and shakes his head. He furrows his brow and tries to find words to articulate the events he has witnessed. "Maybe it's best if you go up and see it for yourself," he says.

"Okay," I agree. "Let's go."

Chet leads Quentin and me back out into the tunnel. There are no windows at all along the long, dark corridors. I know it makes this place safer, but it is still unnerving. We round a corner and the smell of the horse stables intensifies. I scan the doorways we pass, hoping to get a sense of the layout of the building, but it is too dark to see much. If not for the flashlight, the darkness would be nearly pitch black, and it would be impossible to find your way around.

"The lights in the cafeteria were working. Why not the rest of the building?" I ask Chet. My voice echoes off the hard surfaces in the empty hall.

"Those are the emergency lights," he explains. "They run on batteries. Some of them ran out already. I kept meaning to check them all before all this. Pretty soon we'll have to figure something else out I guess."

We round another corner, and Chet shines the flashlight along each of the doors on the left as we pass them. He stops and heads for a door with a sign depicting a stick figure using the stairs mounted in the center. We climb a dark flight of stairs to the second level. The upper floor is carpeted, with white painted walls and glass doorways that lead into a handful of offices. The arrow slit windows on this floor allow just enough sunlight inside to see, so Chet clicks off the flashlight. He leads us down the hall in the opposite direction that we walked on the lower level until we reach a room marked with a maintenance sign. Chet pushes through the door and kicks aside a rolling mop bucket that blocks the way. We ascend a set of metal stairs to the roof, and I have to shield my eyes from the blinding sunlight when the door opens.

Nothing could have prepared me for what I see from the rooftop. In both directions, thousands of abandoned cars clog the Kennedy expressway as far as the eye can see. An army of walking corpses still wanders amongst the vehicles. The scorched remains of several military Hummers form a barricade in front of the toll booths. A couple of corpses cut in half by rounds from the .50 caliber machine guns use their arms to drag what remains of their mangled bodies down the road. I can only imagine what it must have been like when this all started.

"The military started forming that roadblock over there when we first came up top." He gestures towards the toll booth. "They fought like hell, but those boys didn't last twenty minutes. Those things just swarmed them."

Across the expressway, several tall office buildings and hotels billow smoke into the sky. Corpses shamble around inside the shattered windows. The tallest building is about ten stories of reflective blue glass, but a quarter of it has been charred to ashes and collapsed. Now, it looks like something took a massive bite out of it.

"A plane came down over there last night," says Chet. He traces a line with his finger to show the path of the plane, ending at a faint cloud of smoke drifting into the sky. "Clipped the corner of the big building there and went right into that shopping mall. Must have been circling for hours until they finally run out of fuel or something."

"Jesus Christ," gasps Quentin. He leans forward and rests a palm down on the edge of the building as though to steady himself. He cups a hand to his mouth and gazes at the battle sight near the tollbooths in shock.

I cross the roof to check the other side of the building and find the undead have indeed followed us here. It's possible the corpses won't notice me up on the roof, but to be safe I crouch down behind the parapet. Chet does the same. A few dozen of the things wander across the main parking lot below. Hundreds of undead are still drifting along the road making their way toward the entrance. The first one to reach the door begins to bang against the glass and moan.

"Told you they was coming," Chet says. "Sure is a lot of them too."

"We better make sure those doors can hold them," I tell Chet. His face looks a bit pale as he stares out at the oncoming horde of the walking dead. He manages a nod, then backs away from the wall and heads back inside.

"Mind if I ask something?" Chet says as we descend the stairs to the maintenance room. "Where was it you were all headed?"

"I don't know," I tell him. "We were in the cemetery. The place was surrounded by a few hundred of those things. The fences were holding, but it didn't seem like that would last. We were hoping to find some food here and take the highway as far from the city as possible."

Chet pauses on the stairs and waits a moment for me to go on. "That's it?" he asks.

119

"Not much of a plan," I admit. "We thought it might be better where there are fewer people."

"It's just, well, we saw your cars pulling in and thought we were being rescued," Chet sighs. "Or at least, you might be headed someplace safe."

"Sorry to disappoint you," I say. "I don't know that it's safer anywhere than it is right here."

"It's alright," Chet sighs. "I shouldn't have expected as much." We follow him through the cluttered maintenance room and out into the hallway. "You and your group are welcome to stay if you want. We don't have much in the way of beds, but we have plenty of food to go around. It'll go bad before we could eat it all."

Chet flicks on the flashlight and opens the stairwell door. He leads us back down to the ground floor, through the long dark hallways and back to the employee lounge area. The others watch us enter expectantly, waiting to hear what we have to say. I don't know what to tell them anymore. Quentin settles in a chair and stares absently at a spot on the floor.

"Well?" Dom breaks the silence. "What are we doing?"

"Looks like we'll be staying here awhile," I announce. "Lot of traffic on the highways."

Dom sighs and fishes a cigarette out of the pack on the table.

"The good news is we should be safe here awhile. We're much better off," I say. My gaze moves back to Melanie lying unconscious on the couch, and it feels like I'm telling a lie. For what feels like a long time, no one speaks.

"I'm going to go reinforce the doors now," Chet says finally. "I could use a hand." Chet nods to Devin, and the kid obediently follows him out to the darkened the hallway.

"Hey, wait," Joey calls them. He sits on the edge of a table, his legs swinging slightly just above the floor.

Chet pauses in the doorway and turns to look at Joey.

"Where are the swords?" Joey asks.

Chet raises an eyebrow at the question. "In the prop room."

"I told you they were fake," Dom gloats. "Just props." She places a cigarette between her lips and lights it.

"No, no," Chet corrects her. "They're real."

"I knew it," says Joey. He pushes himself off the table and heads for the door. "Where's the prop room?"

"Come on," says Chet. "Give us a hand, and I'll show you on the way back."

Joey turns and looks at me as though asking for permission. I nod, and he smiles at Dom, then he follows Chet and Devin out the door.

"Ugh," Danielle grunts and closes the freezer door. "These ice packs are already warm." She locates a dish towel and turns on the faucet and soaks the rag in cool water before wringing it out. Danielle returns to the couch and brushes the hair from Melanie's face, then rests the damp cloth over the swollen bruise on her head.

"Has she been out this whole time?" I ask.

Danielle nods. "I don't know what else to do for her," she sighs. "If she has something other than a mild concussion..."

"Like what?" I wonder.

Danielle bites her bottom lip for a moment while she thinks. "Well," she begins hesitantly. "It could be an injury to the spinal cord. Worst case scenario would be an injury to the brain tissue. Without a CT scan or MRI though, there isn't anything I can do to help her. We just have to wait and hope she wakes up."

My stomach tightens as Danielle gives the prognosis. "You mean she might not wake up?" I ask. "Like she might die?"

"Don't think that," she says. "She could be completely fine tomorrow." Danielle sees me staring down at the unconscious teenager, and she takes hold of my arm to bring my attention to her. "Remember, you saved her life yesterday. You did everything you could to help her."

The sight of Melanie lying there is too much. I turn and pound my fist on the table behind me so hard it hurts. I don't know why I ever thought I could keep her safe.

"It's not your fault, Blake." She rests a hand on my shoulder. "I didn't want to tell you. I knew you would beat yourself up over it. Melanie will probably recover just fine."

"She'll be fine," I echo softly, not believing a word of it. I collapse into a chair beside one of the tables in the dim glow of the emergency light. I run my fingers over my unshaven facial hair. Then rest my head in my palms, feeling my unwashed hair. I still feel guilty, even though I know I couldn't have done much to prevent what had happened to the kid in the car.

"You okay?" asks Danielle.

"Yeah," I sigh. I gesture around at the room and everything. "This situation just gets better all the time, doesn't it?"

"It's not so bad here," she reasons. "Just a little dark."

"Better than sleeping with the dead," Dom agrees.

"Only two doors to worry about," Quentin adds. "No sweat."

Maybe we could be worse off than we are here. It isn't this place that bothers me so much, I realize, it's that we have no way of getting away from those things. There is nowhere left to run. We just have to wait here to be rescued, or to die of starvation.

"On the expressway, there were a couple of military vehicles," I explain. "Chet said they had tried to set up some kind of roadblock there yesterday, but I guess there were just too many of those things for them to handle."

"So what," says Quentin. "You think the military is just gone?"

"I don't know," I sigh.

"Trust me, that's not possible," insists Quentin.

"But just suppose there aren't any more civil defense forces out there. If we lock ourselves in here, no one may ever be coming to get us out," I say.

"There must be other survivors like us out there," insists Danielle. "There has to be someone who can help us."

"They are probably in the same kind of situation we are," I say. "Or much worse." I regret bringing up the scene on the highway. The truth is, I really don't want to stay here. I don't want to give up on going home and finding my family. I don't want to relinquish what little control we still have over our fate. But I don't know what else to do when every road we take leads to the same dead end.

"I wish we had a better option than staying here, but it doesn't seem like we have anything else," I admit.

"We're lucky we even made it through this so far," said Dom. "We can't keep running around the city, or we will eventually run out of luck."

There is that word again. Luck. I feel my face cringe.

Quentin walks over and pulls me up by the back of my shirt. "Come on," he said. "We need to get some real food in you, and you'll be feeling better."

I sigh and let him lead me out of the room and back down the dark hallway towards the kitchen. He clicks on a flashlight and then glances back at the break room.

"Look, man," he whispers once he won't be heard. "I get it. You're tired of trying to get somewhere and going nowhere instead."

He flashes the light around the hall. "But this here is probably as good as it gets right now. If you can't see that, it's only because you're still looking for something else, something that doesn't exist anymore."

I release a deep breath and expel all thoughts of finding some kind of normality again as the air leaves my lungs. I realize there is no going back to it. I have to figure out how to move on, even when I am trapped in the same place. As we continue down the dark hallway, Quentin directs the beam of the flashlight at the doors we pass until he locates the kitchen. We push through the sliding doors into a room full of stainless steel prep tables and appliances.

"Just what was it you did before this?" I ask Quentin.

He pulls a couple of bottles of beer from a cooler and hands me one without looking at me. He twists the cap off and gulps from the other bottle while he seems to think how or if he wants to answer me. He finishes half the bottle then wipes the moisture from his lips with the back of his palm.

"I worked in a grocery store," he grins.

"Come on," I press him. "You didn't learn to shoot like you do by working in a grocery store."

"No," he concedes. "Didn't pick that up from working there. My old man is a Navy SEAL instructor or was anyway. I was in the training program a while, too. Didn't quite have what it takes, though."

He stares down into the dark opening of the bottle of beer in his hands.

"I would have felt much better yesterday knowing we had a Navy SEAL with us," I confide.

Quentin laughs and shakes his head, and then sets the bottle of beer down on a prep counter behind him and retrieves the flashlight.

"You don't," he corrects me. He pulls open the door to a walk-in refrigerator and shines the light around at the contents.

"I'm just a washed out grocery store clerk," he explains. He hauls out a big frozen rack of ribs and sets it down next to his beer. "But I do know how to cook a mean rack of barbecue ribs."

"That's good because I'm not much of a cook," I tell him.

Quentin twists at the red knobs on the oven and considers the unlit indicator light. I wonder how he plans to cook ribs, or anything for that matter, without power. Quentin glances up around the shelves for several moments, scanning the kitchen items. He locates some large metal catering trays. With his long arms, Quentin lifts a tray off a shelf I would need a ladder to reach, and sets it down on the counter.

"So you weren't a chef," he says. He opens a drawer and glances and pushes some utensils around. "I bet you were an accountant or something like that."

"No, but you're not far off," I say. "I'm a statistician. Or was, I guess."

"Like batting averages and stuff?" he asks.

"Anything with probabilities," I say, not wanting to get into a confusing explanation. "I make predictions based on statistical analysis."

"Sounds pretty boring," he says. "No offense."

"It can be," I shrug. I'm used to that reaction.

"Would have been helpful if someone could have predicted this shit," he muses.

"I'm pretty sure people did predict this kind of thing. They have for the last fifty years. It was a cultural premonition of sorts."

"So what, those people saw this coming?" Quentin locates a large kitchen knife in a drawer and removes it and sets it on the counter, then opens the walk-in refrigerator and disappears inside.

"Well, sort of," I say.

"You mind holding the light?" he asks and hands me the flashlight. I direct the beam while he shuffles around some boxes on the shelves, inspecting their labels.

"It's like someone writing about a plane crashing into a skyscraper before it happens," I continue. "It's just a story to the writer, but then it really happens."

"But that's just a coincidence," he says.

"Right," I agree.

He stops searching through the contents of the fridge and scratches his scalp. "You lost me, man," he sighs.

"A long time ago, I read this book," I explain. "The author researched a history of cultural premonitions and then theorized that perhaps when enough people start to think that a specific kind of disaster will happen, inevitably it does happen."

Quentin grabs a couple more racks of ribs from the fridge while he considers this then shakes his head. He moves through the doorway and sets them down on the prep table. "Are you saying, we like, created this, or something?" he asks.

"We don't know that. We only know we created the concept of walking dead bodies that go around and eat people a long time ago. Then one day, seemingly without explanation, they are suddenly real."

"Sounds like some bullshit to me," he says as he moves back into the walk-in fridge. I follow him with the flashlight beam as he searches the racks of meats and produce.

"Me too, but I've always been a skeptic about everything," I admit. "Now, I'm not so sure, though. I see there are these things out there that defy any reasonable explanation. Dead bodies aren't supposed to get up and walk around. It's not possible according to science. But, nevertheless, it is happening. So we, at least, have to accept that we don't understand as much as we thought."

Quentin lifts a big cardboard box from the shelf and carries it out on his shoulder and sets it down beside the ribs. He slices open the packing tape on the box with the kitchen knife, then sets it down and retrieves his beer.

"It don't really matter," Quentin says finally. "No point in wondering why things are the way they are, man. You'll just go crazy doing that now." He leans against the fridge and drinks the rest of the bottle down. Quentin's dark eyes consider me, and then he shakes his head. He sets his beer down and resumes opening the box on the counter. "Premonitions," he laughs. "You think too much, man. For real."

For the first time that I can remember, I don't see the point in trying to figure out the answer. Even if I can explain what was happening and why, it wouldn't change anything. The realization makes me feel helpless and uncomfortable. I look around for something to do but have no idea how to help Quentin cook without a stove or even a microwave. Nothing works anymore. "I'm going to see if they need help with the barricades," I tell him as I head toward the hallway.

"It's cool," he says as he lights a burner for the catering trays. "I got this."

At the rear doors, I find Chet and Devin have already stacked tons of heavy boxes in front of the loading bay door. If I didn't already know there was an exit there, I would never guess there was one behind the wall of cardboard. It doesn't seem possible that the undead could force their way inside. Getting back out might not be a possibility, but surely we can wait it out until they starve, freeze in the harsh Chicago winter, or rot away. I wonder how long that would take.

"Think we got it blocked pretty good," says Chet. "Nothing's getting in."

Looking at the barricade, I let out a long sigh as though I'd been holding my breath for more than a day. We will all be safe here for a little while. Maybe even for a long time. I can let my guard down for a bit, for now. With that realization, I suddenly feel very drained. I didn't sleep more than two or three hours last night. The stress and lack of sleep are finally catching up to me. The flashlight flickers and then goes black.

"Got some more batteries back in the lunchroom," he says.

"What happens when we use them all?" I wonder.

"We can use some of the propane torches they got around here for the show," says Chet.

"Good idea," I agree. "Thanks again for taking us in."

"It's nothing, really. Not like this place is ours. We just work here. Besides, it would get pretty lonely here with just the two of us."

I can suddenly smell the aroma of cooked meat drifting in from the kitchen. "Quentin is getting some food together. We haven't had a real meal since this started. Hope you don't mind."

"I could eat a horse right now," says Chet. "I was kind of afraid to raid the kitchen yesterday in case this blew over. That's probably not going to happen."

"I am going to see about rounding our group up. How about you get those torches, and we'll meet back in the arena," I say. "You can get to know the rest of our group a bit better."

In the break room, I find Danielle whispering quietly beside Melanie. "Some studies suggest that patients who aren't conscious can still pick up the conversations around them," Danielle says. "A lot of doctors believe it helps recovery too. Keep her company for me for a minute."

Danielle leaves the break room, and I'm sitting alone with the girl. I try to think of something that I could say, but I can't. Finally, I manage to say, "I've got a little girl, too."

I don't even know this child, so I try to close my eyes and imagine what I would say to Abby if I could. "I wish you were never left all alone out there in this chaos. I want to make everything better, but I can't."

I open my eyes, wanting to believe I am going to look down and see Abby there, but it isn't Abby. Just some kid I don't really know. Then I realize the thing that I am thinking about the most is what I would do if she opens her eyes right now, but isn't alive anymore. I put my hand on her chest and feel the slowed thudding of a heartbeat like the seconds of a clock counting down to zero. I wonder if Danielle was thinking the same thing and that was why she wanted me to stay with her. Suddenly her body starts to convulse. She tilts her head back, and her teeth start chattering. Her eyes roll back in her skull. I use my body to prevent her from falling off the couch, but I am afraid to touch her. She is coming back. Or, this is some kind of seizure.

"Danielle!" I yell.

I reach behind my back for the gun stowed in my waistband. I grip the handle and flip the safety off as I stand up, and then point it down at the girl's face. Her convulsing movements lose some intensity, then slow to nothing more than erratic twitches. After what seems like forever, she finally becomes still.

I call to Danielle again, not taking my eye off the girl. Feeling my palm slick with sweat around the handle of the gun, I wait to see her move or open her eyes or something.

"What happened?" asks Danielle as she comes back into the room. She is staring at me, wondering why I am pointing the gun at the girl who looks just the same as when she left her ago. I hear footsteps in the hallway. Devin and Chet appear in the doorway behind Danielle.

"I don't know," I say. "She was having a seizure or something."

Without waiting to hear more, Danielle hurries to the couch, reaching her fingers to Melanie's neck to check the girl for a pulse.

"She's okay," Danielle says. She looks at me still standing there with the gun. "Please put that thing away."

I flip the safety and tuck the gun in the back of my waistband. "I thought she might be gone, or was coming back. I was so close to pulling the trigger."

"It's okay now," says Danielle. "Just relax, I'll take it from here."

"Maybe we should restrain her," I suggest. "Just in case."

"I don't know if that's a good idea. She shouldn't be restrained if she is having seizures."

"But what if she doesn't make it, and turns into one of those things," I say.

"If she has a brain injury already, I'm not even sure she could come back."

It makes sense, but she could still move her limbs during that seizure, so I wasn't so sure I believed it.

"We just need to make sure someone keeps an eye on her," says Danielle. "We need to do that anyway."

"Alright," I say. "But you should take a break and eat something. Quentin made some real food. I'll keep an eye on her."

Danielle looks at me uncertainly. I'm guessing she is a little uneasy about finding me so close to shooting a little girl that was still alive. "You need to eat, too. Go ahead, I can wait until later."

"I can stay with her." I turn to look at Devin. "My little sister has epilepsy," he says. "So I know what to do if it happens again."

"I'll help keep an eye on her too," says Chet. "Just need to turn the horses out in the arena first. They been cooped up for almost two days now."

"Thanks," says Danielle. "Just call if you need anything."

I take the gun back out from my waistband, flip the safety off, and set it on the table. "You know what you have to do if you need it?" I ask Devin.

He looks at the gun fearfully but nods his head.

"Don't touch it unless you need it," I say. I reach into the duffel from the security office, fish around through some batteries and junk food until I find the other Glock in the bottom of the bag.

"I can handle myself," he says firmly. He shoots me a look to tell me he definitely is not as much of a kid as I think he is.

CHAPTER EIGHT

"I wonder where they went off to," I say to Danielle. We sit in the arena, watching Chet lead the horses out by the dim glow of the flashlight.

"Joey is probably off playing with a sword somewhere," Danielle muses. "And Dom just seems like she is glad to have some space. I don't think she likes any of us very much."

Three horses that Chet had lead out so far trot around the sand floor of the arena. They toss their heads back and prance around, glad to be free finally from the stalls. Danielle pours herself a glass of red wine and watches them move. We glimpse each horse only for a brief moment as it eclipses the beam of light then vanishes again into the darkness.

"I used to love horses," she says. She sets the bottle down and takes a sip from her glass. "That one there," she points at one of the horses. "He reminds me a little of one of the horses we had back in Pennsylvania."

"You had horses?" I ask.

"My family used to raise them. Then times got tough, and they had to sell them all."

"Did you ride?"

"Sure," she says. "Wouldn't be much point in having them if I didn't ride them."

"So, why don't you love them anymore?" I ask.

"Because I don't have any to love," she says. "But I guess now I can have any of these."

"I used to love horses, too," I say. "Well, betting on them anyway."

"Was that why you were at the track yesterday?"

"No, I was heading to give a lecture in the city."

"A lecture? About what?"

"About betting on horses."

"Really?" she laughs, not at all taking me serious now.

"Really," I say. I go on to explain about my book and about how I used statistical probabilities to bet on horse races.

"I didn't know they taught classes on gambling at college," she says. "And to think I was wasting my money trying to become a successful doctor when I could have learned how to do something like that instead."

"Seems like my skills won't have much value now, though, given the state of things," I say. For a second, I had been able to forget about all the horrific things going on outside. I was enjoying just talking normally to another human being. But there is no evading the current situation for very long. No matter what we may try to talk about, it always leads the conversation back to the death of everything that mattered to us, and the rise of the dead.

"Looks like I might have to find a new line of work," I say, trying not to totally kill our brief illusion of normality. I take a sip from my glass of wine. Then I realize there is no telling how long we'll have to live, and I take another long drink and empty the glass. I pour another for myself and fill up Danielle's glass.

For a long moment, we just sit watching the horses. For all the time I had spent around them, betting on them, studying their best times and whatnot, this might be the most I've ever really enjoyed looking at them.

"Maybe I'll raise horses," I say.

Danielle smiles and takes a sip of her wine.

"Alright," says Quentin. He steps down the stairs carrying an enormous tray of ribs. "Who's ready for some real food?"

"Finally," teases Danielle. "I could eat a horse."

Joey trails in behind him carrying a big tray with giant roasted chicken drumsticks and wings. He now has a sword sheathed at his belt that clangs on each step as he moves down the stairs. Then Dom appears behind him with some golden herb-roasted potatoes and a stack of plates. Joey plops down on the seat next to me while Dom joins Quentin in the row in front of us. All the seats face the arena, so the three of us in the back are facing the back of their heads.

"We wondered where you two were hiding," I say to Dom and Joey. "Glad Quentin found someone that isn't as inept in the kitchen as me."

"Pssht," Quentin laughs. "They didn't help with shit. I just passed them in the hall on my way with the ribs and told them to bring the rest."

I look at Joey, but he is too busy smiling at the back of Dom's head to even notice me. Then I study Dom, and I realize her blonde hair seems a bit messier than it had been awhile ago. She is trying to ignore Joey. She takes a bite of her potato and sighs. It seems like she can feel him staring at her intently.

It doesn't take me very long to put it together. Something definitely happened between these two while they were off in the building somewhere. Joey nudges my arm with his elbow, then jerks his head at Dom. He mimes a few sexual thrusts in her direction and grins.

Danielle, watching this from the other side of me, laughs so hard she sprays a mouthful of wine on Quentin.

"What the hell!" Quentin jolts upright.

"What is he doing?" Dom asks me. Then her eyes dart to Joey, who sits there smirking and about to burst. "Shut up," she tells him. She turns back around and fiddles with some of the food on her plate.

"I'm really sorry," Danielle apologizes to Quentin.

Quentin looks at Joey, and then Dom. He sits down and grabs up a napkin and wipes at the wine on his arms and neck.

We all resume our meal quietly except Joey. After a minute or so he mumbles, "I banged the lesbian."

Dom drops her leg of roasted chicken on the plate with a thud and buries her face in her palms. No one dares laugh until Quentin with a big mouthful of chicken begins to chuckle, and shakes his head.

"Idiot," says Dom. She turns around to face Joey. "I'm clearly not a lesbian."

"Not anymore," he smiles.

"Ugh," she glances around at the rest of us. "Go ahead laugh it up. If I'm going to die here, I am at least getting a little before I go."

"Little?" says Quentin but before anyone can begin to laugh, we hear screaming and then the sound of the gun going bang, bang, bang.

I push my chair back from the table and hurry up the stairs. I remove the gun from my waistband and flip off the safety as we run down the hall. Quentin holds the flashlight and scans the hallway as we race back to the break room. The employee lounge is dark and empty. The emergency light has shut off. Devin and Melanie are both gone. By the glow of the flashlight, we can see some drops of blood on the floor trailing out toward the hall.

"What the fuck happened?" asks Quentin. He follows the blood with the flashlight, then shines it around the empty hallway in the opposite direction from which we approached.

"It's Melanie," I say.

To make things worse, the beam of the flashlight dims, then flickers. Quentin shakes it, and the light comes back for a moment before we are submerged in total blackness.

"Where are the batteries?" I ask. Someone bumps into me, I can't even guess who, that's how dark it is with no windows in this place.

"I left them in the duffel bag over here," says Dom. She trips over a piece of furniture, and it crashes loudly on the tile floor. "Damn it, I can't see a thing."

Another scream echoes from farther off in the building.

"Did you find it?" I ask Dom.

"No," she whispers. "The fucking bag isn't here."

"Are you sure?"

"No, I can't see shit," she says. "It's not where I left it."

We hear a hoarse moan coming from the other direction in the hall now.

"Keep looking," I say. "We have to try and help them out there. Dom, keep this door shut unless you are absolutely sure it's safe to let anyone in, even one of us." I stop when I hear another noise in the hall.

"The horses," says Danielle. "They're loose."

The clomping of hooves on the tile floor gets louder and louder as the horse rushes by the doorway. I can hear the heavy, deep breathing as it passes.

"Man, this is fucked up," Joey whimpers.

"Shut up," says Quentin. "Blake, we can't just stand here."

"Okay, okay," I say. "Danielle come with me to check the stables for Chet. You guys see if you can track down Devin."

"I don't think we should be splitting up," says Quentin.

"I don't like it either, but this place is too big for that. We have to cover more ground or we won't find either of them before it's too late."

Even though I can't see him, the prolonged silence tells me he still isn't crazy about any of it. Finally, Quentin mutters, "C'mon dumbass," and we listen as he hustles off down the hall alongside Joey.

"You ready?" I ask Danielle.

"No," she whispered. "But we have to go." I hear her tell Dom she'd be closing the door and then the soft click of the lock snapping into place.

We head the opposite way down the hall that Quentin and Joey had gone. Danielle rests a hand on my shoulder to keep track of my movements in the blackness. I squint my eyes trying to make out anything I can, not just looking for a human shape, but anything I might bump into that would make a noise and give away our location. I try to remember where the door is that leads to the paddocks, but I only remember the layout vaguely. I am mostly following the smell of hay and horse shit. My palms get slick with sweat. I try to move steadily, but my muscles tremble from the terror.

I notice Danielle's grip tighten on my shoulder. I wish I didn't have to bring her along, but I may not be able to do any of this alone. Danielle is the only person among us that might have any idea how to corral the loose horses. She is also the only one that can help if someone is injured.

I ease over towards the wall on my left, feeling my way down the hall with my left hand and with my right I am pointing the gun at a wall of blackness. I pause when I feel the cold, steel doorknob.

I really just want to try and call out to Chet, but I don't dare. I don't even know for sure this is the right door, or what else might be around to hear me. I turn the handle slowly, and ease the door open with the weight of my body. The smell of horses wafts over me. For a moment, we just stand in the doorway listening.

I hear the dry, scraping hiss of straw pushed around the floor. There is something in there, which I can only hope is just a horse. I try to squint, but it's useless. I could wave my hand a few inches in front of my face right now and fail to see it. We creep forward down the aisle. I can hear the heavy hooves of a horse in one of the stalls. Faint vibrations emanate through the concrete floor whenever the huge animal moves. There are a few sudden thuds, then a loud bang. Maybe it kicked a stall or ran into something. It must be spooked. I know I am. Since there seems to be no reaction to the sound, I start to feel confident there is no one else in the stable with us. I move a little more boldly down the center aisle between the stalls. "Chet" I hiss into the darkness, but there is no answer.

I lower the gun and finally feel a little release in the tension of my muscles. I can feel the hot breath of the horse on my face, so I know it must be holding its head out in the aisle just a few inches beside me.

"Easy, gal," I hear Danielle whisper, and I realize she is calming the mare by stroking her nose.

The next thing I know, I'm laying flat on my ass. It takes me a second to figure out how I got knocked down. I thought I heard a gunshot but can't be sure. The horse is gone. It must have gotten spooked by the gunshot and came crashing out, knocking us down. I hear a nearby moan. I feel around in the dark for Danielle, finally touching what I think is her arm.

"Are you hurt?" I whisper.

"I don't know," she groans. "I think I'm okay."

"Come on, let's get back to the room." I hold her arm and lead the way back down the row of paddocks. Instead of total blackness, there is just the faintest trickle of light now spilling from an open doorway across the hall that leads to the arena. Silently, we edge close to the door one slow step at a time.

In the center of the arena floor is the flashlight, abandoned on the ground. Dust from the sandy surface plays in the beam of light and swirls off into the darkness. A few feet from the origin of the light, there's an unmoving form that partially blocks the beam. It can only be a body lying on the ground. One of the horses I think at first, but then I realize the body is too small.

"Who is it?" asks Danielle.

"I can't tell," I say. "We need to get that flashlight."

I take a couple of the steps that lead down to the arena. Six-foot high walls surround the oval dirt floor. I stop to scan for another way down other than jumping the barrier. The only other access seems to be the tunnel that opens under the grandstands on our right. I throw one leg over the edge and lower myself down to the sand. I turn around and grab Danielle around the waist to help her down. We both turn back around to see the figure slowly rising from the ground. The person is hunched on their hands and knees now. I still can't tell who it is, or if they are alive or dead. I watch as the dark shape lurches upright, then rises to stand in the beam of the flashlight. I see the black Converse shoes.

"Devin," I whisper, but there is no response. He breathes a quiet moan as he takes a step toward us. I reach behind my back and feel the place where the gun should be. I must have dropped it when the horse knocked us over in the paddocks. I don't dare try and make a move on the flashlight without anything to defend myself. I grab Danielle's wrist, and she follows me up the slight embankment as we enter the blackness under the grandstands. The tunnel curves around to the right. We emerge back up near the door to the stables. We hurry back down the aisles between the stalls and feel around on the floor where I had fallen.

"The gun," I panic. "I can't find it." I find a handful of manure and curse. I wipe the bulk of it off on the ground and start feeling around again.

"Got it," says Danielle.

We get up and head back towards the hall, turning right to trace our route back to the employee room. I debate going back to look for Devin first and put him down, but I doubt he is where we last saw him. More likely he has made his way to the dark tunnel and is going to find his way to us soon. Better to regroup first and figure out who else is still alive.

The door to the employee lounge is wide open. We ease along the wall, and I peer around the corner of the doorway to recon the room. Inside it's still too dark to see much of anything, but it seems empty. I hold the gun out, pointing it at nothing.

"Dom?" I whisper.

A weak groan breaks the silence. I'm about to start spraying bullets when I hear a voice mutter a couple of profanities. It sounds like Chet. I step into the room and move in the direction of his voice. Danielle follows me in and closes the door behind her.

The room is in shambles, and I run into overturned tables and chairs in the dark. Making so much noise is not a good idea, but unavoidable nonetheless.

"Here," grunts Chet. He shoves something off from on top of him in the dark, and I reach down to find him slumped against the wall.

"What happened?" asks Danielle, working her way over.

"That blonde bitch," he laughs. "Cracked me on the head and took off. I think she took the flashlight and the gun."

"What?" I ask because I can't believe what he is telling me. Dom is a little cold, definitely tough, but it doesn't seem that she could possibly be mean or stupid enough to do that. "Did she say anything?" I ask him.

"No, I just came in quiet. Horse got away from me when I first heard the gunshots. I went after it but left the damn arena gate open. Now they're all out there. Came back here and thought the room was empty."

I have a better guess at what caused Dom to attack Chet. Maybe she had attacked him before she knew he was alive. Alone, in darkness, I might very well have done the same. Better not to take any chances when it's your life you're protecting.

Danielle crouches down, checking a gash on the back of Chet's skull as much as the darkness allows. "I can't see a thing," she complains.

"I'm fine," Chet says. He pushes her hand away, and then he grabs my shoulder and gets to his feet. He hangs on a moment longer as though he needs a few seconds to steady himself.

"If you can move we need to find everyone."

"Have you seen Devin?" he asks.

"Yeah," I say, unsure how to relay our encounter with Devin. I pause to look for the words but realize there isn't any need to go on. By the tone of my voice or the fact that Devin isn't with us, Chet pieces it together.

"Damn it all," he sighs.

I am about to say something to try and get us moving again when I hear someone running down the hall, screaming. I creep over to the door, but I can't see anything in the darkness.

"They're inside!" Joey screams. I catch a glimpse of him moving toward us fast in the dark. Every few steps the stupid sword he is carrying clangs against the floor or some object. I expect him to stop, but he sprints right past us. He turns back and yells to us. "Hurry! She opened the damn—"

He grunts, then I hear the sound of his body falling on the floor.

"Joey?" calls Danielle.

I start to run after him, but I hear a harsh rasp, and then Joey screams. He must have run right into the thing that used to be Devin. I pull the gun out but can't find a target. I just point at sounds in the black hall, but the echo makes it difficult to pinpoint. The sword is clanging around on the floor. Joey utters a few curses, and it sounds like he is fighting the thing off for a moment. Then he screams again, a long screeching howl that suddenly stops. I fire a few rounds, hoping I hit one or both of them.

I turn and head the other way down the hall, keeping the gun at the ready. There are at least three corpses loose in here now, and Dom and Quentin are missing. I also can only guess what Joey was trying to tell us, but it sounded like we might have bigger problems as well. I am moving a little faster now even though I still can't see a damn thing, but I want to put some distance between us and the scene down the hall. It won't be long before one or both of them are up again and looking for us. I don't know how, but they seem, even in total darkness, to be able to track us by some sense.

We round a corner and approach the loading bay. I press my ear against the cold steel of the door, but can't hear anything except the pulse of blood being pumped rapidly to my brain. Without realizing it until that moment, I'd already made up my mind we were going to try and get to the cars and get the hell out of there. I have the keys to the cruiser in my pocket. I don't want to leave Quentin behind, but things are going downhill in here real fast.

I step back and slowly push open the door. An amber light washes over my face, blinding me for a moment. It takes me a second to realize the light is from the setting sun. The outer doors are wide open. The door handle is ripped from my hand. Two corpses tumble through, tackling me on the floor before I can even react. I start kicking and throwing fists and elbows. Danielle manages to knock one off of me by kicking it in the head. Chet grabs on to the handlebar of the door and is using all his weight to try and pull it shut or, at least, keep out other corpses that are trying to squeeze through the doorway. I grab the disgusting hair of the dead woman on top of me and start pulling it to the side to try and roll her off. As soon as I make some progress, the clump of blood-crusted hair comes out, and she plunges back down, her teeth finding a home on the side of my face.

I close my eyes, waiting for the pain, expecting it even. I scream so loud I don't even hear the sound of the gun going off. I feel the splatter of lukewarm gore paint one side of my face, and then I feel the dead weight of her body pressing down against me. I open my eyes and shove her off.

Quentin helps Chet pull the door closed, but two of the things have their bodies halfway inside. Several more have their faces or arms in the doorway. I kick one of the things in the face, pushing it back. Another one fills in the gap. They claw at us. Their jaws snap at our arms and legs. Quentin keeps adjusting his grip to avoid their teeth while trying not to lose hold of the handle. We can't hold them off much longer. They are coming in.

"Forget it, man," Quentin screams. "Run."

The front door is heavily barricaded. I doubt we have time to clear the doors and escape before they are on us. It's also possible, even likely, that there are just as many outside that door, too. We have to go up.

"The roof," I say. "We have to make a run for it."

On a three count, Chet and Quentin release the door, and we take off down the long hall. We go back around the corner, and I can see the tide of the undead pouring down the corridor about thirty yards behind us. They pack the passage from wall-to-wall and continue to pile in through the open loading doors, blotting out the incoming light with their bodies.

When we round the corner we are submerged again in the darkness. Devin or Joey could be anywhere around here, but there's no time for being cautious. There are even more of them on our trail now. We pass the employee lounge, and I hear a faint grunt then someone falls over. Quentin swings the light around, and I see Danielle a few feet behind me, laying on her back in a daze. Joey's corpse crawls toward her on the floor. It claws at her while struggling to get to its knees. It grabs at the hem of her shirt, then lunges and grabs at her breast and pulls it's body on her. I kick him as hard as I can in the face, the force of the blow drives his skull back into the wall behind him.

"Keep going," I wave to Quentin. He turns to leave, but the flashlight falls on a bloodstained corpse several paces away.

"Shit," Quentin says as Devin's corpse flails his dripping red arms at him. Quentin steps to the side and the thing crashes into Chet's lower legs. They tumble to the floor. Chet is immediately screaming in pain. I hear his voice intensify when the teeth dig into his flesh. Quentin gets the light steady and fires off two rounds into the corpse on top of Chet.

I struggle to get Danielle on her feet. Even when she opens her eyes, she is still dizzy. The undead swarm rounds the dark corner, and I can hear them closing in on us. Quentin scoops Chet up off the ground and tosses him over his shoulder.

"Come on," urges Quentin.

"Go," I wave him on. I wrap Danielle's arm over my shoulders to help support her. We advance down the dark tunnel, but I can't keep pace with Chet and Quentin. I can only hope we are moving fast enough to stay ahead of the undead.

From somewhere behind us, an explosion rocks the whole building. The foundation trembles and I nearly lose my footing. The blast jars Danielle and she removes her arm from my shoulder. I look back and can see a burning light up the hallway around the corner. A second later, I feel a rush of heat and smell rotten flesh burning. Plaster and dust snow down from the ceiling above us. The closest corpses don't even notice. They just keep pursuing. We continue running. I have no idea where Quentin and Chet have gone. I try to remember how we got up to the roof before, but it's impossible to tell where we are in the dark.

We round another corner and can see the front entrance of the building at the far end of the corridor. The barricade there is still holding up, but faint light flickers as figures assault the glass doors. The stairway should be about halfway down the hall, I think. I slow down enough to be sure I don't pass it.

"Here, Danielle," I call out after I spot the stairway door. I latch onto the handle as a bright flash blinds me. The ground disappears beneath my feet, and then everything goes black. My whole body aches and my ears are ringing. I open and close my eyes but everything is still dark. I wonder vaguely if I'm blind.

"Danielle," I groan. I can barely hear myself, so I say it again. I crawl around in the dark, feeling my way through the dust, stone and rubble along the floor. I feel a hand and grab it thinking I found Danielle, but it's just a severed hand blown off one of the undead. Hands hook around my arm and pull me up, and I yank my arm free, but they latch on again and pull me close. I just want to give up, and let the dead take me right here.

"Get up!" Danielle yells in my ear. I am so relieved I find the strength to get to my feet, and we stumble through the door to the stairs, collapsing on the floor.

"You're fine," Danielle assures me. "Let's go." I cling to the railing and haul myself up the stairs to the second floor. We push through the door at the top of the stairs and find a gaping hole at the far end of the hall above the entrance. I can see the light from outside. It's a relief to know my eyes still work. But it is also pretty clear to me now that someone was blowing holes in the building with bombs or something. In a second, I start to hear gunfire outside, but I can tell it isn't Quentin. These are automatic weapons. I hear something else too, a great whirring noise coming from the far end of the building.

"A helicopter," says Danielle.

It is a helicopter. There's no mistaking it. I want to believe we are being rescued, but it seems impossible. If it was a rescue, why are they attacking the building. I struggle for a moment to make sense of any of it, but then I hear the door to the stairwell on the floor below us slam against the wall. We round the corner and move quickly down the long hallway. We reach the maintenance room and head for the set of stairs that goes up to the roof. I push the handle to open the hatch and am staring at the nasty end of the biggest freaking gun I've ever seen in my life.

"Get back!" The soldier holds the gun on me until he is sure I am not a threat. I just keep my hands up. I am still in disbelief at the sight of the soldiers, but can't help wondering if they are actually here under orders, or if this is some rogue military unit looking out for themselves. He looks me up and down then says into a mic on his helmet, "Team leader, we got two more souls. Sending them up top."

I finally relax a bit, slowly lowering my hands.

"Is there anyone else alive?" he asks.

"I don't know," I say.

He seems only vaguely interested in my response. He jerks his head at the door to indicate he wants us to get moving. Danielle follows me up the stairs past the squad of soldiers getting ready to go into the building. I wonder why they bother when no one else is inside. I watch them file through the doorway as we step onto the roof. Another squadron has taken up defensive positions behind the numerous air conditioning units interspersed along the roof. I see not one, but three helicopters at the far end of the building, and one is still circling the building laying down fire all around it.

I spot Chet and Quentin in one of the helicopters on the building, and we hurry over. One of the soldiers is leaning into Quentin's ear and telling him something that makes him smile. Chet sits in the chopper while a medic bandages the bite wound on his arm.

"What's going on?" I ask Quentin.

"We got lucky," he says. "They didn't even know we were here. Just stopped because of all the food in this place."

That explains what they are still doing inside. We get into the helicopter and Quentin tells me it was some kind of stealth Blackhawk, which is why we didn't notice until they were on top of us.

"Why were they bombing us?" I ask him.

"They weren't trying to bomb us. They were sealing off the points of entry to keep more corpses from getting in."

As I watch the soldiers start coming out, burdened with boxes of food, Quentin tells us the rest of the details he's heard from the military.

"They are taking us back to Great Lakes Naval Station. It's safe there. They are fighting back. They're going to take back the city block by block. They had people just start showing up yesterday, so the whole place turned into a refugee camp. It's fortified for five blocks all the way to the lake shore. Hospital and everything. They got power and running water, too."

It sounds too good to be true. After the last 36 hours, I have a hard time believing that any place is safe anymore. I think of all those people around us at the racetrack when this whole thing started, how many didn't make it. The naval station can't be any worse than what we've already been through.

We lift off and I watch the building recede below us. Once we are in the air, I can see the massive amount of undead surrounding the building now, drawn to all the activity. I notice the Mercedes is gone from the back of the building. I guess Dom made it out of there after all. In some ways, I don't blame her for looking out for herself. But she better hope she never sees my face again.

CHAPTER NINE

The sun sets at our backs as we fly low and fast to the darkening east. I started off just trying to get home, to find my family. Instead, I find myself steadily being pulled farther away from everything that matters. My old life is just a memory, turning to ashes as quickly as the burning city I watch below. Entire neighborhoods are still blazing. Cinders coil into the sky from a building across the expressway, and then it collapses before my eyes. There are so many signs on the rooftops of houses. Most just say HELP or ALIVE. Some of these buildings are on fire as well, and clearly, whoever was alive to make those signs isn't alive anymore.

The Chicago skyline comes into view, just a silhouette of a city against the cooling sky. Looking at it gives me a chill. Instead of the usual electric glow of the city, there are only the fires. One building, maybe the television network, is like a giant torch in the sky. Near the airport, a jetliner that crash-landed on the highway left a smoldering trail of carnage.

The Blackhawk banks and my stomach turns. I start to feel sick. I lean over and throw up on the floor. Everyone looks at me but says nothing. It might be that I have never flown in a helicopter before, but I think something else is what is really making me sick. The scent of things that should never burn fills my nostrils. It's the smell of chemicals, rubber, plastic, and flesh roasting together in an acrid symphony. It's even worse up here in the air.

Finally, the lakeshore spreads before me. The dark surface of the water is massive. The lake extends to the horizon and suddenly vanishes into the night sky. It's like I am looking at the edge of the earth. I know that science would say this is not possible, but neither is dead people that get up and walk around.

We touch down in the middle of an oval track. No one is jogging around it anymore. It has become a small airfield for any aircraft that can manage a landing. Aside from the helicopters, there is a handful of recreational aircraft, a small commuter plane, and a couple of fighter jets.

We step onto the ground amidst a flurry of activity. A refrigerated truck rolls up behind the last helicopter and the soldiers hustle to load up the food. An officer in a pressed white uniform and white hat pulls up in a golf cart and immediately approaches Quentin and leans close to his ear to say something over the noise of the vehicles. The officer waves us over indicating we should get in the golf cart. He stops Chet and points him to an ambulance up near the other end of the track.

Quentin slides in the front seat with the officer, while Danielle and I face the opposite way in the back. We exit the track to a parking lot overloaded with cars, tents, and exhausted looking people. They mill around and choke on the smoky air.

I turn and ask the officer where we are going.

"Captain Black's office is just up ahead," he says, pointing out a long, white four-story building to the left. I remember seeing it as we approached through the air. Snipers perch along the rooftop at intervals, and spotlights sweep across a marble courtyard surrounded by manicured trees and shrubs. From the Blackhawk, I'd seen the giant red and gold star emblazoned into the center of the grounds, lit up like a beacon by the spotlights as though it signified something important. Maybe it just made the place easier for the pilots to find.

I want to ask who Captain Black is, but Quentin looks back and tells me.

"My father." He smiles, an expression I haven't seen on anyone recently. "He's alive."

We follow the officer through the clean lobby, up two flights of stairs and down a long, bright hallway. He taps a couple of times on the window before leading us in. Captain Black, a taller, older version of his son rises behind his desk. He has dark circles around his eyes. An ashtray full of cigarettes sits next to an empty mug with half a dozen brown rings staining the interior. Quentin steps around the desk, and his father stands up and holds out his hand for Quentin to shake. Quentin looks down at the hand before him as though it held a losing wager slip. Then he grips the hand and returns his father's gaze.

"I knew you would be okay," says Captain Black. "I never doubted my boys would round you up eventually, and here you are." His tone is almost condescending, as though he alone was responsible for his son being alive. To think of what he had gone through to get here, to the only person he had left in the world, and greeted with a handshake. It made me dislike the man immediately.

"Good to see you too, sir," says Quentin.

Sir? The sudden change in Quentin is striking. He stands more rigid and upright as though at constant attention. I try to catch his eyes but notice they only glaze over everything, as if he is subconsciously trying to avoid seeing everything around him. My hands clench as I watch. We could all be dead tomorrow. This old man has the chance to reunite with his child against all odds, and yet, he seems indifferent.

"Have a seat, please," he says to me and Danielle and gestures to a few chairs across the desk. "I suppose I owe you two my gratitude as well for helping my son along the way."

"Not at all," I say. "If anything, Quentin saved our asses more than a few times."

"Very good," he grumbles. "My boy always means well." He sits back and retrieves a box of cigarettes from the desk. He puts one between his teeth and brings a flame to it as he takes a long draw. He continues to talk to Danielle and me directly, acting as though his son were but another piece of furniture in the office.

"Welcome to Great Lakes. I am sure you both must have a lot of questions, most of which I can't answer, so I will just brief you on our status." He paused to take another long drag from the cigarette.

"This installation represents the only territory under government control in the state. We have running water, and power to four of our primary buildings. We have fortified the area from Nimitz hospital to the lakeshore, approximately fifteen square miles. However, we have suffered heavy casualties in the process. About four thousand of our active duty personnel are still ready for action. Though that same number are injured, and nearly twice that many killed in action or missing and presumed dead."

"We have a civilian population close to ten thousand. If they can make it here, we let them in. However, we do not have the assets needed for any search and rescue operations. All our operational resources are deployed for perimeter security or procurement of provisions. To be blunt, we have more mouths than we are equipped to feed."

He pauses to suck on the cigarette again.

"Our next initiative is to reorient our civilian population to combat support roles. This is the only way to maintain the troop levels needed for security. Everyone here must learn to fight, every man, woman, and child. That being said, I am glad to have you all on board here."

He tapped out the cigarette in the ashtray and rose to indicate the completion of his briefing.

"Does anyone have any idea what's causing this?" asks Danielle.

"That's not something I can answer. I am just a soldier, Miss…"

"Danielle," she says.

"Danielle. All we know for sure is that it isn't some infection. The initial fears of a spreading pandemic only exacerbated the situation. It is, as of now, still an unexplained occurrence."

"That doesn't make any sense," she insists.

"I told you everything I know," he sighs.

"How can we find out if someone is here?" I ask him.

"We have yet to establish a protocol to document incoming personnel. Frankly, it's low on the list of priorities. It's not such a big place. If you ask around you will find them. Assuming they are here, of course." He tries on a smile, but it doesn't fit well. Instead, he just tugs at his tie like the collar of his shirt is too tight. He shuffles a stack of reports into a folder with a classified stamp across the front of it to politely indicate our time is up, but I have more questions.

"Do you have contact with other outposts? What about Washington?" I ask. "Is it this bad everywhere?"

The last question seems to make him wince. He places the folder down on the desk and stares down at it a moment before he composes his response.

"This is as good as it gets right now. I lost a lot of good men just holding this place together. A lot of good men. Those bureaucrats, trapped in their bunkers under Washington, they can't save anyone now. Now if you'll excuse me, I have to get back to work here. Lt. Commander Reynolds will show you to your quarters so you can get cleaned up and rested, and he will be available tomorrow to help you get situated."

We rise from our chairs and start towards the hall. Quentin stops to give the Captain a salute before closing the door, which his father acknowledges with a slight nod and a sigh.

"Your dad is kind of an asshole," whispers Danielle.

"No shit," says Quentin. "I been saying that to him for years."

I can't help feeling like this place will never become a refuge or stronghold. Maybe just the future site of humanity's last stand. I don't want to acknowledge it, but I am clinging to the hope that I might actually find my wife or daughter here. I know the odds are pretty slim of that happening, but even if it's unlikely, it's not impossible. I have to look. I am exhausted, but I know I won't be able to sleep until I have looked everywhere for them.

CHAPTER TEN

Lieutenant Commander Reynolds brings the golf cart to a stop at a building around the corner. It looks to be a large barracks. Several soldiers sit on the front steps and eye us as we follow the sergeant through the glass doors to the lobby. He presses a button to call the elevator.

"This building is the only housing with power, air conditioning, and hot water," he tells us. "It only houses the soldiers, but with all the casualties it is essentially half empty."

"I don't understand why all those people are stuck outside if there is space here," I say.

Reynolds pushes a pair of round glasses up the bridge of his nose. "The captain thought it would be best to reserve these facilities for those civilians that volunteer for service. Sort of an extra incentive. For now, you can all enjoy your own rooms for the night. Tomorrow Captain Black is looking to begin recruiting from the civilians."

The doors slide open, and we ride up to the third floor. We emerge in the middle of a long, narrow hallway with white utilitarian walls and identical pine doors every ten feet. The rooms are differentiated by the simple black numbers above the peepholes. The sergeant leads us down to room 362 and opens the door with a plastic key card.

"This will be you, sorry, I didn't catch your name."

"It's Blake."

"Blake. You can just call me James." He hands me the plastic key card. "Showers are down at the end of the hall. If you need anything, I am down in room 101, right next to the lobby. Your friends will be next door in 364 and 366." He points to Quentin and Danielle in sequence to the room numbers. "The other fellow in your group will be at the hospital this evening."

I walk inside and eye the simple desk and chair in front of the window, flanked on both sides by a twin bed. A locker sits at the foot of each bed, with a sticky residue still on the empty nameplate.

I turn to see Reynolds retreating to the hall, pulling the door closed behind him. I walk over to one of the beds and sit down. The indented pillow reminds me I am using a dead man's bed and I forget my urge to sleep. I get back up and lean over the desk, turning the blinds to see out the window. The scene is a side view of the marble courtyard with the star and the headquarters is off to the left. I glimpse my faint reflection in the window pane, covered in dust and grime from the explosions earlier. I stare at my hands, noticing the sooty gray layer over my skin. I go to the bathroom and flinch at the reflection in the mirror. I look like a corpse. Dried blood has crusted around a few minor scrapes on my forehead and neck. My hair is greasy and powdered with filth. I run the sink and wash my hands, splash water on my face. Black fluid is what goes back down the drain.

I unbutton my shirt and fill the sink again with fresh water and some hand soap from a plastic container next to the faucet. I have a white undershirt on, and I peel this off and rinse it out in the sink, too. Then I hang both shirts up to dry in the locker. I find a gray t-shirt with U.S. NAVY in blue letters across the chest. I debate putting it on, but instead, I lay it on the back of the chair by the desk and sit on the bed. I pull my cell phone out of my pocket and look at the shattered screen. I set it down on the desk. Then I pick it back up and toss it in the wastebasket on the floor. In the quiet room, I stare at the round white face of an old alarm clock on the desk and only hear the sounds of sporadic machine gun fire from the distant front lines. It's almost ten at night now. About 40 hours from when this all started. Just 40 hours. It seems like an eternity.

A knock on my door startles me. I get up from the bed and open it and find Danielle in the hallway.

"I'm sorry," she says. I catch her glancing at my chest, and then she blushes and looks down. She is wearing an identical shirt to the one I found in the locker in my room. Her hair is still dripping wet, and I can see a puffy bruise at the top of her forehead. "I didn't mean to wake you."

"It's okay. I wasn't asleep," I tell her. I move aside to let her in the room. "Is everything okay?"

"Oh, yeah," she says. "I just don't know if I can be alone right now."

"I know what you mean." I should be tired, but my thoughts keep my mind moving. I retrieve the shirt from the chair back and pull it on.

"I want to stop thinking about everything that is happening, but I can't. It's all I can do when I am alone." She punctuates her last thought with a sigh.

"I was about to go out and have another look around. I'd appreciate some company if you're up for it."

I can tell she knows the reason I want to look around. She looks at me a moment, and I suppose she is deciding if I actually want company, or if I feel obligated to let her stay with me.

"I know they probably aren't out there, but I have to look for them anyway."

"Of course," she says. "I'm glad to help you look."

We go down the elevator to the first floor and head for the door to the front steps. There are still several soldiers hanging around outside of the entrance, smoking and drinking beers. They don't seem as bothered as the civilians we encountered. I overhear a soldier wearing a cowboy hat telling a story about the time someone named Jervis accidentally shot a camel.

"All that shit we were in, and the only thing that ever got to the bastard was shooting that fucking camel," he finishes to a chorus of suppressed laughter from the other four soldiers. They stop when we move down the steps, trying not to look directly at us.

At the street, I look in each direction trying to decide which way to go. Other than the people we saw in the parking lot between the landing field and the headquarters, I don't have an idea where we should start looking.

"You two lost?" The voice of the soldier calls to us. He flicks his cigarette away and walks down the steps toward us. He wears a tan cowboy hat and camo fatigues with FLETCHER stitched on the left breast of his shirt.

"Would you know how we get to the hospital?" I ask him.

"Sure," he says. "You don't want to go there, though."

"Our friend is there," I say.

The soldier seems to consider this a moment then he points out another building to the Southwest that has all the windows illuminated.

"That's it," he says. "But you don't want to go there. Take my word for it. You have to get clearance anyway unless you're in for treatment."

The other soldiers stare down at us with accusing expressions that make me a little uncomfortable.

"Don't mind the grunts up there," Fletcher whispers. "It's just kind of strange for them, seeing you move in here. And, wearing the clothes from some of our guys that just died this morning."

I definitely feel awkward now, but I don't say anything.

"They'll have to get over it, though," Fletcher goes on. "Lot more of that will be going on soon enough. Anyway, best place to be on the base is right here. Take my word for it. Stay away from the fences." He points and makes an arc from the south to the west and up to the north. "Nothing to see but corpses out there."

"Well, we appreciate your advice," says Danielle. "We are trying to locate someone, though."

"Suit yourselves." He turns to climb the steps, and then he pauses and eyes Danielle. "If you need anything just come find good ole Chuck in room 304. That's me."

He gives her his most charming cowboy smile and goes back up to join the other soldiers.

We head across the lighted courtyard toward the parking lot that we saw when we arrived. I glance up at the buildings. Snipers track our movements from the rooftops. We cross the service road that passes in front of the headquarters and into the gloom of the parking lot on the south side of the building.

There are people piled in truck beds, on the roofs of RV's, and even just laying out on thin blankets in the grass. Most of them are just as filthy as we were when we arrived, and they clearly don't have access to the kind of facilities we were given. Some of them eye us curiously in our military shirts. A delirious woman runs over and clamps a hand around my arm. She clutches a photo of a child in a hockey uniform.

"Please, help him," she cries. "Someone needs to get him from school."

"I'm sorry," I stammer.

"He's alone out there," she points to the city. "Please go help him."

A man I presume to be her husband comes and retrieves her, apologizing. He leads her back to the trunk of the minivan they are living out of now.

Here and there amongst the refugees, I spot a child. There aren't many, and the sight of each one troubles me. They all seem to have the same tired, traumatized stare.

We get to the end of the row of cars, and I realize then the lot curves around and spans the entire rear side of the building. People don't just fill the parking lot either; the refugee camp extends down a grade and across a wide road and into the golf course beyond. All the way to the lake, it looks like a massive junkyard with thousands of people living amongst the battered vehicles. The camp is lit up at night by makeshift guard towers, snipers with spotlights perched atop the raised booms of utility trucks and fire engines. Military and police vehicles weave through the rows of cars, soldiers with machine guns ready for anything.

We walk from row to row looking into every unfamiliar face. Half a dozen bikers in leather jackets sit drinking hard liquor from bottles. An old man pushes a cart around, picking through empty cans of food that seem to be lying everywhere on the ground. Another man stares at me while he urinates in the space between two parked cars. The whole place is already starting to smell of rotting food and human excrement.

The more we see of the place, the more I am hoping I don't find my family here. I realize there will be no fight to take back the city. The military can't handle the people that are alive inside the base, let alone the millions of undead that are wandering the streets. I wonder if the captain has any idea how desperate the situation is outside.

A brunette woman without pants stumbles between the rows of cars, clutching a bloody wound in her abdomen. Blood soaks her ripped shirt and trickles down her thighs. She collapses on the ground a few feet in front of us, her face smacking the hard surface of the road. She lies motionless. Her wavy hair masks her face. Danielle moves to help her, but I pull her back a few feet. Several other people get out of their cars and look on as a spotlight locates the woman's body. No one moves as a squad car comes around a corner and approaches the scene.

A petite cop gets out of her car, removes the pistol from her holster and moves cautiously toward the body on the pavement. She crouches down beside the woman, then pins the body to the ground by planting her knee on the woman's back as she checks for a pulse. She stands back up and then fires a round in the back of the woman's skull. Without a word, the cop turns and goes back to the squad car. She grabs a rope attached to the cruiser and ties the body to the bumper. The cops reverses down the aisle and drags the body away. No questioning the witnesses or pursuing suspects. Nothing. Case closed.

"What is going on here?" Danielle whispers.

"I don't know," I sigh.

"I can't believe no one is doing anything about it," Danielle says. She looks at the people nearby as they turn their backs away.

"I guess they all have bigger problems to deal with," I say.

"I never imagined there'd be a place as horrible as this," Danielle whispers. I look over and can see she is crying, her lips quivering. I put a hand on her shoulder, but she turns and sobs into my chest.

"I've seen enough," I tell her. "We should go back now."

"No." She lifts her head, wiping at her eyes with her fingers. "We've come this far. Let's finish looking."

As we move through the cars, the hours pass, and people begin to settle into their shelters for the night. The sounds of constant gunfire from the barricades rattles in the distance.

A dog appears suddenly alongside us, a big, scruffy terrier, wagging its tail, panting, oblivious. It stops to sniff some empty tin cans and selects one to piss on. It runs back to catch up with us, and Danielle bends down and scratches the top of its head between the ears. It rolls onto its back, and Danielle rubs it on the belly. The dog gets up and runs off ahead, stopping here and there to beg for food until the people chase it away.

In between the unfamiliar hopeless faces, my eyes keep going back to the dog. I cling to the sight of its constantly wagging tail amidst all this despair. The dog doesn't remember the horrible things it witnessed yesterday and doesn't fear what might become of it tomorrow. The dog lives only in the moment. I envy the stupid animal because it is a stupid animal.

At the back of the golf course, in the last line of the vehicles, I spot a long, yellow school bus. I try not to get my hopes up, but as we approach it to my amazement, the lettering on the side of the bus reads, LYONS ELEMENTARY.

"That's Abby's school," I tell Danielle. We hurry to the door of the bus, but I can't see anything inside the interior. I bang my fist on the door and call her name. The door swings open, and a frightened woman stares down at me.

"I'm looking for my daughter," I stumble over the words. "Abby Wakefield."

The woman holds a finger in front of her lips and exits the bus. "Please, they're sleeping inside. Your daughter goes to Lyons?" she asks.

"Yes."

"What grade?"

For a second, I can't even remember, and then it comes to me. "Second grade."

"These kids are all in sixth grade," she says. "I'm sorry."

I can't believe it. She has to be on that bus. For a single moment, I had hope that I would find her there against all odds. I let myself believe that fate was a real thing and that I had been dragged through hell for a purpose, to find my daughter. Only to have it turn out to be a sick coincidence. Another statistical improbability, unrelated to any grand design. But it didn't feel like that. I felt like a character in a novel that the author was fucking with.

"How did you get them all the way down here?" I ask the woman.

"These kids weren't in classes. They were going on a field trip to the planetarium," she says. "We were just very lucky."

Lucky. I lose the strength to stand anymore and have to lean against the bus.

"I got a call through to the school when this first started. Some of those things were already inside. They were trying to lock down individual classrooms. It sounded pretty bad, so we didn't head back there. That's all I know."

Danielle comes over and starts to lead me away. "Sorry if we woke you and the children."

"It's fine. I'm really sorry I don't have your little girl with me here. I hope you find her."

The door of the bus squeaks closed, and we start the long, quiet walk back to the barracks. I can only guess at the time, but it must be one or two in the morning. The soldiers have vacated the steps out front. We call the elevator and return to the third floor. I use the swipe card to unlock my door, and Danielle follows me in.

"We can check the hospital tomorrow," she says, watching me collapse onto the mattress. She sits down on the opposite bed. "I want to see how Chet is doing, too."

I mumble some words of agreement, but I am so exhausted I can barely form a sentence.

"Are you sure you don't mind sharing the room?" she asks.

I hear the question but I am already drifting off to sleep, and I say nothing at all.

CHAPTER ELEVEN

The next thing I know, I open my eyes and see Quentin standing in my room having a whispered conversation with Danielle. It's light outside. The bright sunlight leaks through the window shades onto my face. I hear Danielle telling him about our walk through the camp last night.

"This place isn't safe," she says. "Not at all. I think it's only going to get worse. The people out there are desperate. You need to talk to him again."

"Talk to him," says Quentin. "Right. In case you didn't notice, he doesn't really give a shit."

"Well, we better figure out a plan when things go bad here," says Danielle. "Because it's about to happen."

"You don't know that," he says. "There's food, water and electricity here. This place is worth fighting for."

"She's right," I interrupt. I sit up and look at the clock. It's just after eight. "That's no army out there. Those people aren't soldiers. If I can find a way out of this place, I'm leaving before things get out of control."

"And go where?" Quentin asks.

"I don't know," I say. "I like my chances better when I'm on the move. That's how we survived this long. When we tried to hole up, we were nearly eaten alive."

"The only family I have now is here," Quentin says. He plants his fist on the desk and leans forward, looking across to the headquarters. "I don't understand why you think it's better to keep running."

"No one expects you to come with," I tell him. "I expected to be going it alone."

"But you're not," says Danielle. "And we're not leaving Chet here unless he decides to stay. So you have time to think about it anyway." She tilts her head towards me as she says this and raises her eyebrows, a look I know from years of marriage means don't even think about going against me.

A knock on the door breaks up the conversation, and I open it to find Lt. Commander Reynolds in his pressed white naval uniform. His face is clean shaven, and his trim brown hair is clean and neatly combed. I catch a scent of some strong aftershave or cologne. If you saw him, you would never believe the human race was on the verge of annihilation. Maybe that is the point. He looks past me and notices Quentin and Danielle in the room as well.

"We have a situation," he says. "Captain Black ordered me to get you to headquarters immediately."

"What kind of situation?" asks Quentin.

"An urgent situation," Reynolds says in a flat tone. Soldiers walk back and forth through the hall, some dressed in fatigues, loaded with packs and headed to the line, others in robes and towels headed to the showers.

"I just woke up," I say. "Just give me a minute to take a piss." I turn toward the bathroom door, but the officer clears his throat.

"I'm sorry, we don't have a minute," he says.

"Fuck," says Quentin.

It's clear the situation Reynolds mentioned must mean that we are in immediate danger. We follow him down the hall and toward the elevator. The soldier in the cowboy hat we spoke to the previous night is in the elevator car and spots us approaching so he holds the door. He pinches the tip of his hat down in greeting to Danielle.

"Hi Chuck," smiles Danielle.

"Morning, miss," Chuck nods.

I watch the lighted numbers as we pass the second floor. When we reach the lobby, we follow Reynolds out to an armored Humvee parked out front. No golf carts today apparently. The air is humid, the kind of muggy summer days I have always hated in Chicago. I notice there is a lot of gunfire coming from the direction of the hospital.

"Did they get inside?" Danielle asks Reynolds as he opens the rear door for us.

"It's happened before," he says. "We have always driven them back out again. We had to retake that hospital once already. Lost the whole medical staff, though. We're preparing to evacuate just as a precaution." He closes the door and gets in behind the wheel. The soldier in the cowboy hat, Chuck, gets in the front passenger seat, so I guess he's with us now, too.

As Reynolds starts the truck, I lean forward to ask him a question. "How are you going to evacuate all these people?"

"We aren't evacuating at all yet," he says.

"But if you had to," I push the point, wanting an answer.

He accelerates toward the end of the block. "We have a few large yachts anchored just offshore. Only room for maybe eight or nine hundred. It would be impossible to evacuate all of them." He takes a right around the corner, pulling up behind another Humvee parked in front of headquarters.

"Don't worry, though, it'll be fine," he says. "If there is a problem, the Captain ordered us to take you out on one of the helicopters with us." He gets out of the car, and we follow him up the front steps. Some soldiers are piling sandbags around a couple of serious looking machine guns at the base of the steps. The snipers on the roof keep their attention focused west, watching for any sign of a breach. A couple of the Blackhawk helicopters circle a battle going on near the hospital building. It doesn't take any military training to see that things are becoming desperate at the station.

We follow Officer Reynolds downstairs to a storage area, which now serves as the armory for the base. An armed guard keeps watch over a gate and salutes Reynolds when we approach. Reynolds swipes his card and unlocks a cage door, nodding to the sentry.

"What are we doing down here exactly?" I ask.

"My orders were to get you ready for evac," says Reynolds. Then he adds, "In case the situation degrades." We stop at a caged window in the middle of the long hall, with a supply clerk stationed beyond it.

"If you will all let the private here know your measurements, we will find you some more suitable clothes," says Reynolds. "There's a locker room down the hall for you to change. Sorry, there won't be any time for showers just yet. Lieutenant Fletcher and I will round up some supplies and be back to collect you in ten."

The cowboy and Reynolds leave us, and we tell the young clerk our shirt, pant and shoe sizes, which he jots down on a slip of yellow legal paper. The soldier begins collecting items from shelves and racks in the storeroom and piling the neatly folded clothing on the counter.

"This is crazy," says Danielle. "Why are they giving this stuff to us?"

"My father thinks he owes you for helping me," says Quentin. "He feels obligated to return the favor."

"Favor? It feels like I'm being enlisted," says Danielle. "I'm no soldier."

"We are all soldiers now," I say. "We don't really have a choice. But we're not getting this gear to fight. This stuff is to give us a chance to survive."

I grab up a pair of uniforms and the boots off the counter and walk to the locker room. Danielle goes on the opposite side of the aisle of lockers, and we change into the uniforms we were issued. One set was black and the other a green camouflage. I picked up the black pants with large cargo pockets, but Quentin tells me to wear the other one.

"Black is for night only," he says.

I kick off my leather shoes and strip out of my tattered dress pants and pull on the uniform. I button the top right over my Navy t-shirt. I find these separate pads which I don't understand until I watch Quentin strap one around his kneecap, so I do the same. I look down at my outfit and feel sort of ridiculous like I am some kid dressed as a soldier. I look down at the floppy hat and decide not to put it on. I lace up the pair of tan boots.

Danielle walks around from the other side of the lockers, her dark hair now back in a ponytail. She looks like she has aged ten years in a matter of days. She is still bruised and has several slim scabs along the right side of her face. Instead of just an attractive young woman, she also looks every bit a hardened soldier too.

"You look ridiculous," she says to me. Then she looks at Quentin. "You look better this way."

The door opens, and Reynolds and Fletcher come in with assault rifles slung over their shoulders. They each carry enormous rucksacks full of god knows what. Food and ammo, I imagine, but there must be a whole lot of it. I look at the heavy packs hoping they don't expect me to lug one of those around everywhere.

"Holy crap," says Danielle. "I hope you don't expect me to be able to carry all that."

"Hopefully, you won't need to," smiles Reynolds. "If you're all ready, let's load up and go see the captain."

We lug the gear back up the flight of stairs and as we approach the lobby I can hear the sound of gunfire just beyond the doors. We go outside, and I can see the corpses lining up at the hurricane fence beyond the courtyard.

"The damn bastards got the hospital again," says Chuck.

I notice a look of concern cross Reynold's face as he stares off at the horde pressing against the flimsy barricade. Troops are pouring out from the barracks now, some only half-dressed, spreading out into the courtyard and spraying the bodies at the fence with bullets. The snipers on the roof are firing more slowly, but steadily and without end. From this distance, I can only make out the massive size of the crowd. There are hundreds of thousands of corpses trudging forward like a glacier of rotting meat. It's just a matter of time before they topple that fence and there isn't enough firepower here to hold them off.

"We better hurry," says Reynolds. He opens the trunk, and we heave the heavy supplies and assault rifles into the back. Quentin is already running up the stairs for the door by the time the last pack is loaded. We follow him up the stairs and down the hall to the captain's office.

"We need to get the fuck out of here now!" Quentin pleads.

Captain Black stands behind his desk, looking out the window at the courtyard beyond. The captain has changed from his dress uniform into some battle fatigues. He has a pistol holstered at his waist and has traded in his cigarettes for a big cigar that he chews between his teeth. He turns and looks at Quentin, and grins. I have to wonder if the guy is losing his mind.

"Those fucking things are going to be all over the place any minute," Quentin urges.

The captain walks around the desk and puts his arm around Quentin. "Calm down there, son," he says. He speaks with a mellow voice like he is reading a child a bedtime story. He withdraws the cigar from his mouth so he can speak more clearly. "It's time you go with the Lieutenant Commander."

"What are you talking about?" asks Quentin. "There's too many out there. We need to evacuate now."

"You are being evacuated," he says. "I have orders to hold this base at all costs. We will fight to the last man." The captain removes his hand from Quentin's shoulder and walks back around the desk. He withdraws his pistol from the holster and pulls back the action.

"No," says Quentin. "I'm not leaving you to die here."

"I can't leave my troops to die here," the Captain says. "You can see that, can't you?"

"Then I'm staying to fight them, too," Quentin says. "I'm not leaving you either."

The captain's calm demeanor fades for a moment. His brow furrows and when he sticks the cigar back between his teeth his jaw clenches as he bites the tip. For a brutally long moment, he just stands there, staring at his son.

"You still don't get it," he says. "These men are willing to lay down their lives to protect those people back there. So that some of them can survive. And I can lead them down that road because I know that you can survive this. I can't do it for nothing." His eyes are glassy but fierce and determined.

"Pop," says Quentin.

"Get on that chopper, boy," the captain growls. He nods at Reynolds and turns around and faces the window again. One of the Blackhawks is circling the fence, firing rockets into the crowd of undead. The sky erupts into a burst of flame and chunks of flesh and bone. The building trembles beneath our feet.

Reynolds salutes the captain, then steps out into the hall. Danielle follows him, and I walk out behind her. Quentin remains a moment longer, staring at the back of his father. I want to get the hell out of there, but I stop in the doorway and wait for Quentin. He opens his mouth as if to speak then seems to change his mind. He glances down at the floor and shakes his head.

"So long, Pops," he says. Then he backs out of the office, and we move quickly down the hall.

CHAPTER TWELVE

We come down the stairs into a crowd of people rushing in every direction. Soldiers are coming up the stairs from the armory laden with assault rifles and ammunition. Several soldiers block some civilians at each of the corridors. More people try to push through from doors that face the rear of the building. The sounds of machine guns outside continues to build. We push through the front doors behind a squad of soldiers.

The courtyard is teeming with the undead. Bodies and limbs constellate the ground, but the horde continues onward toward the building, stumbling over the fallen bodies. The dead have already overrun the barracks. Corpses pour into the entrance unopposed.

Some soldiers bust out windows in the upper floors and take up firing positions. Glass fragments rain down around us.

I take this in as we file through a firing line of troops on the stairs. The last line of defense before the dead reach the headquarters and the thousands of people sheltered behind. The large machine guns at the sidewalk chew through long belts of ammunition. I reach the passenger side of the truck and wait as the others get in and scoot to the driver's side. I notice a young soldier stops firing for a split second as he eyes us getting into the vehicle. For a second, I think he is about to come running over to get in too, but he squints one eye and looks down his sight and begins firing again. I hear the Captain's voice from what sounds like a radio somewhere.

"Pace your shots," he says. "Conserve your ammo. Hold those lines and give them hell boys."

I look up and realize it isn't a radio at all. The Captain stands between a pair of soldiers in the open window of his office, barking into a bullhorn and gesturing urgently.

"Nuts to butts!" he yells. He stops for a moment and watches as I get into the truck and shut the door.

Fletcher whirls the vehicle in a tight u-turn, and then I am pushed back against my seat as tires wail and the armored Humvee zips down the road. The dead along the far edge of the street grab for the truck as we go past. The soldiers keep the line, still firing furiously, and a few wayward rounds pepper the side of the vehicle. Who knows, maybe they are pissed off to see us escaping while they fight a battle with the dead they have no hope of winning.

We reach the end of the main building and roll past the parking lot. The vehicles nearest the road are all abandoned. The people have all moved toward the lake, hoping to reach the offshore boats, which I can see now in the daylight. I can hear the screams of panic coming from the lakeshore and see people diving into the water and swimming for the boats.

A Blackhawk lifts off from the middle of the track and flies low over the cab of the truck. Chuck pulls off the road and into the grass. He steers over the packed dirt toward the last helicopter waiting in the middle of the field. I panic when I notice the blades are already circling, but the helicopter does not take off. A half dozen armed soldiers have taken up positions around the helicopter. We have to weave through several dozen bodies riddled with bullet holes on the ground. Once or twice the truck bounces as we roll over one.

Fletcher brings the Humvee to a skidding halt about thirty feet from the swirling blades. Fletcher pops the trunk, and two of the soldiers run over to assist with packs.

"Let's move," says Reynolds.

I get out of the back and duck my head instinctively as I hurry towards the chopper. I look inside and notice that other than the pilot there are two other passengers seated in the rear of the helicopter. A woman around my age with long blonde hair, wearing dark aviator sunglasses and a black sleeveless top with camo cargo pants. She seems unconcerned about the whole situation. To my surprise, I notice as I step into the cabin that she is casually reading a thick, paperback novel. The other passenger is an older man with a graying beard wearing a dirty white dress shirt and a bow tie. The old man keeps turning his head nervously back to look at the road and the horde of undead that can't be far behind us.

Danielle takes a seat next to the blonde woman. I sit across from them next to the old man in the bow tie. Quentin takes the seat next to me. Fletcher is next to the other pilot, strapping on a helmet. He turns back and points to indicate a rack above my head where several other helmets are stowed. I grab a couple down and hand one to Danielle, and put the other on myself. I hear Fletcher's voice through the headset in the helmet.

"Those belts are there for a reason," he says.

I strap the belt around my waist and wait for what feels like an eternity for the soldiers to board. One of them mans a giant machine gun mounted on the open door.

"Get us the fuck out of here," one of the soldiers yells into the microphone. "They're coming our way."

The rotors seem to accelerate, kicking up dirt and grass from the field. The moment before we lift up a small creature darts through the cabin door.

"Holy shit," screams a voice over the intercom.

My heart races momentarily, my fingers ready to free the safety belt from my waist.

"Everything alright back there?" Fletcher asks.

"Yeah man, it's just a dog," replies a soldier with a laugh. "Good pooch."

The helicopter slowly ascends off the ground, and the soldiers up front move the dog back to the rear to keep it away from the doors. I notice it's the same dog that followed us around all last night. I get a hold of it by the collar and scratch it on the neck. I notice the metal tag on the collar with "STITCH" engraved into the aged blue surface. The helicopter banks to the left and we make a wide arc around the station. The courtyard is just a sea of the undead now. The corpses have overrun the soldiers and flood through the entry of the main building. The wave of undead flows through and around the headquarters, working their way towards the shore. Thousands of survivors flail in the water. They fight to get aboard the boats already overloaded with people. The mass of corpses slowly works its way through the giant parking lot behind the building to a crowd of people still standing on the shore. They can choose to get eaten alive or drown trying to reach the boats. As the dead move closer, more and more people plunge into the water. They swim for the boats even as the ships begin to sail slowly away.

"All those people," sighs Danielle.

I am thinking about the kids on that school bus. It seems wrong that we are flying out in this helicopter while those kids are stuck on shore. I can only hope they made it to the boats.

The helicopter banks again and circles before flying off to the west with our backs to the morning sun. We watch the horrific scene that is playing out, and that we are totally powerless to stop.

I feel bile creeping up my throat and my stomach churns. It is only partially from the movement of the helicopter. I lean forward and heave, but since I haven't eaten in eighteen hours, hardly anything comes out.

"Stop puking in my helicopter," Fletcher says over the intercom. I look up to see all the soldiers laughing. They just saw me doing the same thing yesterday. Now, I'm doing it again. I'm turning into the guy that pukes every time he is on the helicopter. That's my thing.

I sit back in the seat, feeling a little light-headed. The old man has his head tilted back and stares up at the roof blankly. The blonde woman turns a page of the book she is reading. It's a copy of The Stand. She is reading an apocalyptic novel during the apocalypse. Now I know the world has completely gone insane. I glance back up and realize she has noticed me staring at the book. She smiles so slightly that I can't tell if it was intended to be amicable or if she was enjoying my apparent astonishment.

Beside me, Quentin sits so rigidly and quiet in his seat, I had almost forgotten he was there. He stares out the window, not even noticing the dog sniffing at the leg of his pants. I see his lips move and realize he is talking angrily to himself. I debate getting his attention somehow, maybe asking if he is okay. Instead, I decide to leave it be for now. Nothing I might say could make this mess any easier for him to deal with anyway.

After only ten minutes or so in the air, we set down on the rooftop landing pad of a hospital building. We get out of the helicopter once the soldiers have cleared the roof. The place looks deserted, but sure enough, a couple walking corpses approach the sliding doors to the hospital and try to grab us through the glass.

They press their pale faces and palms crusted brown with dried blood against the barrier. It's almost worse to look at them when you aren't running away. When you stare at them longer than you should, you notice too many gory details, like the congealed fluids seeping from the gnawed off parts of their bodies. You start to focus on the way their eyes have clouded over. Or the way their pupils don't move so it seems they are never looking at you, even when they are. The corpses stare past us like we are not actually what they want. We are just something in the periphery to tear apart on the way to some indistinct, unquenchable desire.

"Don't worry," says Fletcher.

I flinch at the sudden sound of his voice. I am still tired and hadn't even noticed when he walked up behind me. Seeing my reaction made him smile.

"Easy boss," he says. He jerks his head toward the Blackhawk. "We won't stick around long enough for them to bother us. We lost contact with another bird. Since we were the last ones out, we'll see if we get any radio contact before we vacate the area. We'll be back up in twenty."

He starts to walk away, but I say, "Hold up. Where are we going?"

"Hardened site. Bout twenty clicks southwest of here."

"Hardened site?" I ask.

"An underground bunker owned by the United States Army at the Manhattan installation."

"I never knew there was an army base down there."

"That's kind of the point," he grins. He tosses his helmet back in the bay of the Blackhawk and replaces it with the cowboy hat.

Quentin hasn't left his seat in the chopper. He stares off at the skyline of the city. The dog runs past my leg, panting and excited. It's almost strange to me to see anything that can be so optimistic regardless of everything going on. After realizing I was not up for playing, the dog runs back to Danielle on the other side of the chopper.

The blonde woman remains in the Blackhawk, turning pages in her novel. The old man, though, has made his way over to the glass doors and studies the corpses.

"Who are those two?" I ask Fletcher.

He glances over to see if the woman is paying attention, and then he jerks his head to indicate the blonde and says, "Spooky in there is CIA."

"Spooky?" I ask.

He turns around and sits on the floor of the helicopter, so his back is to her. "Says her name is Jessica Lorento, but that's probably a fake. Spooks never use their real names, so we just been calling her Spooky or J-Lo behind her back."

"And the other guy?" I ask.

"Charlie Foxtrot?" he asks. "That's just her luggage. Some lab geek she is hauling to New Mexico to try and figure out what all this shit is. Unfortunately, he's all ate up."

"So he's, what, some kind of doctor?" I ask.

"Radiation expert," he says.

"Radiation?"

"Fuck if I know," Fletcher shrugs. He reaches into a pack beside him and pulls out two water bottles and hands me one. "They probably don't know either."

I twist the cap off and take a long drink. I feel the warm liquid slosh around my empty stomach. Though drinking the water only makes me feel even hungrier, I take another long pull, downing half the bottle.

"What do you think this is?" I ask him.

He looks over at the undead lurking by the doors and considers it a moment. "I think this whole thing is Charlie Foxtrot. That's what we say when something is completely fucked. Just like that old man over there."

Fletcher takes a drink from the bottle, wipes at his mouth with a forearm and caps the water.

"You get anything, Wiz?" Fletcher asks the co-pilot.

"Negative, Fletch," answers the other pilot without turning. He flips some switches and starts the engine.

Fletcher lifts up his left boot and ties the laces.

"Sorry to ask," he says, "but is that your hammer over there?"

"Hammer?" I ask.

"The girl," he says. "Is she with you?"

Once I realize what he is getting at, I say, "No, I'm married." I glance down at the ring on my finger and twist it around. Then thinking about it I say, "I was married."

"Sorry to bring it up," he says. He stands up and grabs his helmet from the helicopter. "Just like to know the situation."

The rotors begin to churn and Fletcher straps on his helmet.

"Okay ladies, we're bugging out," he says.

Officer Reynolds walks over and gathers the old man from the entrance. He leads him back to the helicopter by the arm. The old man glances around at the soldiers and helicopter with an expression of stunned confusion, like he was just seeing the soldiers and helicopter for the first time. He hardly seems to be capable of figuring out where he is, let alone how to fix this mess.

We strap back into our seats and lift off from the roof of the hospital. The corpses stand in the doorway, still reaching for us as we drift away in the sky.

CHAPTER THIRTEEN

The streets we travel above show the extent of the destruction of the past couple days. Most of the fires have burned themselves out, but the air still smells and tastes of ash. Entire city blocks have been incinerated. Figures, some of them charred, shamble along every street. A couple of times I can see the corpses swarming around a house or building where there might be survivors. One man sitting on the roof of his house waves as we pass overhead, but the helicopter is full, and we keep on going. Even a war could not have created this much devastation in such a short time.

We pass over the airport, the planes are motionless on the ground while zombies wander around the runways. They look up at our helicopter flying overhead. It's a relief to be back in the suburbs, which are slightly less horrific than the city. There are still a lot of undead, but nothing like the hundreds of thousands that surrounded the naval station. They congregate on the main streets and around buildings, but some side streets seem relatively clear. We pass over a forest preserve where I don't see any at all.

The helicopter touches down in the middle of an enormous grassy field, along the Des Plaines River, just southwest of Joliet. Though I had only seen a single barb wired fence along the perimeter, there were very few corpses around it. From where we are, there is nothing but prairie grasses and trees visible in any direction, so I can't imagine we could attract much attention. The nearest town is maybe five miles away, and there are several large farms on one side and the river on the other. It seems like a secluded location.

We unload the helicopter, and I throw one of the heavy packs over my shoulders. It weighs a good seventy or eighty pounds, not including the assault rifle, which I also sling over a shoulder. We walk single file through the field, following one of the soldiers along.

"Everyone, keep your eyes peeled," whispers Reynolds. "It should be clear, but don't assume it is."

We walk about fifty yards east and come to a blast door embedded in the earth, almost invisible amongst the tall surrounding grasses. It leads down a flight of stairs to another thick steel door next to a keycard lock. The lead soldier swipes a badge and following two quick beeps the lock disengages.

We file into another room that seems like an airlock of some kind, then through another doorway into a small storage room. It's a relief to see the halogen lights on the ceiling. Somehow this place still has power. The soldiers carry their rifles but drop their packs, so I follow their lead and set my gear down on the floor. My shoulders ache just from that short walk from the helicopter.

"What is this place?" Danielle asks.

"This site was part of Project Nike during the Cold War," says Reynolds. "It used to house Army surface-to-air missiles before the Air Force took over air defense fully and the sites were decommissioned. Well, officially anyway. As you can see, it's still here. It's been refitted to protect against chemical and biological attacks, in addition to a nuclear strike. The SEALS just happened to be up here doing some training exercises when the shit hit the fan."

At the opposite end of the room from the door we just came through is another door, which Reynolds opens. We step into a concrete hallway and follow Reynolds to the left until he stops and opens a door on the right. He leads us into a spacious room with a kitchenette, television, a few couches, a ping pong table and a long mess table.

"This used to be the missile bay. There's sleeping quarters off each of those doors," Reynolds says. "It's pretty cramped, but this is the most secure facility in the area. We have food, electricity and satellite communications with what few remaining military installations are operational."

Some of the soldiers head over to the fridge and pass around cans of beer. The air smells stale, but I am relieved to finally be in a place that seems impossible to breach. We are actually safe here. The muscles in my shoulders relax and I feel like a giant weight that I have carried since the beginning of this mess has finally been lifted. I walk over to one of the doors and open it to find spartan living quarters, only a bunk bed and an alcove for storing clothes.

"The boys will get you some chow and make sure you get settled," says Reynolds. He looks at Fletcher, who gives him a nod. "I'm going to show Agent Lorento to the com room to see if we can reach Washington and New Mexico." Lorento follows him out the door, pausing to look back at the doctor as he studies his reflection in the screen of the television on the wall.

The old man has clearly lost it. Seeing his strange behavior, I remind myself not to relax too much. He seems elderly and frail, and if he suddenly kicks the bucket, things could get nasty in here in a hurry. Aside from that, he is definitely not thinking straight, which I already know can mean trouble for everyone.

Aside from Lieutenant Fletcher and the co-pilot, Wiz, seven other soldiers flew in the helicopter with us. I recognize a couple of them from the night before, when we saw Fletcher outside the barracks. Since a few guys don't seem as big as some of the other soldiers, I assume they are part of the helicopter crew. I haven't really been paying much attention to any of the insignia on their uniforms, but it isn't too hard to figure out. The other five soldiers all look rough and fit, and I have no doubt any one of them could kick my ass. These guys have to be the SEALS. The SEALS stick together, and the helicopter crew hangs together. While there is a mutual respect, there is still a definite division.

"Throw a couple pizzas in, Hernacki," Fletcher orders one of the SEALS. "And don't drink all my beer."

The youngest looking of the SEALS grabs two boxes from the freezer and turns on an electric toaster oven in the kitchenette.

"You guys okay with that?" Fletcher asks us.

Just the mention of the word 'pizza' has me salivating. Quentin looks over at the other soldiers, then to me, and without a word, he walks into the room behind me and lays down on a bunk.

"That would be perfect," says Danielle. "I'm starving."

"You two want a beer?" he offers. He hands us each an ice-cold can. It's cheap beer. I probably would have even turned it down a couple of days ago, but a lot has changed since then. I crack the top and taste the cool foam that bubbles out the opening.

The room begins to fill with the aroma of the warming pizzas. Chuck, Danielle, and I sit around on the couches. The helicopter crew plays some ping pong while the SEALS sit around the table with a deck of cards. I watch the old man as he moves from door to door, opening each one and then scanning the identical sleeping quarters as though he was looking for something.

Within a few minutes of drinking the beer, I can even relax a little more.

Chuck tells us about how they were working on special ops training with the SEALS and the stealth helicopters. They flew mock missions around the Chicago area at night, then monitored the media and internet to gauge how well they could avoid detection in an urban environment.

"Nobody ever gets to see these helicopters we've been flying around in. There's only a dozen or so out there," he says.

He smiles at Danielle, and I can tell he is hoping his story has impressed her. She smiles back.

"So what about this place?" I ask. "How'd you end up here?"

"We had to have someplace low profile to keep the Blackhawks. Since this place isn't even officially in service, we got clearance from the Army to conduct training exercises here this month."

"If all this is top secret, or whatever, should we even be here?" asks Danielle.

"I doubt it matters anymore," he says. "They got bigger problems now."

Hernacki brings over one of the pizzas and sets it down on the table. I extract a slice for myself and bite into the warm, melted cheese. It's so hot that I burn my tongue, but I don't even mind. I devour the piece in five bites, wash it down with a swig of beer and then take another slice.

The room grows quiet as everyone eats hungrily.

"Don't get too used to this," says Fletcher.

I savor the last of the crust, sucking the oil and parmesan crumbs from my fingertips.

"So how long will the supplies here last?" I ask.

"Not very long," he says. "For all of us, maybe a couple of weeks. We won't be here that long, though."

"Why not?" I ask.

"We still have orders from Washington to get Charlie Foxtrot over there to New Mexico." He points to the old man who is now in the room where Quentin is resting on the bed, and stands there staring down at the sleeping man.

"That seems like a waste of time," says Danielle.

"Indeed, it does," says Fletcher. "But orders is orders."

Reynolds and Agent Lorento return to the room. Lorento sighs and goes over to retrieve the old man and ushers him across to another room.

"Bad news," says Reynolds. "Washington has gone dark."

Fletcher looks up at him.

"I can't get anyone at the White House or the Pentagon," says Reynolds.

"What about New Mexico?" asks Fletcher.

"Still operational, but it sounds like it's FUBAR. Some private led a mutiny. Fragged the commanding officers. Told me he is running the show now."

"So?" asks Fletcher. "What now?"

"We have standing orders," says Reynolds.

"Fuck orders," mutters Fletcher. "There is nobody left to give a damn if we follow orders or not."

Agent Lorento exits the sleeping quarters, closing the door behind her. Fletcher and Reynolds stop talking as she approaches.

I shoot a glance over to Danielle to catch her attention and she grimaces, which I take to mean she is as concerned about our situation as I am. Since we were rescued and brought to the Naval Station, every decision has been made for us. We had no control over anything, and the military personnel have these conversations like we aren't even in the room. It seems like we are mostly just extra cargo they have been ordered to transport.

"So when do we leave?" Lorento asks Reynolds.

Reynolds glances over at Fletcher and says, "2200 hours."

Fletcher groans.

"Is there a problem?" asks Lorento. She folds her arms in front of her chest and shifts her weight to one leg. The room grows silent as everyone listens. Even Quentin gets back off his bunk and ambles through the doorway to see what is going on.

"There is," says Fletcher. "I ain't flying to New Mexico."

"Lieutenant," Reynolds starts, but Lorento cuts him off.

"You have direct orders from Admiral Livingston to get me and Dr. Schoenheim to Area 51 by any means necessary."

"That was yesterday," says Fletcher. "The situation has changed."

"Nothing's changed," insists Lorento. "The order was never rescinded."

"Probably because there isn't anyone alive to rescind it, lady," Fletcher growls. "The situation has changed. You don't have a pilot."

"Check your tone, lieutenant," orders the Lt. Commander. "Respect the chain of command."

"Reynolds," Fletcher says. "With all due respect, you need to wake the fuck up. This whole mission is FUBAR just like Dr. Charlie Foxtrot in there. If I thought there was any chance that by getting him to New Mexico we might turn this thing around, hell, I'd be the first one lined up to get on that bird."

"Look," begins Lorento. "We all have a job to do, whether we like it or not."

"No. We don't work for anyone. Not anymore."

"I still work for America, and right now my country needs me. We can't just sit here hiding in a hole in the ground. We need to do whatever we can to make things right."

"There is no goddamn America. Can't you see that, lady?"

Lorento rolls her eyes and growls. Fletcher picks up his cowboy hat from his head, tilts his head back and then rests the hat over his eyes.

"We are leaving in ten hours, Lieutenant, with or without you." She picks up the last slice of pizza from the plate on the table while giving Fletcher a look of disgust. He doesn't seem to notice from beneath the brim of his hat. Then she retreats to the room where she left Dr. Schoenheim and slams the door loudly behind her.

"You sure got a way with the ladies," says Wiz. Not bothering to look, Fletcher salutes him with a middle finger.

"You can choose to stay or go," Reynolds informs us. "Our orders were just to get you someplace where you can safely wait this out. The rest of us," he pauses to glance sidelong at Fletcher, "still have a job to do."

"Fucking A," chimes in one of the SEALS.

"You've got weapons and supplies to last you a few weeks until we can relocate you to a permanent facility."

I can tell that Reynolds doesn't really want us to go. Just more civilians to try and look after. That is all right with me, too, as I am wary about the situation in New Mexico.

"If anyone else here has a problem with our mission, well, I'm not going to shoot anyone for dereliction of duty. I have my own doubts, but I am going to see this through. We can die in a hole in the ground, or we can try to do something to turn this thing around. So just think about that before you decide."

Reynolds looks around the room at the soldiers. Then he walks over to the table, grabs one of the beers and proceeds to another of the sleeping quarters, closing the door behind him. Once he leaves, a few of the SEALS glance back at Fletcher. He remains still and seems to be dozing beneath his cowboy hat. After a few seconds, they return to their card game, talking not too discretely and with some bravado about finishing their mission instead of hiding under a rock. Within a minute or two, they are again joking and griping over their cards.

The helicopter crew picks up some darts and chucks them at the board mounted on the wall. They talk amongst themselves, occasionally stopping to glance back at Fletcher sitting on the couch. Whatever they decide on, I am pretty sure they will stick together. If they don't agree to go, I wonder who will fly the helicopter.

I walk toward the room where Quentin is lying down and jerk my head to signal Danielle to follow me inside.

"You okay?" I ask him, just to try and say something to engage him again. We need him now as much as ever to give us an idea what is really going on. He will know if we should stick with the SEALS and go to New Mexico, or if we stand a better chance by staying behind. We have supplies here, sure. But we'd be on our own until help arrives, if help ever arrives.

"I'll be fine, man," says Quentin. Stitch hops onto the bunk and squirms beside Quentin and pants loudly as he pets him. Quentin sits up on the bed and makes room by sliding toward the pillow. Danielle sits next to him, and I close the door before sitting on the edge of the cubby along the opposite wall.

"Did you catch all that out there?" I ask him.

He nods but doesn't reply.

"What do you think?" I ask him.

Quentin thinks about it a moment.

"Will we be safer in New Mexico?" asks Danielle.

"No," he says. "If what they said about it is true, the undead might be the least of our worries in New Mexico."

"So we stay," I say.

"We stick together," confirms Danielle. She forces a smile at Quentin, which sheds a ray of light through his gloom. "Family," she adds.

The word stings. These are the only people left I know in the world. A few days ago we didn't know each other. Now these people are the only thing keeping me going.

CHAPTER FOURTEEN

I wake up when the noise of the troops in the common area stirs me from sleep. I feel as good as I have felt for several days. Though there isn't a clock in the sleeping quarters, I guess I must have slept at least five or six straight hours. I can smell coffee and bacon, which helps motivate me to sit up on the bed. I notice Quentin has left the room already.

I was so tired I fell asleep in the camo fatigues. I undress and switch to the black uniform. The cold concrete floor motivates me to hustle. I lace up the boots and follow the inviting aromas of real food out to the common area.

The soldiers are already scraping the crumbs off their plates and into the sink. I worry I slept too long and missed out on the food.

"About time you woke up," says Quentin.

The four SEALS that just finished eating walk past me and out to the hallway back toward the storage room. I take a seat across from Quentin, trying not to covet his plate of food while I wait for my own.

"What time is it?" I ask.

"2100," he says.

"You sound like them," I say.

"Sorry," he says. "It will be easier to use military time in here. No natural light. It can get confusing whether it's night or day."

"Is there any of that left?" I ask.

"I can make more," answers Fletcher from the kitchen. "Coffee is on now."

A door on the other side of the room opens up and Lorento steps out.

"Come on," she urges the doctor, but he just stands in the dark.

"I can't leave without my pants," he says.

She sighs and shuts the door.

"Everything alright?" asks Fletcher, peeking up from a skillet of eggs he is scrambling.

"Did you see what Dr. Schoenheim did with his pants, Lieutenant?"

"His pants?" he asks, holding back a shit-eating grin. "How am I supposed to know what he did with his goddamn pants?"

"You were out here the entire time we were sleeping. Surely you must have seen him come out of the room."

"I'm a real sound sleeper," Fletcher says.

"Bastard," she grunts. She looks accusingly at Quentin and me, and then storms out into the hallway.

Fletcher walks over and drops a plate of scrambled eggs and bacon in front of me, and I thank him. I always used to order my eggs over easy, with some toast to dip in the yolk. Now, any kind of real, fresh food is beyond reproach. I pour some black coffee from a pot on the table. There is nothing to put in it but powdered creamer packets. I don't even care. I drink it black and hope it abates the slight headaches I've had from a lack of caffeine.

"Enjoy it," he says. "We'll have a hell of a time finding any more. It's MRE's from here on out." He heads to the couch behind me and groans as he takes a seat.

"Danielle get up yet?" I ask Quentin in between a mouthful of bacon.

"Still out," he says. His plate is empty, and he wipes the crumbs from his mouth with a paper napkin while he watches me eat like an animal. Quentin crumples the napkin and tosses it on the plate a leans back in his chair. He rests his hands on his satisfied stomach.

"You look like shit," he says with a smile.

The comment makes me pause as I shove a piece of bacon in my mouth. Quentin has already taken a shower and shaved. Aside from that, he has come through this whole ordeal without looking any worse for the wear. Not even a scraped knee.

I've been nearly blown up twice. I can feel the bruises on my back, the crusty scab from a cut on my lower lip that burns as I chew every bite of food. My face bristles with stubble, and I notice the scent of my body odor over the strong smells of coffee and bacon. In spite of everything, this is the best I have felt in days.

"Thanks," I grumble.

"It's an improvement," he says. "You look kind of tough now."

"I look like I got my ass kicked, you mean."

"Well, yeah," he says. "But it looks like you put up a fight at least."

I hear white noise coming from the television and turn around to look. Fletcher flips through a few channels broadcasting nothing. Not even any test patterns or automated emergency updates.

"Thought maybe there'd be something through the satellite," says Fletcher. He hits a button then a movie begins playing.

"How are you doing?" I ask Quentin.

"Don't worry about me, man," he says, turning his attention from me to the television. "I'll be fine."

I can tell he is far from fine because we are all far from fine. We are in that place where hopelessness and misery and loss pursue us until we can't even remember what normal felt like. Even the fake gunfire on the television disturbs me. The sounds give me visions of brain matter spraying out the head of a walking corpse. It's really some movie about Vietnam. The soldiers are all smoking grass and surfing in the middle of a war zone like they were all a couple of beers short of a six-pack. I wonder how long it will be before my psyche has had enough of reality.

"How can you watch this?" I ask Fletcher.

"Only movie we got down here," he says. "You don't like it?"

Instead of making a big deal out of it, I decide to get up and take a shower. The bathroom has two green shower stalls, a toilet, a urinal and two sinks below a wide mirror. The room smells of chemicals and urinal pucks.

I grab a folded towel off a shelf above a linen basket that is nearly overflowing. There are sample bottles of generic soap and body wash from the collection on the shelf below. I strip and hang my clothes on a hook on the outside of the shower door and turn on the water. Before stepping into the stall, I reach my hand into the shower to test the temperature. The hot water stings and steam fills the room.

For a while, I just stand there. The pulse of the water soothes my muscles. I examine the bruises and cuts on my body, and they are numerous. Looking at the one on the side of my torso makes me wince. I prod it, and then grind my teeth from the pain. I probably have some bruised ribs. Hopefully, they aren't cracked. I am glad I didn't notice how bad the injury was until now. If I'd gone to the hospital with Chet, I wouldn't be alive.

I lather the body wash across my face and close my eyes. I try not to think about anybody that died. If we hadn't gone to that restaurant, maybe they would all still be alive. Maybe Melanie, Chet, Devin, and Joey would have lived if it wasn't for us. I know that's all bullshit, but I can't help but feel partly responsible. If I had only kept the situation under control, things might have been different.

I rinse the shampoo out of my hair, then cut the water. I dry myself with the towel and wrap it around my waist. I look in the mirror at the cuts on my forehead and jaw. It almost looks like road rash, but it's from a million pieces of cement that exploded in my face. The cut on my lip does make me look a little tougher. Though I am not tough enough to try my luck shaving over the many scabs on my skin.

I get dressed and head back out to the common room. The movie is still on, but I feel good enough after a shower that I do a better job of blocking it out. Quentin has joined Fletcher on the couch, and they are playing cards. I notice the clock on the wall reads quarter after ten. It feels like morning even though it is late at night. Being down in this bunker is already screwing with my connection to the world above.

"Did the rest of them leave?" I ask.

"Yup," says Chuck. "Maybe ten minutes ago."

"How can you stay behind? I thought the military was all about brothers in arms." I realize my question might have come off wrong when he slaps down a couple of cards on the table. I decide to change my approach. "Just curious what made you want to stay."

"Those guys are sticking together. I barely know them. Their pilot was killed two days ago. I haven't flown missions in years. It's just a job, okay? You feel bad you didn't show up for work this morning?"

"I didn't mean anything by it," I say.

"Nah, I'm sorry for snapping," he says to the hand of cards he's holding. Fletcher waves a dismissive hand. "Of course, it bothers me a bit. Not having a helicopter bothers me too. But I'm not planning on dying like those poor bastards back at the station."

"We're just as dead down here," I say. "It'll just be a slower death."

"Fuck that," he says. Then he tilts his head back from Quentin. "What you got?"

"Straight," says Quentin, displaying his cards on the table.

"Son of a bitch," grins Fletcher. He tosses Quentin a can of beer.

The warmth of the shower dissipates, and I can already feel the soreness returning. I shuffle over to the open couch adjacent to the others and stretch out across the length of the cushions.

"Your deal," says Fletcher handing Quentin the cards. "You want in?" he asks me.

"No," I say. "I don't gamble."

"We're just playing for the rest of the beers," he says. He grabs a six pack of beer off the floor and tosses it beside me on the couch. "Come on. Play a hand."

I look over and see a couple of cards lay at the edge of the table. I pick them up. A six of hearts and a nine of hearts spread out in my hand.

"Check," I say.

"Let's make it two beers this round," says Fletcher. He puts one of his five remaining cans on the table. Quentin adds a beer, and then I add one from my cache as well.

"Blake," says Fletcher. "I don't know about you, but I don't have plans to die down here at all. It's not as bad out here as it was in the city. It's spread out. We can move around. Hell, we can probably go out there and pick up anything we want."

Quentin places three cards on the table facing up. Side-by-side appears a six of clubs, an ace of hearts, and a jack of hearts. They both look at me, awaiting my play.

I only have a pair of sixes, which is pretty terrible. I do have four cards towards a flush, though, and with two cards coming, I've got coin-flip odds of making my hand. I decide to see the next card.

"Check," I say.

"I'm feeling lucky," says Fletcher. He adds another can to the collection on the table.

Quentin tosses his cards aside, giving up. He deals another card. The king of spades.

"Say you're right," I say. "Then what? We hide down here until the apocalypse blows over?"

I try not to let my face betray my reaction to the cards on the table. With only one card left, the odds are pretty bad that I will make my flush. My pair of sixes doesn't have a good statistical chance either based on the other cards in play. I take my time to hopefully convince Fletcher I am contemplating a raise.

"Check," I say.

He looks at me a moment. Then he puts the rest of his six pack in the center of the table.

"I'm all in," he smirks.

"Fuck," I grumble, then toss my cards down.

Fletcher slides the cheap beers over to his side of the table.

"What did you have?" I ask him.

He flips his cards over to reveal a four of clubs and an eight of diamonds. He beat me with nothing.

"Nice bluff," Quentin laughs.

"Sometimes life gives you a shitty hand," Fletcher says. "We're all stuck with a real shitty hand too, but I'm not about to fold. The only way we have any chance is to play this out as though we think we are going to win anyway."

"Alright," I concede.

"If we're smart, and we're patient, we can survive this," he says. He looks over to Quentin, who nods in agreement.

Door hinges squeak, and I hear the sound of paws running over the concrete floor behind me.

"I think he has to go out," says Danielle.

I turn around and see her squinting into the light.

"I got it. Come on, pooch" says Fletcher, abandoning the deck of cards in the table. He scoops up his cowboy hat and places it on his head. He pats his leg, and the dog follows him toward the hallway. "There's some coffee and a plate for you on the table, doll."

Once he is gone, Danielle asks, "Did he really just call me doll?"

It's one of those stupid questions that isn't really a question. The only time someone asks a question like that is to make sure you notice something they thought was important.

"Breakfast is on the table, doll," I smirk.

Danielle rolls her eyes at me, which, for a second, reminds me of my wife. I stop smirking and avert my gaze. I can only pretend that reality didn't happen for so long. Eventually, some random thing reminds me that those parts of my life were real and that I'm never going to see any of it again.

"It's cold." Danielle stands next to the table, picking at some bits of scrambled egg with her fingers. "How long was I asleep?" she asks.

"We ate a couple hours ago," says Quentin. "It's around eleven, probably."

"In the morning?"

"At night," he says, then he gets up from the couch to turn off the television. He could sense it is still bothering me.

I get the urge to look around the installation a bit more. There doesn't seem to be much to do other than driving yourself crazy thinking about things you'd rather not think about. I don't care for ping pong. Maybe there are some books or something around here someplace. Anything to keep me from dwelling on the thoughts I want to avoid.

"Did you check out the rest of this place?" I ask Quentin.

"Not yet," he says. "You want to have a look around?"

I get up off the couch and follow Quentin towards the hall.

"You coming?" I pause to ask Danielle.

"I'm going to get a shower first," she says, pouring herself a cup of cold coffee. "Okay." I almost call her doll again but decide not to. It didn't seem to go over too well the first time.

CHAPTER FIFTEEN

The underground facility is nothing more than several other rooms connected by a long, dimly lit hallway. The generators are in a utility room down the right end of the hall. The room also holds a fuse box, a water heater and filtration system, and a complicated air conditioning or treatment unit. We open a door across the hall to find a small closet with a mop, bucket, some towels and spray bottles.

"Not much going on down here," says Quentin.

"No, there isn't," I agree.

"Just the essentials," he says.

We go into the communications room, which is across the hall from the common area. There is a big control board that seems to control the entire facility. There are readings for fuel levels, power usage, air quality. There are also several video monitors that cycle through a series of cameras recording the interior and exterior of the bunker. I watch Fletcher on one of the screens, smoking a cigarette outside. The dog sniffs around the overgrown field. The night vision cameras show their green shapes and eerie eyes. Several enormous phones sit on a charging terminal. The huge devices remind me of the first cordless phones ever made. An old radio with a shining silver microphone sits next to a shelf of boring looking manuals. I pick up one that's titled, SURVIVAL FM 21-76. Real catchy. There are similar books for things like first aid, guerrilla warfare, and boobytraps. I decide to hang on to the survival book since I haven't found anything else to read. At least, it'll help kill some time down here.

"You know what all this stuff does?" I ask Quentin.

"Most of it," he says. "The rest of it doesn't seem too complicated." He looks over the board.

"It's like being on some spaceship," I say. "I'm afraid to touch anything." I stare at the changing images on the monitors. I like being able to see everything and to know that everything is all being monitored and controlled in this little room.

We exit the communications room and head to the other end of the hallway. Just past the storage room, there is a small exercise room with a treadmill, some free weights, and a stationary bike. The next door we open reveals a small washer and dryer with some spare bedsheets and towels folded neatly on shelves. Across the hall, we open the door to a supply room. There are racks along the wall stocked with assorted rifles, knives, handguns, and ammunition. I spot some shotguns, some grenades, there is even an RPG. Aside from the weapons, there are tons of first aid supplies, clothes, food stores, and countless bottles of water.

"God damn," breathes Quentin. He picks up a package of white underwear and some socks. "There must be enough in here to last us, at least, six months."

The heavy door closes in the next room. The sound of the dog panting echoes in the hall. We leave the supply room and head back to the storage room. Fletcher digs through a large rucksack.

"We got some company out there," he says. He pulls out a pair of night vision goggles. "Must have been drawn here by the helicopter."

"How many?" I ask.

"Can't see in the dark, man," he says. "I can hear them out there, though. Creepy as shit."

I completely forgot it was the middle of the night already. Being down here is really going to take some getting used to.

"You need a hand?" asks Quentin. He grabs up one of the assault rifles and the helmet beside his pack.

Fletcher looks at Quentin.

"If you're up for it," he says.

I gather up the assault rifle I had carried in. It's a little heavier than I expected and I hold it awkwardly. Fletcher watches me.

"You know what you're doing with that?" he asks.

"No idea," I admit.

"How about you sit this one out," he says, without even bothering to make it sound like a question. He walks across the room and reaches for my pack, pulling out a two-way radio and turns it on. "Keep eyes on those screens in the control room."

I put down the assault rifle and take the handset from him. Fletcher doesn't really need me to monitor the screens. It's just something to get me out of the way. As much as I feel completely inept, I am more relieved than anything. I realize I am totally unprepared to go out there and stalk the living dead in total darkness.

"I don't think any of them breached the gate, but just keep checking," he says. "We don't need anything sneaking up on us."

"Got it," I say, turning to head to the control room.

"Blake," he says, as I make a turn to go down the hall. I wait while he straps a helmet on his head. "When we get back, we'll go over some shit, so you know what's what. Sound good?"

"Alright," I mumble, so it comes out as an apology. "Good luck."

I pass Stitch in the hall on my way to the control room, and his excited tail smacks my leg as I go by. He stops and looks back at me before running to tag along with Quentin and Fletcher. Even the dog is more help than me. I sit down in the swivel chair in the control room, putting the radio and the survival manual down on the workspace.

I pick up and flip through a few pages of the manual while I wait. Scanning the contents, I encounter a list of skills I don't have. Now my life could depend on them. The lives of the few remaining people I know could depend on them, too. I don't want to learn them, but I am determined to now. There is no way I am going to be a liability.

"Hey."

The sudden voice jars me, and I knock the radio over as I try to swivel around and put the manual down.

"Sorry," says Danielle. She runs her fingers through her dripping hair. "Where is everybody?"

"Quentin and Fletcher went outside. Fletcher heard some of those things out there while he was out with the dog."

"You can see everything in here," she says. She leans over the table next to me, looking at the images on the monitors. The scent of the soap or shampoo coming off her distracts me from whatever else she is saying. I am wondering how we all use the same soap, but it smells more intense coming off her skin.

"What?" I ask.

"Are you okay?" she says.

"Yeah," I say. "I was just... distracted." I look down and twist the ring on my finger to straighten it out. A knot tightens in my gut. I feel guilty about the things I won't even admit to myself.

"Are there a lot of them out there?" she asks again.

"I don't see very many," I say. "It seems like they are all outside the fence still." I point to one of the screens with a camera focused on the perimeter fence. Four figures grasp the barricade, pressing their bodies and faces against the metal.

"Why don't we just leave them there if they can't get in?" she asks.

Before I can think of a logical answer, the radio squawks and I hear Fletcher whispering through the speaker.

"Blake, you copy?" he says.

I grab the radio off the table and click the button on the side. "Yeah," I say. "Loud and clear."

I see them just outside the exit on one of the screens. Fletcher looks up at the camera as he speaks.

"What do you see out there?" he asks.

"I see four of them on the north fence," I answer.

"There's two miles of fencing there," he says. "I need you to be more specific."

I check the screens again, waiting for the camera angle to come up where I spotted the corpses. There must be some way to switch them manually, but I can't figure it out. "About a hundred yards from the northeast corner," I say.

"Okay, we're moving out," he whispers.

When the camera on the main entrance cycles back around, the two men are gone. I listen to them talking quietly over the radio.

"Watch our six," Fletcher orders Quentin.

Danielle taps me on the shoulder and points to another screen. There are two more corpses on a different camera that covers part of the east fence. I click the button on the radio.

"Fletcher?" I say.

"What is it?" he asks.

"There's two more about midway on the eastern fence."

A long pause.

"I don't have a visual, but I hear them," Fletcher finally responds. "Will check it out on the way back. Over."

I look around at the control board in front of me, trying to read all the various controls and locate something that might work the cameras.

"What are you looking for?" asks Danielle.

"There has to be some way to switch through the cameras manually."

She reaches up on top of one of the screens and pulls down a remote. Danielle hits a couple of buttons and cycles through the cameras that cover the perimeter. She stops it on the camera that has a view of the four corpses along the north fence. Feeling a little stupid for not being able to figure that out myself, I thank her for the assistance.

"They're nuts to go out there at night."

"Maybe it's better," I say. "At least, they have night vision. Who knows how well those things can see in the dark."

Unfortunately, the night vision also makes it all too easy to see the physical state of the undead outside. I watch a huge man in overalls with a hand and forearm chewed to a pulpy mess. It clings to the fence with the only good hand it has and flails at the barrier with the phantom hand. A disemboweled woman in a tattered and stained nightgown drags her intestines through the weeds. The other man, he is more of a boy, really, is stark naked. His lower jaw is missing from his face. The last corpse sports a motorcycle helmet.

I wonder if I should mention the helmet to Fletcher. I am pretty sure a helmet won't stop a bullet to the head, though. Before I can pick up the radio to make the call, I see one of the four figures along the fence flop back. The naked boy lands hard on his back and is still.

"Short, controlled bursts," whispers Fletcher.

I hear a muffled series of taps. The woman in the nightgown and the guy in the overalls collapse in the grass. Over the radio, it sounds like they are taking them out with a typewriter. The suppressed shots are exactly like the sound of someone typing snippy words with the keys.

"That fucker is wearing a helmet," Quentin gripes.

A few more rounds pepper the helmet, lodging in the cracked surface.

"Damn thing must be kevlar," says Fletcher.

The radio goes quiet again. I watch the motorcycle rider assault the fence with renewed intensity. Fletcher emerges onto the screen from the right. He retrieves a pistol from a holster strapped to his thigh. He slips the muzzle through the fence, and tucks it into the bottom of the helmet and pulls the trigger. Brain matter spatters the face shield and the corpse drops to the ground.

"Target down," breathes Fletcher as he exits the screen.

I stare at the image on the screen. I can't take my eyes off the bodies on the ground. It isn't the same watching it on these screens. At first, it doesn't seem real, so I become absorbed in the violence. Once the action cuts to a new scene, the story will go on. Except those bodies don't move, the scene will never change. The corpses of the people will remain lifeless in the grass, and they will always be there for as long as I keep watching.

"Proceeding to the east perimeter," whispers Fletcher. "You still got eyes on the other ones?"

"Yeah," I say. I manage to pull my eyes away from the bodies on the screen and search the control panel to try and pull the east perimeter up on the monitor. Danielle stares at the corpses too, but she snaps out of it then and finds a switch that brings up the camera outside the east perimeter.

They are two young women with long, dark hair, wearing long, dark dresses. They aren't clawing at the fence like the others, just loitering side-by-side along the edge of the road. Their blank eyes stare up at the camera. I swear it's like they can see us somehow.

"They're twins," I mumble.

One of them has a face that is half devoured. She has lost an ear, and her cheek has been eaten away leaving her teeth and jaw entirely exposed. The other sister had her throat ripped open. Her head lolls slightly to one side.

"It's like they're looking at us," says Danielle.

"That's impossible."

"What else could they be doing?" she says.

"What's wrong?" asks Fletcher over the radio.

"Nothing," I say. "These two just aren't acting like the others."

"How so?" he says.

"They're just staring at the camera," I tell him.

There is another long pause.

"You sure they're dead?" Quentin asks.

"They're dead," I say. "They're all messed up."

"Alright base, we'll check it out. Over," whispers Fletcher.

"Roger," I respond. "Over."

The pale empty eyes continue to stare at me. Now I want to switch the screen off. If I don't have to look at them, it will eliminate the terrifying power of their presence.

"Wish they'd hurry up. These two are freaking me out," says Danielle.

"They weren't doing that before were they?" I ask.

"No they were walking down the road," says Danielle. "I wonder what made them stop."

I try to come up with a rational explanation, but I find nothing. They were heading north before. If they heard the other gunshots, they should have kept heading north. I haven't seen any of them show any signs of intelligence before now. So what the hell is this?

After several long minutes, bullets pierce their craniums sending the twins down to rest among a splatter of gore upon the ground.

"All targets down," says Fletcher. "We're heading back now, base. See you in ten."

CHAPTER SIXTEEN

"They saw a light on top of the camera," says Fletcher. "That's all. Nothing to freak out about." He unstraps his helmet and sets it down on one of the benches between the storage lockers. The dog, collapses down beside my boots, panting deeply, it's tongue lapping at the air as though to drink it. I reach down and rub the dog's soft, exposed belly wishing I could have that kind of trust in the people around me.

"It's like they saw us," Danielle protests. "Didn't that seem at all weird to you?"

"Define weird," says Fletcher. He waits a moment before he adds, "The whole fucking world seems pretty damn weird to me right about now."

Danielle looks to me, but I can tell Fletcher is not thrilled about the topic and decides it's best to let it drop. He grabs some more supplies out of the pack and deposits them into a nearby locker.

"If we're all done here, I'd like to eat something." He tosses a package to Danielle, then another to me.

We follow him to the common area and tear open our MRE pouches on the mess table. I have a pouch marked as jambalaya, which I've never actually eaten before in my life. I was surprised to see it also contained a pound cake, a cracker with peanut butter and jelly, some dried fruit, and a dairy shake. There was another pouch with coffee, salt, chewing gum, and even a moist towelette.

Quentin gave us a quick rundown of how to use the flameless heater by adding water to a bag containing a sodium and magnesium pad to generate heat. It took like fifteen minutes to warm the little bag of jambalaya.

"When we go out, this is how we eat," says Quentin. "We don't make any fires out in the open that will draw more attention to ourselves."

"When we go out?" Danielle asks. "Why would we go out? We have everything we need down here, right?"

"We won't sit in here and twiddle our thumbs all day until it's all gone," interrupts Fletcher. "We need to requisition medical supplies, not to mention more fuel and water. There's a lot of stuff out there now, but it won't last forever."

"Plenty of it has probably been looted already," adds Quentin.

Fletcher nods in agreement.

"That's right," he says. "So eat up, doll. We got work to do."

I take the bag out of the heater and put a spoonful of jambalaya in my mouth. I gag and have to try hard to swallow the nasty concoction down.

"This is fucking awful," I groan.

"Just like mom used to make," says Quentin and I notice he is eating the same meal as I have. It doesn't seem to bother him at all. Maybe I just don't like jambalaya.

"I'll save the jambalaya for you from now on," I say. I extend my pouch toward him, and he takes it and inclines it against his open beer while he finishes his portion. I stare at the sorry wheat cracker and withered dried fruits, then shove them back in the bag. Getting some real food might be a good idea. I don't know if I could get used to eating this stuff on a daily basis.

I use the hot beverage bag to heat some water the same way as the food. The only part of these meals I seem to enjoy is heating them. I watch as the others finish their pouches while I make my coffee. I add the pouch of instant grounds to a bag of hot water and shake the mixture. I retrieve my mug that is still sitting on the table from breakfast and pour the coffee. It tastes about as bland as any coffee I've ever had in my life, but it's better than nothing.

"I wouldn't mind if we hit up a coffee shop too," I say.

Fletcher points his empty spoon at me. "Now you're talking," he says. "I have my mind set on finding a liquor store."

"I don't suppose this place has any supplies for feminine hygiene?" asks Danielle.

"I didn't see anything in the supply room," I say.

I look down at the dog who is eyeing us from beneath the table, waiting patiently for a morsel to fall. I hand the dog the cracker and several pieces of dried fruit from my MRE. It inspects them on the floor, then reluctantly eats them one at a time.

"The pooch probably won't complain about getting some real dog food either," I say.

"Well damn," says Fletcher. "We got plenty to do now then." He drops his spoon into the pouch and heads toward the kitchen to throw it out. He steps out of the room and returns a minute later with rifles slung over his shoulders and a couple of large knives and handguns. He hands me one of the pistols, then passes the other along to Danielle.

"This is your new best friend," Fletcher smirks. He pulls his own version out of his side holster and attaches the suppressor to the muzzle. "It's an MK23 SOCOM .45 with a suppressor. This is going to be your primary weapon."

Fletcher meticulously shows us how to take it apart, clean it, and load it, and makes us do it over and over until I want to use the damn thing to shoot the hard-headed bastard.

After what seems like the millionth time I take the thing apart, Fletcher asks Quentin to take over and leaves the room. I put the damn gun together again and lay it down on the table.

Quentin looks at the weapon and gives me a smile.

"I think I got it," I say.

"It's your ass," he warns.

I'm not sure if he means Fletcher will give me hell for disobeying, or that I better know how to take care of the firearm. Fletcher doesn't intimidate me. He knows a lot more than I do, or even Quentin, about how to survive in this mess. Right now, I want to learn from him, so I deal with this condescending bullshit. Still, I'm not about to let him start to think he can order us around like we're his new recruits.

"I want to shoot this thing," smiles Danielle. She points the gun at the wall, squinting down the sight. "I really want to try it."

"Well, let's gear up and we'll go out." Fletcher watches us from the doorway. "I just checked out the perimeter. There's one or two out there we can use for some target practice."

With a helmet strapped on, a pack over my shoulders and the MK 23 gripped tight in my hand we exit the bunker into the dark of night. It's getting close to five in the morning, but with the recent time change, the sky has yet to show any signs of daybreak. There is just a sliver of the moon visible above. I pull the night vision goggles over my eyes, and I can see again.

We walk up the steps and exit out into the silent field. We move slowly through the tall grasses, crouched and scanning the surrounding landscape. I follow Fletcher toward the western fence line. Danielle trails behind me, and Quentin watches our backs.

"Don't get lazy," orders Fletcher. His voice is like a whisper in my ear over the radio. "There's miles of fence. Never assume the perimeter is still secure."

His tone kind of annoys me. It's not like we haven't had to fight these things off for several days already. Still, he knows a lot more about the art of killing, I guess.

We walk single file. Stitch moves swiftly alongside our formation, keeping his body low to the ground. About one hundred yards from the fence Fletcher pauses and holds up a fist. We wait and watch as two figures wander along the road.

"Alright, showtime," he says. Fletchers gestures to Danielle and me. "You two work your way up to the fence and take those two out as quietly as possible. We'll cover you from here, then rally to your position."

I keep crouched and move forward slowly, checking the ground for any sticks or objects that may cause me to trip and give us away. We move right up to the fence unnoticed. I look through the chainlink and realize these aren't just corpses. They're kids. A girl with blonde pigtails, torn corduroys, and one shoe follows a slightly older boy wearing a baseball hat. Neither of them can be older than nine or ten.

"I got the one on the left," whispers Danielle. "The girl."

Maybe she thinks this will make this easier for me. The girl looks nothing like my daughter, but it makes me imagine Abby wandering the streets like this kid. I lower the handgun.

"It's okay," I whisper. "You have a better angle on the boy."

"You sure?" she asks.

I nod and lift the firearm up again.

"Let's move this along," Fletcher groans over the radio.

I ignore Fletcher, and wait while Danielle takes aim at the dead boy.

"Ready?" I ask.

She nods.

Two suppressed shots drop the corpses on the road. The bodies lie motionless on the asphalt. I lower my gun and stare at the small shapes. In spite of everything we've been through, nothing compares to pointing a gun at the head of a dead child and pulling the trigger. I can't swallow. My tear ducts burn. I close my eyes, but the image of the scene is already imprinted onto my memory.

"Good shooting," says Fletcher. "You two were born to kill."

I open my eyes and see Danielle still has her gun raised toward the road. I reach over and put my hand on her wrist, lowering the weapon.

"I spent my whole life learning to keep people alive," she says. "It was all I wanted. Now, I just wish they'd stay dead." She sniffs and wipes a sleeve below her nose, then returns the pistol to the holster.

Quentin and Fletcher are making their way to us through the brush, still scanning the terrain for any other indications of the undead. Over their heads, I can see the hint of daybreak emerging in the eastern sky. I remove the night vision goggles and look around in the dawning blue light.

"Shit," says Quentin when he gets close enough to see the bodies of young children on the road. "Those were just kids."

"They aren't kids," says Fletcher. "They're fucking zombies."

"You shouldn't have sent them," Quentin says. He strides ahead of Fletcher to hurry toward our position. "You knew those were kids out there. You saw them on the camera, and you sent them to take care of them anyway."

"So?" asks Fletcher. He shakes his head in frustration. "I don't see why that's such a goddamn big deal. Christ."

I put the MK23 back in the holster and stand up. I don't know if Fletcher was testing us to see if we could put down these children. I don't really care. It wasn't shooting them that bothered me. It was seeing them shambling alone in the dark road. I know if those were my kids, I would want them put to rest. I blink to bury an image in my mind of Abby, wandering through the halls of her school like that. It is too horribly vivid.

Stitch is first to reach us at the fence and does a lap around us before settling down next to Danielle and licking at her face. She instantly smiles and rubs his scruffy neck. Quentin stalks up to the fence, raising his arms in a show of confusion.

"It's okay," I tell him. "We were going to have to come up against something like that eventually. Better now than out there." I tilt my head at the other side of the fence.

"Guess you two don't need any target practice after all," offers Fletcher. He removes the goggles and tries on a smile. He looks down at his boot, toeing a spot of dirt. "Sorry, by the way. I underestimated you. Both of you."

"Don't worry about it," I say. "Really."

"They are tough," he admits to Quentin. "You weren't lying."

The songs of birds signal the approaching morning. Far overhead, I can hear the bickering of a flock of geese on their return flight north after the long winter. The air is crisp with the scent of fresh buds on the trees. Life proceeds, all around us, as humanity breathes a final death rattle. Through a fog so thick I can feel it caressing my face, we head back toward our bunker. The hole in the ground seems more and more like a grave we are already living in. We're all dead. Sure, our hearts beat, and blood flows through our veins. Whatever that means. It isn't the same as living anymore.

It feels good to get back inside and pull off my pack and gear. I'm not in shape for this kind of thing, especially with the injuries I've endured the past few days. My shoulders and back ache and I can feel a headache coming on.

"We'll head back out at dusk," says Fletcher. "There's a strip mall with a pharmacy and a gas station about two miles west. I saw it on our flight in."

"We'll have to go under the expressway, Fletcher," says Quentin.

"Yeah," he sighs. He opens up one of the lockers along the wall and places his helmet inside. "Might get a little thick around there, but we can get through."

Stitch wags his tail, but the dog is the only optimistic one in the room. We follow his wagging tail into the common area and collapse onto the couches. Stitch hops up next to me and curls up into a ball.

The second hand of the clock on the wall makes a few circles as we sit in silence. Fletcher picks up the remote from the table and turns the television on again. The movie starts over. He pulls the tab on a can of beer and takes a big gulp.

"Can we not watch this?" asks Danielle.

"There isn't anything else to do, doll. Unless you want to play some strip poker."

"Doesn't all this bother you?" she asks him. "How can you just sit around drinking beer and watching television like nothing's happening."

"And what do you propose I do about it?" he asks.

Danielle folds her arms and leans back in her seat. "I'm not saying you should do anything about it. Just stop acting like you don't give a shit."

Fletcher takes a long swig of his beer, and then he picks up the remote and shuts the television off. He lifts the deck of cards off the table, then puts them back down.

"I drink and watch the television because I give a shit," he sighs. "It won't do any good to drive yourself nuts thinking too much. That's the last thing you should do."

"It's not that easy," says Danielle.

"You got family out there?" he asks her.

She nods her head.

"Where?" he asks.

"Pennsylvania."

"Mom?" he asks. "Dad?"

"My dad and my brothers," she says.

"You talk to them since this started?"

Danielle shakes her head.

"I got a brother, too," he says. "Ain't a minute that goes by that I'm not thinking about him."

Quentin shifts in his seat then he leans forward to grab a beer off the table.

"Where's he at?" asks Quentin.

"Fort Collins," says Fletcher. "Colorado. At least, he was. We have this old cabin up there in the mountains, been in the family for years. That's where he was heading."

"Is that why you didn't want to go to New Mexico?" I ask him.

"That's part of it," he says. He looks down at the deck of playing cards on the table. "I told him I'd meet him when I could get out there."

"This place," I say. "This cabin. You think it's safe there?"

"It's real out of the way," Fletcher says. "There's a lake between the cabin and the city. Mountains for miles on the backside. If he made it there, he's alive. Jimmy is a tough son of a bitch." For a moment he chuckles at the memories of his sibling, then, with a sigh picks up his beer and drinks.

I can't tell whether he really believes his brother is still alive, or if that is something he is choosing to believe in order to keep himself going. I guess if he believed it, he wouldn't be here with us in this place, hiding from reality.

"Listen to me going on like I'm the only one with any problems here." He rises from the sofa and walks toward the kitchenette. "Might as well get some chow then get some sleep."

We go through the routine of preparing the MRE meals. I decide to go with a sloppy joe and thank god it's not as bad as the jambalaya. We sit down at the table and wait while our food heats in the bags. The slow process takes forever, and my stomach complains about the wait.

"Where were you guys when this whole thing started?" Fletcher asks.

We tell him about the train station. About our brief stay at the racetrack and the security building. We recount our trip to the cemetery and how we finally went to the restaurant where the military picked us up. It was still hard to believe what we'd been through and survived, but it was just as hard to tell it again. There is no way to tell the story without mentioning the people we lost. I'd been trying to forget about them. It probably sounds callous to say that, like they didn't matter as much as the rest of us. I just can't deal with the guilt.

I devour the whole meal, even the dried fruit pouch and the stale wheat cracker with peanut butter as well. I'm still hungry afterward, probably because I hadn't eaten much before. I warm the water and stir in the packet to make apple cider. I breathe in the steam and savor the spicy scent as I sip it.

"This is good," I say, hoping to change the subject. "I only ever drank this stuff in the fall. We'd take Abby to this farm every October. Pick out a pumpkin. Go on a hayride, all that typical stuff. They had the best hot apple cider, though, like they made it right there. They put some caramel and whip cream on it. I used it to keep warm while I waited for Abby and Amanda to go through the haunted house. That stupid thing wasn't even scary, but it made Abby cry every time. I probably should have gone in there with them." I stop talking at the end of the sentence, but it sounds like there is more to the story. There's one more line I can't bring myself to say. That I wasn't there for them before all of this happened either.

I blink my eyes and stare at the tin cup and the tangy orange liquid cooling inside it. I look up and see them all staring at me intently, probably wondering if I'm about to lose it or something.

"This isn't anything like that stuff," I say. I take a drink of the cider, and then I get up to toss out the trash and rinse the cup. Quentin eyes me curiously as I fill and dump the water.

"I don't know about the rest of you," says Fletcher. He rises from his chair and collect the wrappers on the table. "I'm ready to call it a day."

"It's not even ten in the morning," says Danielle.

"We need to be ready to move at nightfall, doll. I don't know about you, but I haven't slept much at all in the past few days, and it's time for a reckoning." Fletcher tosses an empty can of beer into the trash can and it clangs against the metal container. "By the sound of it, you could all use a little extra rack time too. Need to be sharp out there."

CHAPTER SEVENTEEN

There's nothing to do down here in this bunker but think. Even though it has only been about twelve hours since I awoke, I wouldn't mind going back to sleep. That sounds easy enough, but whenever I close my eyes I see all the things I don't want to picture. Before all this, I read stories about people dying every day. While they were sad and all, I didn't ever sob over the fate of some strangers. But now, just being human means something again. If we could find people and save them, we had to do it.

"This is bullshit," Quentin blurts.

His outburst startles me. For a moment, I'd forgotten I wasn't alone.

"We can't live like this," he continues. "Sitting around here. Not doing shit about a goddamn thing. Waiting until it's too late."

The rest of us still believe we have family out there. We distract ourselves with thoughts of getting back to them. Quentin doesn't have those kinds of thoughts anymore. I can't imagine what he is thinking now.

"Too late for what?" I ask.

"For everything."

I wait for him to go on.

"There's still people out there," he says. "I know you saw them too when we flew in."

"Yeah," I say. "I saw them too." I picture the desperate guy stranded on that roof that was trying to wave at our helicopter.

"We know what will happen to them if we don't do something."

"Yeah," I say.

Quentin sighs. For a long time, we lay there, saying nothing. Eventually, he snores lightly on the bunk above me. A groan from my stomach urges me up from the bed. I shuffle out to the kitchen and pick out another MRE to eat. I dump my water in the heating bag and read the Army survival manual while I wait for the spaghetti and meatballs to heat up. I try to distract myself with anything. I read the same few lines over and over again. My thoughts keep going back to the world outside, the people that could still be alive out there. When my mind focuses on something, it refuses to let go until I surrender to it, like a Chinese finger trap.

I pick up the packages of food and move down the quiet hall to the communications room. In the dim glow, I sit and watch the security screens. A storm has erupted, darkening the midday sky outside. More corpses are already drifting down the roads along the perimeter of the facility. They plod through the thick sheets of rain like abandoned ships at sea. They have no course or destination. They just drift around, carried by some unseen current. Lightning strikes and illuminates the effigies of humanity. I wait for the sound of thunder, but I hear nothing except the sound of air arriving and departing my body in the quiet depths of the bunker.

I spoon a mouthful of bland spaghetti into my mouth. It doesn't taste too awful if you try not to think about it. It's nothing like going out to an Italian restaurant, though, that's for sure. I wish I had some garlic salt to make it taste like something.

Another flash of lightning makes the security monitors flare. It is a hell of a nasty storm. This kind of weather always terrified Abby. The lightning made her inconsolable. It drove me nuts. I tried telling her the odds of being struck by lightning were astronomical, but that didn't matter. She would always feel like it was aiming for her, and the only thing that would help was holding her until the rain stopped.

I could never understand her fear before, but now I think I do. Sometimes knowing the odds doesn't matter. I know my best chance of surviving the day is to stay inside here as long as possible. The odds of surviving very long out there are pretty bleak. It's just a matter of time for all of us. Just a matter of time.

While I might survive a whole lot longer down here, it won't be much of a life. Locked away from the world, playing ping pong until I die in this hole in the ground. Watching everything through these television monitors, oblivious. Scavenging for anything that sustains us a bit longer, or makes us feel more alive. We'd be no more alive than those dead people out there.

I guess that's how I lived my entire life. Waiting for a day when things will get better, a magical tomorrow that will never come. Not willing to take a chance on the things that matter most, because the fear of what may happen if you're wrong.

At that moment, I realize I'm not afraid anymore.

I've lived my entire life like I was dead already. I've got nothing left to lose.

The rain outside has stopped. There's this one corpse on the road. A bald, gangly man dressed in a black and red flannel shirt. It lingers near a puddle, staring down at its reflection like Narcissus. Except what this thing sees is a hideous face, the flesh ripped away on one side from the chin to the scalp.

At last, my eyes ache to be closed, and my mind relaxes. Sleep will come easier now. When I wake up, I will set out to look for my family.

CHAPTER EIGHTEEN

I am the first one to wake up. I shower and quietly get dressed and ready to go. I debate leaving before anyone wakes up, but I can't bring myself to do it. Even though I have decided I will head out on my own, it doesn't feel right to slip out while they sleep. I visit the supply room and load my pack with some extra rations. I stuff some extra ammunition and clothes in the bag, and inspect the shelves for anything else that might come in handy.

"Won't need all that," says Fletcher. His voice startles me, and I wonder how long he has been standing in the doorway. "We won't be gone more than a few hours. Don't need the extra weight slowing you down out there."

I can't think of any reasons to explain my loaded pack except the truth, so I just nod and sling the heavy bag over my shoulder. Fletcher studies me curiously as I pass him and then follows me back to the main room.

Quentin is already dressed in his black fatigues and devouring his breakfast. Stitch eyes him hopefully from beneath the table. Fletcher pulls out a chair and lifts his foot to rest on it while he tightens the laces.

"You sleep okay?" asks Quentin. He pours some instant coffee from the heating bag into a tin cup and slides it toward the seat beside him.

"As good as I have in a while," I say. I unsling my pack from my shoulder and gulp the warm coffee down in several swallows without enjoyment. A door opens, and Danielle emerges from her room in black fatigues, her auburn hair back in a ponytail.

"When do we leave?" she asks.

"It's getting dark," says Fletcher. "We should move now. It shouldn't take more than a couple hours, but I don't want to risk being out there when the sun comes up."

We follow Fletcher to the storage room and grab our weapons. I take the .45 and stow it in the holster secured to my thigh. Fletcher hands me one of the assault rifles. The thing is enormous and has a suppressor, a scope, and a mounted flashlight.

"That's an M4A1," he says, reaching down to pick up another one for himself. His has two barrels. The bottom has a pump action grip like a shotgun. "Just in case we run into a crowd."

I sling the strap over my shoulder, and then Fletcher slides the card. We file out the open door to the darkness beyond. I don't feel the fear that I had felt each time before when I knew we were going to encounter the dead. I just want to get moving. I want to help them get their supplies, and then maybe find a vehicle and head north towards Abby's school. It's not much of a plan, but even the best plans don't work out like they're supposed to anymore.

I pull down my night vision goggles before we move through the whispering field. The wet grass sways in the breeze and my boots sink into the damp earth. Stitch jogs along the side of us, pausing to lap at a puddle or sniff the ground every few feet. The dog seems to be able to sense when the dead are close. Maybe it's just the canine sense of smell, but the scruffy hairs around his collar will stand on end when the dead are near.

We approach the only gate in the perimeter fence and gaze out at the empty street beyond. Fletcher removes a ring of keys from his pack, selects one, and inserts it into a padlock that secures the chain around the gate. The chain rattles as he fumbles with the lock and slides the links through the fence. I scan the road again and spot a couple of figures emerging from the dark corn fields about a hundred yards up the road.

"God damn," mutters Fletcher. He pries the gate open and the rusty hinges whine.

The noise draws the attention of the corpses. They shamble forward more quickly now, moaning and raising their arms. Fletcher works to secure the gate while Quentin and Danielle crouch down in the tall grass along the road.

"Blake, get down," urges Fletcher.

I glance back at him, then return my gaze back to the approaching undead. There are still just two of them in the road. Both of them have dusty jeans and reflective vests that glint in the moonlight. One of the dead things still wears a hard hat. They must have wandered over from a construction site around here.

"I'll get them," I say. Inexplicably, I don't even feel the need to whisper out here. I start walking toward them while I remove the .45 from the holster and attach the suppressor to the barrel.

"Stand down, Blake," hisses Fletcher. His breathing sounds labored through the headset. "I can take them out from here."

I ignore the sound of his voice. I stop walking several feet from the first staggering corpse. It lunges toward me, and I slide to my right and trip it with my left foot. It lands hard on the pavement. It doesn't even have the sense to use its arms to break the fall. I shove the knife under the back of its skull, and it goes still. I hear the one with the hard hat closing in behind me. There is no time to pry the knife free. I turn as the corpse in the hard hat tries to grab my shoulder. It lunges as I aim the .45, so I use the handle to hit it in the face with all the force I can manage. The hard hat falls to the street, making just the kind of clatter that I was hoping to avoid. The thing keeps coming. It latches a hand on each of my shoulders and tries to pull me close enough to bite. I drop the gun just so I have two hands to fight it off. I manage to turn the thing so its back is to the other corpse on the ground then I push it backward over the body as hard as I can. When it loses balance, I drive it down to the pavement. There is a wet slapping sound as the back of the thing's skull bounces off the street. The weight of my pack nearly pushes me within reach of the open mouth. I sit up and grab the head of the thing with both hands and slam it back to the pavement as hard as I can. Then I lift the head of the corpse up and bring it down again and again until the skull fractures. I stop when I hear the soggy sound of soft tissue hitting against the hard surface of the road.

It isn't until I stand up that I realize Fletcher, Quentin and Danielle are standing a couple of feet away. They don't know what to make of my violent outburst. Danielle looks ready to cry. I avoid their eyes and locate the gun I dropped on the street.

"What the fuck was that about?" asks Fletcher.

I bend down and pick up the gun. The reasons for what I did seem clear to me. These damn things have taken everything I didn't appreciate until it was gone. The sight of them, the mockery of the human beings they once were, broke something inside of me. I try to find the words, but it seems like it would take too long. So, I make something up instead.

"Conserving ammunition," I explain and walk away before there is time for anyone to question my reasoning. I can feel my hands still shaking from the adrenaline coursing through my body. Drawing air into my lungs feels harder than it should, and the sound of my breathing seems so loud in the silence of the night.

I hear my name whispered. The soft voice makes me think of Amanda calling to me, and I get the haunting feeling that she has witnessed what just happened. Guilt turns my stomach, and I stop and lean over and throw up.

"Blake," whispers Danielle. She catches up to me and puts a hand on my shoulder.

"I'm okay," I cough and wipe the vomit away from my mouth. "Let's keep moving."

The streets are black and empty and slick from the rain. We move towards the tunnel beneath the highway. Some wrecked or abandoned vehicles clog the dark passage. Fletcher holds up a hand as an echoing moan comes at us from the darkness. The night vision goggles only allow us to see so far into the blackness, and there is no telling what awaits behind the vehicles. We won't know what we are walking into until we are in the middle of it.

"Maybe we should go around," suggests Quentin.

"Sounds like there's only one in there," reasons Fletcher. He tilts his head and listens closely. "Maybe two or three at the most."

"I don't like going in there blind," Quentin sighs.

I stare into the darkness. Drops of water trickle down through the cracks in the highway and splatter in puddles on the pavement. I hear the faint sound of shoes scuffing along the street. There could be dozens of them in there. Whatever lies in the depths of the tunnel isn't what I fear any longer. The only thing that scares me is living the rest of my life in fear. I would rather face anything than go on like that. I will keep going forward no matter what gets in my way.

I step cautiously into the tunnel. I am conscious of every sound of my movements. A hand falls on my pack, and I pivot back to see Danielle right behind me. I slow down my pace. The others follow her slowly in a single-file line. I feel something brush against my leg and glance down, but nothing is there. I look around and spot Stitch ahead of us. He trots along, pauses, cocks his head at us and keeps going.

To the left, I see a bare-chested figure hovering a few yards away. It vacantly stares upward into the darkness. There are hunks of flesh missing from its forearms and midsection. It takes a step and drags its other leg across the ground behind it. I hear someone behind me misstep, their boot crushing a piece of glass that crackles beneath their weight. The sound echoes off the concrete walls.

The corpse off to the left turns toward the noise. I stop moving and wait and hope it will lose interest. I scan the darkness and notice another figure further off to our right. As it closes in on us, I spot another figure emerging from the darkness behind him. More sounds of movement bounce off the walls of the tunnel making it impossible to guess how many more there could be down there with us.

"Move," urges Fletcher.

The nearest corpse rasps at the sound of his voice and gropes at us blindly in the dark. I hit it in the face with the butt of the rifle and break into a sprint. Moans seem to be coming from every direction in the tunnel now. The focus of the goggles blurs when I run. The jittery image is little help to my eyes, and I stumble over a body lying on the ground that I never saw. I get back on my feet and keep rushing forward. Suppressed machine gun fire erupts behind me.

"They're all over the fucking place," screams Quentin into the radio. The corpses close around us in all directions. I can see the distant light of the other side of the tunnel now, and I head for it as fast as I can, knocking several corpses to the ground that stagger in my way. I spot Stitch waiting for us down the road. He cocks his head and stares at me as I emerge from the tunnel.

The body of a falling corpse from the highway above crashes onto the asphalt beside me as I turn to look back into the darkness. The sound of the body smashing into the ground makes me stop in my tracks and look up. Two more of the dead tumble over the rail and I stagger backward to get out of the way. The crunching collision of bones and dead flesh splattering on the street paralyzes me with horror. I spot Danielle and Quentin as they race out of the tunnel, avoiding the bodies falling to the ground around them. Stitch wags his tail when he sees them. More and more corpses keep leaning out over the railing until gravity pulls them down to the ground. Most of them keep moving, dragging their mangled bodies toward us.

"Where's Fletcher?" I ask.

No one answers. We stare at the tunnel and wait and listen as the corpses keep coming towards us.

A gunshot echoes in the darkness of the tunnel. He must still be alive. I shrug off my pack and drop it to the ground.

"If I'm not back in two minutes, leave," I say. I run back towards the tunnel, making my way through the bodies strewn across the street. Instead of trying to elude the undead in the darkness, I drop every last one of them I see. I stop moving when I see Fletcher on the ground. He struggles beneath several of the dead. His body is face down, pinned to the street by the weight of the corpses and his pack. He blindly slashes away at the things with his knife. I can't be exactly sure what I'm aiming at, but he is dead anyway if I wait around all damn day. I fire off several shots taking down one of the corpses as I approach. I smash the stock of the rifle into the back of the skull of another, and then get the last one off him by shoving it with my boot. I put a few rounds into each of them until they stop moving.

Fletcher's helmet has been knocked off, and I look around on the ground for it. His panicked eyes dart around in the darkness as he feels for his rifle. The sounds of gunfire reach us from outside the tunnel. Fletcher locates his rifle, and then struggles to his feet, keeping his weight off his right leg. I try to see if he was injured or bitten, but I notice instead the figure approaching from behind him. I raise my rifle and fire a shot over his shoulder. The corpse falls to the ground.

"I lost my helmet," he says. "I can't see shit."

"Forget it. Can you walk?" I ask him.

"Yeah," he groans and hobbles over the pavement.

I spot several corpses about ten yards away. We'll never make it out of here at the pace he is moving. I shoulder my rifle and grab his shoulder. I hear a low growl, and then a bark from inside the tunnel. The sound draws the attention of the corpses away from us momentarily.

"We have to move faster," I say. "I'll carry you." I squat down and carry him over my shoulder. The weight is almost too much. Adrenaline must be giving me as much strength as I've ever had in my life. There only seem to be a handful of corpses left in the tunnel. They are easy to avoid, but carrying Fletcher through the bodies on the ground proves difficult. The night vision goggles help me see in the dark, but they take away much of my depth perception and peripheral vision.

"Put me down," barks Fletcher as we reach the edge of the tunnel.

I drop him on the ground, and he curses when his feet must bear his weight again.

"You okay?" Danielle asks. She rushes over and puts a hand on his shoulder, but he shrugs away from her.

"I'm fine," he grumbles. "Just twisted an ankle. We need to keep moving." He limps ahead of us down the street while I pause to scan the road. The dead stagger towards us through the brush along the highway. The shopping center is only a couple of blocks away, but the moans of the dead converging on our location urge us to pick up our pace.

I look back into the darkness of the tunnel hoping for some sign of Stitch.

"Blake," Danielle wraps her fingers around my arm. "There's nothing you can do. We have to go."

"I know," I let her lead me away, and we hustle to catch up to Fletcher and Quentin. I stop when I hear the sound of panting behind me. I turn and see Stitch trotting a few feet back, tongue lolling out a corner of his mouth. He sits and looks up at me with his head cocked to one side. I reach down to pat his scruffy head, and he winces, startled by the touch. Then he relaxes, and stops panting.

"Good boy," I tell him. He stands up and wags his tail as he runs to catch up to Danielle.

CHAPTER NINETEEN

The sight of the dark and shattered windows of the ravaged strip mall is a let down after we nearly lost our lives trying to get here. Even though I had expected to see the stores looted, the place looks demolished. The gas station at the corner had burned to the ground. Soaked papers and garbage clutter the walkway along the storefronts, but the area seems clear of undead. I doubt there will be much to scavenge from the raided pharmacy, but the liquor store seems surprisingly untouched. Several cars riddled with bullet holes occupy spaces in the lot. If any of the dead owners are still around here, I might be able to find the keys and get one running. After dealing with the corpses we encountered in the tunnel, I'd rather be traveling in a car if possible. I scan the road behind us to find a crowd of corpses that have followed us from the highway.

"We have to get inside," I say. "Those things won't take long to catch up." I just want to get through this as quickly as possible so that we don't end up trapped here. I want to get on my way home before it becomes impossible.

"We'll check the pharmacy first," Fletcher whispers. He hobbles towards the shattered sliding glass door, which is held open by a dead body sprawled on the ground. Fletcher peeks his head inside, then moves out of the way to let us pass. The smell of rotting food and death is almost more than I can bear as I straddle the corpse on the floor and slip inside. It's dark inside, but enough light slips in through the store windows that I can see the front of the building is clear of any movement. One of the clerks lies dead on the counter next to the register. His dried blood splatters the glass of the cigarette case along the wall. I want to search him for car keys immediately, but I decide to wait until after we finish clearing the store.

"Spread out and grab anything we need," says Fletcher. "I'll watch the door. Five minutes and be quiet."

Danielle takes Stitch and heads toward the aisle of pet products on the right and Quentin heads towards the food aisles on the left. After a moment of thought, I decide to head back to the pharmacy and try to find some antibiotics. I head down the seasonal aisle of the store, pick up a couple of bottles of lighter fluid and a battery-powered camping lantern and shove them in my pack. Nothing else of use remains. The opposite side of the aisle is toys and candy for Easter. I start to move on, but then realize I saw something else and turn around. A plush monkey sits on a shelf of cheap gifts. The kind of thing I would always have to buy for Abby when she was a toddler. Even though she grew out of that a few years ago, the stuffed animal just made me think of her for some reason. I pick it up and shove it in the pack, then sling the strap over my shoulder and hurry toward the back of the store.

The door to the pharmacy is locked, so I set the rifle and pack down to climb the counter and hop behind it. The moment my feet hit the ground, I hear a noise from the back of the room. It sounded like a plastic bottle hitting the floor. I quietly lift up my rifle from the counter and wait for another sound, but I hear nothing.

The tall shelves make it impossible to see much of what is behind them. I want to go back over the counter and get the hell out of here. After a few long moments of silence, I decide to continue my search of the pharmacy. There isn't a lot of time to waste. I crouch down and move along the ends of the aisles and peer slowly around each corner. As I approach the last aisle, I hear another noise. Something scrapes along the floor. It freezes me in my tracks. I steady the rifle and get ready to turn around the last shelving fixture. I take a deep breath and peer around the corner. I scan the workstations in the back corner. Nothing. I release the breath I'd been holding and lower the rifle.

I begin rifling through the contents of the shelves looking for penicillin or something of the sort. I find some amoxicillin tablets and realize I need to find some bottles to store them from the cabinet. I turn back to grab them, and something smashes me in the head. The goggles get knocked from my eyes, and I fall back into the shelves and topple the whole fixture over. As my eyes adjust, I struggle to see anything in the darkness. I grope around and try to bring up the rifle when I realize the person that hit me is alive.

"Leave me alone," she screams.

At the last second, my vision returns enough to see a lead pipe heading for my face. I deflect it away with my arm, and it clangs to the floor. The woman who swung it at me turns to run when I reach for her. I manage to snatch the hood of her black sweatshirt. She lets out a scream and spins and flails her arms at me. After a brief attempt to try and quiet her, I clamp my hand over her mouth and push her back until she is against the wall.

"I'm not going to hurt you," I explain.

She turns her head so she is looking away from me and I feel her muscles relax as she sobs. Her eyes focus on something behind me, and I turn to see Quentin and Danielle beyond the pharmacy counter.

"Everything's okay," I tell them. I relinquish my hold on the young woman. "What's your name?"

"Natalie," she whispers. Her breath is stale, and her voice is dry and raspy. She wipes at her bruised eye with the sleeve of her stained sweatshirt. Her lower lip looks like it split open not too long ago. She flinches when I raise my hand to push some strands of the long dingy blonde hair from her face.

"I'm Blake," I say. "These are my friends, Quentin, and Danielle. No one here is going to hurt you. Okay?"

She stares at Danielle for a moment before she nods her head.

"Is anyone else here?" I ask her. She looks unsure how to answer me.

"I'm sorry I hit you," she apologizes. After everything she has been through, she speaks without a hint of feeling in her words. I set my pack on the ground and reach inside for a bottle of water, twist off the top and hand it to Natalie. She snatches it from me and drinks eagerly from the bottle.

"Who did this to you?" I ask. As if in response, I hear the sound of a heavy door closing in another room. Natalie startles at the sound and clutches my arm. A distant, carefree whistle echoes through the building.

"It's him," the girl gasps.

As the whistler moves closer, the tune becomes almost distinguishable. Natalie digs her fingernails into my arms. She tries to pull me towards the counter.

"We need to go," she pleads. I shake free from her grip to ready the rifle, but she keeps pulling at my arms. I raise a finger in front of my lips, and she quiets.

"Stay here," I command her. "We won't let anything happen to you." I start towards the counter, and she slumps down along the wall.

"Don't leave me," she whimpers.

I slip out the pharmacy door and join Quentin and Danielle on the other side of the counter. Stitch presses his body against

Danielle's leg. The scruff bristles on his neck. I peer around the corner down a long aisle of band-aids, toothpaste, and mouthwash. The cone of the flashlight illuminates the aisle followed by the shape of a man. He crosses the back aisle and heads towards the front of the store.

"What's going on back there?" Fletcher whispers through the radio. "Who turned on that light?"

"We got company," Quentin transmits.

"How many?" Fletcher asks.

"Just one," Quentin responds. "He's alive, but he's not friendly."

Quentin gestures for us to move towards the man from different directions. I nod, and then he slinks away down the long aisle that leads towards the beverage cases. I ask Danielle to stay put in the back and keep her eyes on the girl. She nods and clips a leash on Stitch and brings him with her through the pharmacy door.

I step cautiously along the back aisle of the store. Hundreds of small items cover the floor. Any of them could potentially spell disaster. If I happen to knock a bottle of vitamins across the tiles, the noise will give away our presence immediately. I take cover along the endcaps, easing slowly around the corners to be sure each aisle is clear before crossing. I wait a few seconds, hoping the man might start to whistle again and make it easier to locate him.

"Hello?" a voice calls out. It sounds like Fletcher. What the hell.

There is a long silent pause that seems like it will never end. I hear the noise of heavy boots walking on the floor. Fletcher isn't even trying to keep quiet. I peer around the corner, and I spot the man crouched about halfway down the aisle behind a display of reading glasses. He is focused on Fletcher up in the front of the store, so I watch him for several seconds before retreating around the corner. Fletcher is picking through the shelves, dropping objects intentionally on the floor.

"Don't move!" The man tries to sound intense, but his voice quavers slightly. I hear the cocking of a pistol hammer.

"Hey, easy there, fella," says Fletcher. His soft voice sounds genuinely surprised and afraid. "I'm not looking for any trouble."

"I said, don't move," the man growls.

"Okay," Fletcher concedes. He stops his advance and keeps his hands raised. I realize he is just distracting the man so that one of us can catch him by surprise.

"How about you slide that big ass gun over here," the man says.

Fletcher slowly brings a hand around to the rifle strap and begins to lift it over his head. "Let's just talk this out," says Fletcher.

"What you got in that pack?" the man demands.

"We're all on the same side here, right?" smiles Fletcher. "I can help you."

I tighten my grip on the rifle and prepare myself to round the corner and creep up behind this guy and crack him on the back of the head with the stock. The thought occurs to me to shoot him instead. I turn the corner, but when I aim the weapon at his back, I can't pull the trigger. I move cautiously across the floor, avoiding the bags of candy and potato chips that are scattered all around in the dark.

"What are you supposed to be?" the man sneers. "The cavalry?"

A candy wrapper crinkles beneath my boot and the man whirls around. His shock quickly turns to fury, and he levels the pistol with my head. I duck instinctively and lunge to the side. I bring the rifle up to my shoulder, but before I can pull the trigger, there is a spray of gunfire. The man crashes back into the half empty rack of chips behind him, then tumbles to the floor. Fletcher stands for a moment with his rifle still pointing at the spot where the man had stood. Then he pulls the strap back over his shoulder and advances down the aisle. He stops and looks down at the dead man and nudges the gun away from the man's hand with his boot.

"Why didn't you just shoot him?" Fletcher wonders. He bends down and retrieves the pistol, ejects the clip, then snaps it back in. Fletcher tucks the gun into the pack, then removes his .45 from the holster. He gazes back at the man on the ground once more. Then he fires another silenced round that pierces the man's skull. "He didn't have a second thought about shooting you."

I watch the fresh blood pooling around the body of the man on the ground. His stubbled face is dirty and expressionless. A knot twists in my stomach and I feel a furious hatred for the dead man for being someone that truly deserved to die.

Fletcher walks over and grabs a handful of my shirt sleeve and helps pull me up. Quentin rounds the corner of the aisle and looks at the body on the ground and the two of us standing beside it.

"Let's go," says Fletcher. "There's too many out front. We'll have to go out the back."

"Wait," I say. I remember the clerk by the register and turn to run towards the front of the store. I hear Fletcher mutter a curse behind me, and when I turn to look, I see they are following me. "Just go," I urge them. "I'll catch up."

They ignore this and pursue me to the front counter where I shove the dead clerk to the ground and begin digging through his pockets. The gunshot must have been enough to get the attention of the ones outside because I hear Quentin and Fletcher open fire on the other side of the counter.

My hand closes around a set of car keys, and I yank them free of the trouser pocket. I get up to leave and notice that dozens of corpses are pushing towards the door, stumbling over the fallen undead that Fletcher and Quentin have already taken out. Fletcher waves for me to go and waits until I run past him. Quentin continues firing into the gathering dead until they press through the door, then he shoulders his rifle and follows us to the pharmacy.

"What the hell was that about?" Fletcher screams.

I ignore him and keep heading towards the pharmacy counter at the rear of the store. Once everyone is in back, we shove over a tall shelving fixture to block the door to the back of the store. The pharmacy has a drive-thru window that leads to the back alley of the store. Danielle jabs the glass with the butt of the rifle until it shatters. She pokes away the remaining glass around the edges then shoulders the rifle. Stitch hesitates when she picks him up and sets him on the counter, so Danielle pushes his butt until he finally jumps out to the alley.

"Hey man," growls Fletcher. "You almost seriously jammed us up back there. You mind telling me what was so fucking important?"

Natalie climbs through the window next and waits in the alley while Danielle throws her pack down.

"I had to get these." I show Fletcher the set of car keys. I shrug my pack off my shoulders and set it down on the ground.

"We don't need a car to make it back," says Fletcher.

"They're coming," interrupts Quentin. He readies his rifle on the pharmacy counter. Danielle jumps out the drive-thru, and I hear her grunt outside when she lands in the alley. I lift my pack up and push it through the window.

"I'm not going back," I admit. I climb on the counter and exit the building. The back of the strip mall is wide open. There are several cars parked in the back of the stores, and all I can do is hope this is where the employees park. I click the unlock button on the car key and the taillights on a nearby red Honda Civic flash on and off.

I shoulder my pack and walk toward the car. I press another button that pops the trunk. I throw my gear down on top of a couple of rags, half a bottle of motor oil, and a few dirty towels.

"You're leaving?" pleads Danielle. She runs over and grabs at my shoulder.

"I'm sorry," I sigh. I hate apologizing, especially when it's for something I haven't even done yet.

"What's going on?" she demands.

I close the trunk and look back. Fletcher drops out of the window, cursing as he lands on his ankle. He might also be cursing at me. Quentin pokes his head through, sees me standing by the car. Then he tosses out his pack and makes his way out of the building.

"I have to go look for my wife and daughter. I can't spend the rest of my life wondering if there was more I could do. I know it's a bad idea."

"It's a terrible idea," Fletcher confirms. "Worst idea ever."

"Don't be stupid, man" Quentin urges.

"I'm not asking anyone to come with me," I explain. "It's something I have to do." My hand pulls open the handle on the car door, and I rest the rifle on the passenger seat.

"I'm coming, too," says Danielle. She is already lifting the trunk open and tossing her pack inside when I turn around. Danielle gives me a look to let me know she won't take no for an answer as she moves around to the passenger side of the car. Stitch follows along at her heels and climbs in her lap in the passenger seat.

"Fuck it," mutters Quentin. He leaves Fletcher's side and ambles over to the car.

Fletcher watches Natalie slowly wander to the car, too.

"Hold on a minute," he pleads, the desperation in his voice made his words come with more volume than he intended.

The first of the corpses from the parking lot emerge at the end of the alley. The one in the lead stops in the middle of the alley and turns to pursue us. Fletcher looks back at the approaching dead, and then gives me a cold stare as he strides over and tosses his pack in the trunk.

"Let's go then," he grunts as he gets into the crowded back seat.

I get behind the wheel and turn the key and listen to the familiar sound of the engine turning over. With the headlights off, I accelerate down the alleyway and out to the intersection and head north through the darkened streets toward home.

CHAPTER TWENTY

For what seems like a long while, we ride through the suburbs in silence. The world is a dead place now. Corpses occupy every street, shambling down the middle of roads filled with bodies and trash. To navigate the streets, I have to weave slowly through abandoned cars while avoiding the corpses that grope at our vehicle as we pass. Sometimes they manage to grab on somehow, and I have to drag them several blocks before they eventually fall off. Occasionally, a street is too congested to navigate, so we have to backtrack and try another route.

The road ahead looks congested with dozens of corpses and abandoned cars, so I take a left turn and then go right on the next driveable street. Danielle rolls down the window to let the dog hang his head out, feeling the cool rush of air along its tongue. She strokes the back of his neck as she keeps her eyes open for obstacles in our path.

"You have any idea where you're going?" Fletcher asks.

"North," I say.

His soft, disapproving laugh makes me look up at the rearview mirror to try and see his face in the back of the dark car. With the lights off, the dashboard is dark and all I can see is the dark outlines of the passengers in the back. His irritation with the situation is still clear, but I decide to ignore it for now. I didn't force anyone to come with me.

Danielle turns around in her seat and shoots Fletcher a look with more sting than a whole nest of wasps. Fletcher lets out a deep sigh, and I feel his knee jab into my back as he settles quietly back in his seat.

"Are you doing okay?" Danielle asks Natalie. After a long moment with no response, Danielle asks again. The girl doesn't acknowledge the question at all.

"Did you kill him?" Natalie asks. Her words sound hard and hollow and tired.

When no one else responds, Fletcher says blandly, "He's dead."

"Who was he?" probes Danielle. When the girl doesn't answer, Danielle tries a different approach. "How did you end up at the pharmacy?"

"My boyfriend was a diabetic," Natalie begins. She tells us the story of how they left home to search for insulin. Without insulin, the chance of her boyfriend surviving for more than a few days was pretty slim. They were searching the pharmacy when that man appeared with a gun. They begged him to let them go, but he made her tie her boyfriend to a chair. She watched while the man beat him. The guy even cut out one of his eyeballs and threw it at her to watch her scream when it landed in her lap.

The story made me wish I had the chance to shoot the man again.

Then he did things to her. She hesitated and stuttered as though she had buried the horrible event so deep that there was no way to dig down and bring it out again. It's not a story I want to hear either, but it feels impossible to ask her to quit telling it.

Natalie screams when the car crunches over an object on the road. I clench the steering wheel and pray the tires are not damaged.

"We're going in circles," complains Fletcher.

"No, we're not," I insist.

"I'm pretty sure we passed that diner a couple times already," he says.

I glance over at the darkened restaurant on the left. It appears vaguely familiar. It's possible we passed it before, but it looks like a million other diners, too.

"You don't know where the hell we are," Fletcher says.

"I do," says Natalie. "I know exactly where we are."

"Do you know how to get to Route 59 from here?" I ask.

"I think so," she says. She directs me down a side street and right at a gas station on the next corner.

"Hey, man," Quentin taps my shoulder. "Is there enough gas in this thing to get us there?"

With the lights off, it isn't so easy to check the gas gauge. I hadn't even thought about it either. I find the controls for the lights to the left of the steering wheel. I turn a dial to the right, and it lights up the dashboard and running lights for the car. The street is momentarily bright from the headlights, and I check the gauges and quickly shut the lights back off. The gas gauge shows less than an eighth of a tank, not nearly enough to get us all the way to the northwest suburbs.

"It's running pretty low," I say.

"How low?" asks Quentin.

The gas light blinks on in the dashboard console.

"Pretty close to empty," I admit.

"Great," huffs Fletcher.

"That gas station back there looked pretty empty," offers Quentin.

"The pumps won't work without power," counters Fletcher.

"Maybe we can switch cars," suggests Quentin. "One of these has to have some gas."

"You going to volunteer to go find the keys too?" Fletcher asks Quentin. "We're going to have to hoof it when this thing runs dry."

The thought of the slow journey on foot causes my jaw to clench. We already spent most of the night making the trip to the pharmacy and finding the car. The blue numbers on the dashboard clock tell me it's a little after three in the morning. Within an hour, the sky will begin to grow light and the car will be out of gas.

We might need to find a place where we can stop for a few hours and rest, especially if we're going to be hiking the rest of the way. Maybe we can go looking for another ride, but who knows what we might have to go through to get one.

I reach another congested dead end and have to reverse and head back to the last street we passed. When I put the car in gear and begin to accelerate, something bangs on the trunk of the car. My first instinct is to push the pedal down more, but when I hear a voice, I press hard on the break.

"Please don't go," pleads the voice of a teenage boy. It cracks with desperation.

"Just keep going," Fletcher urges me.

"He's just a kid."

"We don't have room for anyone else," he groans. "It's like a fucking clown car already."

I put the car in park and roll down my window while resting my other hand on the gun. I hear Fletcher curse and the sharp snapping sound as he reloads his rifle.

"What are you doing out here, kid?" I ask.

"I saw you guys drive by," he struggles to regain his breath. He must have been chasing after us awhile. His eyes scan the interior of the dark car.

"Are you alone?" I wonder and scan the road for signs of trouble. After the pharmacy, I'm having a hard time trusting anyone. The kid in the filthy Pencey College shirt seems desperate and afraid, but maybe that is exactly what makes him more dangerous than I think.

"I haven't seen anyone else for days," he says. "Please take me with you guys."

"Car's full, kid," Fletcher barks.

"Come on," he pleads. "I'll ride in the trunk."

"Trunk's full too," Fletcher adds.

Glass shatters in a shop window along the sidewalk. A corpse tumbles out through the window of a thrift shop into the shards on the pavement. We don't have time to sit around. I jerk my head, and the kid runs around to the passenger side and piles into the crowded backseat next to Natalie.

I press the pedal and get the car moving again, backing around a corner then shifting to drive and accelerating down a cross street.

"What's your name, kid?" I ask.

"Kyle," he says. "What are you doing?"

I hear the sound of fabric rustling in the backseat.

"Easy, college boy. Just checking you for weapons," Quentin explains. "Nothing personal, but we already ran into some trouble this morning, and I'm not in the mood for any more surprises."

I see a sign for Route 59, and I take a left turn onto the road. This four-lane road leads straight up towards home and my family. It's the road Amanda would take every day on her way to work, and if we can get far enough, the road winds right passed Abby's school. I spot a gas station that looks deserted along the right side of the road. I slowly pull the car to a stop between the pumps. For a long moment, I stare at the car dealership across the street, and the rows and rows of new automobiles parked outside.

"The pumps won't work," Fletcher reiterates.

I open the door and get out of the car. I slide down the night vision goggles and flip them on to try and see through the darkened windows of the building across the street.

"I don't think we need gas," I grin. "I think we need a bigger car."

CHAPTER TWENTY-ONE

We stare into the open garage door of the service department. Though the sky outside is slowly turning from black to indigo, the inside of the vast building is still immersed in darkness. Quentin slides his night vision goggles over his eyes and takes the lead inside with Danielle behind him. Fletcher and I stay outside and cover Natalie and the teenage boy who bites his nails and rambles nervously. Stitch parks himself beside Natalie and pants and licks at her hand when she pets him.

"Man, I'm so glad these guys picked me up," Kyle says. "I was trapped in my car since this whole thing started. Thought I was going to die in there."

He sits down next to Natalie on a bench in front of the building.

"You don't seem like you belong with them," he whispers. He glances over to see me keeping an eye on them. "They picked you up too?"

Natalie looks at him a moment, then returns her attention to the dog that is nuzzling her fingers.

"What's your name?" he asks.

Instead of answering Natalie gets up and crosses her arms and paces back and forth in front of the building. I stay posted at the corner of the building, keeping an eye for trouble coming from either direction. She looks like she wants to tell me something but can't find the words.

Several suppressed rounds echo inside the building. The dealership lot still seems quiet, but unfortunately, there is no fence to the street. If we make too much noise, we could end up in a really bad situation. They could come at us from every direction, and there is nothing to slow them down at all.

"You guys need a hand in there?" I hear Fletcher's voice through the headset speakers. There is a long silence and then another burst of suppressed rounds echoes inside the garage.

"I think we got them all," Quentin answers once the gunfire subsides.

"Hurry up and find some keys," Fletcher urges. "We got company coming."

I turn around to scan the area around Fletcher, and it doesn't take me long to see them with the night vision goggles. A large group of corpses is milling around the closest intersection. Luckily, they are moving slowly towards the Honda we abandoned at the gas station. I left the headlights on, thinking it might help draw attention away from us. For now, the dead seem oblivious to our presence at the dealership across the street. I poke my head between the cars to get a look further down the block and notice there are more of them several blocks away, slowly heading in our direction.

I really wish they would hurry up with those keys. This scene could get messy if we stick around much longer. It's a relief when Quentin's voice crackles through the headset and reports he has found the office where all the keys are.

"Just grab a bunch and get out here," I plead.

The radio clicks on, and Quentin announces they are heading out, but then stops abruptly. "I heard something," he says. The next thing I hear is the sound of Danielle screaming inside and assault rifles firing wildly. Bullets ping off metal, and a car alarm howls in the garage. I don't hesitate to sprint to the garage entrance.

"Quentin?" I call through the mic on the headset. "Danielle! What's going on?" I race through the garage trying to trace their location by the sounds of their rifles, but the car alarm is blaring and the sound bounces off the high metal walls.

A door on my left flies open and Danielle nearly knocks me over as she backs out the door and fires wildly into the hallway. She holds down the trigger until her clip is empty then slams the door shut.

"Where's Quentin?" I ask.

"He's trapped in there," she cries. She clutches at my arm and pulls me toward the exit.

I glance back at the door and already the fists of the undead begin to claw at the other side. It won't be more than a minute or two before the mass of their bodies is enough to knock the door off the hinges. I follow Danielle out of the garage and look around, but I can't spot anyone. They're completely gone. The corpses are already making their way through several rows of cars between the street and the dealership. We have to get the hell out of here.

Danielle taps my arm, and I follow the direction she is pointing and see Fletcher already moving away from the building with Natalie and Kyle. They are crouched down and scurrying behind a long row of cars. We take off after them, but once we reach cover behind the cars I stop and turn around and look back at the building. The corpses have entered the garage and are swarming towards the sound of the blaring car alarm. At least, that is drawing most of them away from us, but a couple of corpses notice our exit and move slowly towards our location.

There is no sign of Quentin at all. We wait for a moment behind the cars, listening for the sound of the rifle or anything to indicate he is still alive in there. The car alarm continues to blare, making it impossible to hear anything else. The sound draws more and more corpses to the dealership. There must be hundreds gathering around the lot.

"What happened in there?" I ask Danielle. Her eyes are watery, and she struggles to catch her breath and speak.

"We thought we got them all," she says. "But there were so many in the dealership. They were locked inside the office with the keys. They came pouring out as soon as we opened the door. Quentin went down under a pile of them. I tried to shoot them, but there were so many. He told me to get out and tried to lead some of them the other way."

The blaring alarm finally runs to the end of the sequence of piercing sounds and shuts off. The air fills with the dull moans of hundreds of undead. The sky is slowly becoming the bruised purple shade that precedes the dawn. Within a few minutes, we won't need to use the night vision goggles to see, and we will lose the cover of darkness.

I spot Fletcher at the end of the lot with Kyle and Natalie. They dart across the road to an alley a block away. Stitch trails behind them, pausing in the middle of the road to look back. Then he breaks into a run back in our direction. A moment later, Fletcher pokes his head around the corner of the building, and he spots us crouched behind the car. He waves an arm emphatically to urge us to hurry. We have to move. If we wait here any longer, the throngs of undead will close in around us.

I take one last look back at the dealership and consider running back inside. There are just too many now, and even if I am willing to risk my life to help Quentin, I'm not willing to get Danielle killed. I sling the rifle over my shoulder, and we make our way through the cars towards the alley. The sick feeling in my stomach begins to set in then when I face the reality that Quentin is gone. The only person responsible for this is me. I hate myself for allowing any of them to risk their lives by staying with me.

The sound of the assault rifle cements my feet to the ground. I look toward the alley but then realize the sound is coming from the other direction. I swing around toward the building and after a moment, I see a figure rounding the rear of the building. Quentin moves backwards, limping slightly and firing into a crowd of corpses trailing behind him. The elation I feel at the sight of him only lasts a moment before the adrenaline takes over, and I raise the rifle and head back towards the building. Stitch brushes passed my leg and weaves through the cars. He barks loudly, drawing the attention of some of the dead as he moves. The things are spread all over the lot now, shambling up and down the aisles of cars.

We take cover behind an SUV about fifty yards from Quentin and focus on clearing the way for him. I waste bullets, spending three or four rounds sometimes to take down a corpse. The amount of ammunition we are expending could come back to haunt us later, but all that matters to me right now is getting out of this.

Finally, Quentin reaches the vehicle, and we retreat to the alley. We have to stop several times to create a path in front of us and slow the crowd of undead at our backs. Inevitably, some of our rounds miss their targets. I shoot the window of a nearby vehicle and set off another alarm. Danielle looks over at me and rolls her eyes. I just shrug and keep shooting. By now there are hundreds of corpses converging on us anyway. This whole thing turned out to be a very bad idea.

We meet up with the rest of the group, and then we keep moving up the alley alongside the thickening crowd of corpses on the streets. After a few blocks, the alley dead ends at the back of a parking lot. Fletcher shoots out the lock on a loading door, and we take cover in a low-end mattress store. We stay in the stockroom because the front of the building is floor-to-ceiling windows. At least, we have a clear view of the street and can easily assess the situation from inside.

Stitch hops up on the first mattress he sees and walks in circles. He sniffs the padding, then lays down in a tight coil. I drop my pack next to him and remove a water bottle and gulp half of it down at once. Fletcher crawls up to the front window, careful not to attract the attention of the crowd of corpses out in the street. He checks to make sure the front entrance is locked, then retreats to the rear of the store.

"We should be safe here awhile," Fletcher whispers. "At least a few hours."

I retrieve one of the MRE's from my bag and rip open the outer packaging. I remove a candy bar and the crackers and save the rest of the food for later. I tear open the candy bar and begin devouring it. I notice that Kyle is staring at me hungrily, so I toss him the package of crackers. He fumbles with the plastic, then tears at the package with his teeth to get it open.

"When was the last time you ate, college boy?" Quentin asks him, handing him a bottled water from his pack.

"A few days ago," Kyle says.

"Go easy then," Quentin suggests. "We don't need you getting sick out there."

I finish the candy bar and lean back against the wall, and watch the stumbling figures out in the road. The sun is coming up now and casting the long shadows of the dead across the windows of the store. Every so often one of them almost seems to stop and stare at the storefront until I am sure it has some idea we are inside, but all of them eventually wander away except one. There is a middle-aged woman in a kitchen apron splattered with blood that lingers just beyond the door. It gazes at the glass, and I wonder if it is looking inside or if it is merely staring at its reflection. After the first five minutes, I just want her to leave. Some of these things just creep me out more than the rest of them do.

"You sure you don't want to head back?"

I turn my head and find Fletcher crouching beside the mattress. He is digging through his pack and taking stock of what remains of the ammunition. He pauses and looks up to see my expression.

"I didn't think so," he says. "But you should know if we run into trouble like that again we aren't going to be able to shoot our way out of it."

"You don't have to come," I remind him.

"You didn't have to come back and get me out of that tunnel either," he says. "I guess this will make us even."

I stand up and begin reloading the food and ammunition into my pack. "If we keep moving, we should be able to get there by early tomorrow morning," I suggest. No one else looks particularly eager to get going again. They watch me loading my pack in silence. Even the dog is staring up at me while it continues to rest on the mattress. I worry that if I allow myself to stay here even a moment longer, I might not have the will to start moving forward again.

I look over to notice Danielle is putting a new magazine in her rifle and readying to leave. Reluctantly, Quentin pushes himself up off the floor and hauls his pack up onto his shoulders. He looks worn out, but he gives me a small smile to let me know he is okay to keep going. Stitch rouses from the mattress and shakes himself briskly on the bed then hops down to the floor and stretches his legs. Once everyone is ready to go, I push the back door open slightly to peer into the empty alley. I spot a gap in the wooden fence along the back of the alley and we cut through into the backyard of a subdivision. We keep moving north alongside the road that will take me home.

CHAPTER TWENTY-TWO

The day is warm, and the neighborhood streets are quiet and empty, and if you can manage to ignore the bullet holes in the cars and the bodies that are rotting on the ground, it might almost seem like any ordinary day. Except the moment you let that happen, you're dead. We walk in silence mostly, always aware of every small noise we make. By avoiding the main road, we travel with relative ease. For some reason, the side streets contain significantly fewer corpses than the main roads. They seem to crowd the same places they used to crowd. I could almost believe this shows some kind of mental attachment to their former lives, but the truth is that they were likely drawn there by the last humans that survived.

There are plenty of cars parked in driveways along the road, and I debate the possibility of checking the houses for keys. The roads are so difficult to navigate that I think we might be better off traveling on foot. As midday approaches, the streets begin to seem more familiar. We reach a vast nature preserve that I recognize instantly. The woods runs along the highway through several towns, before it eventually ends at the expressway. We cross over Route 59 and follow an entrance into the preserve.

After several minutes of walking without the slightest trace of danger, I shoulder my rifle. We stop for lunch at a pavilion. I sit down at a picnic table and heat up an entree from the MRE. Since we are several miles from the road, we don't worry about the smell of the food or the sound of our voices giving us away. Stitch discovers a tennis ball and convinces Danielle to stop eating her lunch and play fetch. For a few minutes, I sit back and close my eyes and savor the feeling of the sun warming my skin.

The tongue of a dog lapping my face wakes me, and I open my eyes to Danielle giggling on the ground next to me. I wipe a thin film of sweat off my face and am immediately angry with myself for falling asleep.

"How long was I out?" I ask her. I get up and take a sip of water and begin to gather my gear together.

"Maybe a half hour," she says.

I'm already regretting the time lost. It's been a long time since we slept, but I have to keep pushing ahead. I look around at the tired, dirty faces around me and can tell no one wants to move yet.

"We can't keep going like this," Danielle says. "Everyone is exhausted."

"I know," I sigh. "I'm tired as hell too. I have to go, though."

"How much farther is it?" she asks.

"Maybe ten miles," I guess. I know exactly how to get home from here. The route will take me through more nature preserves and undeveloped land. It seems like the least dangerous area we've encountered, and I can probably make it there by myself if I avoid the main roads. I've been wrong about that kind of thing before. I won't blame any of them if they decide to stay behind, but I have to keep moving. "Once we get over the expressway, it's a lot of open farmland. We might even be able to get there before dark."

"Then what?" asks Fletcher.

I am not sure how to respond, I haven't thought past getting home. I can't allow myself to think beyond that moment. "I guess, we'll just see what we find first."

We set out again on a gravel trail that meanders through the preserve to the parking lot that borders the expressway. The lot is full of empty parking spaces. The frontage road that leads to Route 59 looks deserted as well. The expressway is still a nightmare. Corpses wander through a junkyard of automobiles that spans the entire eight lanes of traffic.

"Holy shit," says Kyle as he looks down upon the scene for the first time. He turns and looks at Natalie, who looks terrified. The rest of us have seen this before. We are maybe two or three miles west of the medieval restaurant. Hard to believe we went through so much to end up back where we started almost.

"How are we going to get across there?" asks Natalie. "This is crazy."

"We can try and go down to that overpass," Fletcher suggests, squinting his eyes to peer into the distance. The closest overpass is, at least, a mile to the west, and located near a huge shopping center and movie theater. He takes a pair of binoculars from his pack and holds them to his eyes. "Don't look like that way will be much better, though."

"We go across here," I say. "There is another forest preserve on the other side. It's the best chance we have."

For a long moment, no one says anything.

"They're packed together pretty tight down there," says Quentin. He crouches down and rests his rifle across his knee looking for the best possible route across. "It won't be a walk in the park; that's for damn sure."

"We don't have the ammo for this," Danielle says. "There's too many."

Fletcher returns the binoculars back to his pack and removes a cutter to make a hole in the high chainlink fence that separates the forest from the highway. "We stay together and keep low," he says. "Draw as little attention as possible. Don't shoot unless you have to. We can do this."

Fletcher finishes cutting the hole, and then we move through to the other side and down a small hill of thick weeds toward the highway. The uneven ground is tricky to manage, and I nearly lose my balance trying to shift the heavy pack on my shoulders. We reach the bottom of the hill and crouch behind the concrete divider that separates the easement from the highway. I can smell the overwhelming odor of the dead on the other side. Stitch sniffs the air. The hair on his neck bristles.

"Oh my god, oh my god, oh my god," Natalie murmurs softly. I look past her to see Fletcher give me the nod; then he rises to his feet and disappears over the wall. I hop the barricade, and then wait as the others make their way onto the highway. We follow Fletcher through the maze of wrecked and abandoned cars. We pass by a corpse pinned to the side of a sedan by the grill of a pickup. It claws at the metal and opens its mouth when it catches sight of us approaching. It won't be able to grab us, so Fletcher keeps out of reach of the corpse and moves past it. This maneuver seems to be the best option until the thing begins to bang loudly on the hood of the pickup while struggling to grasp at us. I turn and fire a round through the skull of the thing. After its head smacks the hood of the truck, it is quiet and still again.

I hold my position for a long moment, hoping the noise has not alerted more corpses to our presence. We have a long way to go across the expressway, and who knows how long it will take to weave through the mess of cars. I lower the gun and turn back when I glimpse something moving in the periphery of my vision that stops me cold. A corpse claws at the window of the sports car behind me.

The teeth snap, and there is a dull thud as the thing hits its skull on the glass.

I feel a momentary flood of relief with the realization that the glass separates the corpse from my face. The moment doesn't last long. As the zombie struggles to reach me, it lays a hand on the horn of the car. The blaring sound sets my heart racing.

"Shit," Fletcher growls. He springs to his feet and begins selecting targets and firing round after round.

"Run!" Quentin urges as he stands up and opens fire as well.

I push Natalie forward and wait as she climbs over the crumpled hood of the car. I scurry over behind her, and then bring the rifle up to fire into a handful of corpses making their way toward us between the lanes of traffic. Danielle drops down behind me and takes out several zombies coming from the opposite direction.

Natalie and Kyle remain crouched between the cars. They look too scared to move. "Keep going," I urge them, and then I climb on the hood of a taxi cab and begin firing at several corpses on the other side. I feel something brush against my leg and ready the rifle to put a bullet in whatever was about to grab me, but I look down to find Stitch. He hops down and disappears beneath the undercarriage of the next car.

I remove the empty magazine and replace it. There is only one more before I have only the handgun. We'll never fight our way across the highway. The crowd of corpses closing in on us continues to grow faster than we can shoot them down. With every moment that passes the chances of us making it across seem to get worse. I reach the concrete median and begin to climb over to cross into the westbound lanes, but a hand grabs hold of my shirt and pulls me back. I turn, ready to fight to free myself, but realize it is Quentin.

"Head down!" he screams and pulls me toward the ground behind the median.

I look around and try to understand what he is warning me about. From the roof of a car Fletcher throws something across the median in the direction of a cluster of corpses. Then he shoves me to the pavement and drops down beside me. A series of concussive blasts on the other side of the concrete shock me senseless. Behind the ringing in my ears, I hear a voice telling me to run. I turn around and start to pull myself over the concrete divider when I notice the street looks like a bomb went off. Several cars have exploded, and the blasts sent pieces of jagged metal flying in every direction. The skeletons of several scorched cars are smoking on the pavement, but otherwise, the road is relatively clear of the dead. Coughing on the smoke, I make a run for the other side of the expressway.

Once I reach the fence, I shrug my pack off and toss it up and over the top and start to climb. I have no idea how close any of the walking dead might be behind me. After I pull myself to the top of the fence, I can only muster the strength to swing my body over and drop down to the ground below. I land hard on the unforgiving ground. My exhausted legs buckle and I roll over onto my back and gasp for air. The incessant high pitched tone is all I can hear for a moment; then the sound of a dog barking far away.

I push myself upright and see Stitch digging in the dirt at the base of the fence. Everyone else is still climbing over the top, so I grab the chainlink and pull it up as much as I can until he can squeeze his body underneath. I collapse back on the ground and watch the others climb down the fence. For several minutes, we all rest on the ground and stare back at the expressway. The walking dead continue their slow pursuit of us, and they converge on our position on the other side of the fence. The first of them to reach the barrier has a face that is charred black on one half and still smoking. The smell of burnt, rotting flesh motivates us to find the strength to get up and start moving again.

CHAPTER TWENTY-THREE

After half an hour, the ringing in my ears finally begins to subside but leaves me with a splitting headache. I squint my eyes and pinch at the bridge of my nose as if I could squeeze the pain out of existence with my fingers.

"Here," says Danielle. She nudges my arm with a bottle of aspirin. I take it and down a couple and thank her when I hand it back.

Our pace has slowed since crossing the expressway. Aside from the exhaustion, the nature preserve on this side of the highway doesn't have any trails to follow. We have to push through marshes and fields of tall grass and densely wooded acreage.

"These fucking mosquitos, man," Kyle whines and slaps at an insect on the side of his neck.

"At least, it's just the bugs trying to bite your scrawny ass out here, college boy," laughs Quentin. "I'd take that any day."

The sound of crickets begins to fill the air as the sun drifts downward toward the western horizon. We stop when we come upon a small stream about a hundred yards from the road. I drop my pack and bend down to splash my face with water.

The forest preserve ends up ahead, and we'll have to take to the street as we head towards town. It will be too hard to move through the woods in the night, and the road runs through a sparsely populated stretch for the next several miles. We scout the street to be sure it is clear. No sign of anyone, alive or dead. It doesn't seem right. Though there aren't many houses or businesses along this stretch of the road, it was used by lots of people traveling between towns and would get congested during rush hour. Amanda usually took it to get to work from Abby's school. The last thing she said was that she was stuck in traffic. It just didn't make sense, and I felt more anxious now than ever about what I might find ahead.

"You okay?" Danielle asks me.

A million different scenarios play out in my mind now as I wonder what might have happened to my family. As desperate as I am to find them, I dread facing the likely outcome that I may not find any trace of them. I may even find something much, much worse. These thoughts cause me to slow down, and when I look up to respond to Danielle, I realize I've dropped well behind.

"Yeah," I lie. "Just a little tired."

Danielle looks at me long enough that I can tell she knows something else is wrong. After everything we've been through, I still have a hard time telling her what bothers me. It's not in my nature to willingly show any sign of weakness, even when it's obvious. She seems satisfied when I force a smile on my face and decides not to pry any further.

"These houses are amazing," she says to change the subject.

"Hold up," Fletcher interrupts. "We got something up ahead around the bend."

I try to squint into the bright setting sun to see. I can't tell what it is, but a long metallic object appears to be blocking both lanes of the street. That would explain why there are no cars at all. Whatever it is must have been here since this whole thing first started.

Fletcher removes the binoculars from his pack and peers into them. "Looks like a semi truck," he reports. "Overturned."

He passes the binoculars to me, and I take a look down the road. The giant tanker lays sideways across the pavement. I spot two corpses in police uniforms stumbling around in front of it, but the street is empty otherwise. There's no telling what might lurk behind it. The safe bet would be to get off the road here and hike through the woods again.

"Want to go around it?" Fletcher asks.

"Let's get a closer look first," I suggest.

We approach the truck cautiously, eyeing the woods surrounding the road for any movement but the scene remains quiet. All I can see on the road are several empty squad cars and the tanker. The police officers notice us as we close the distance, and we draw them away from the truck before taking them out. Usually, a tanker truck like this would be carrying fuel or some chemical, and we have to assume it could still hold something hazardous.

I creep along the front of the truck and poke my head out to look down the street. More squad cars barricade the street a hundred yards up the road. Behind the police vehicles is a line of cars as far as I can see. Amazingly, the area seems free of the undead, so I wave to let the others know it's clear before I move around the corner of the truck. I take a couple of steps, and then I spot the long shadow on the ground from something standing on the other side of the diesel engine. I jump back on the passenger side of the truck and hold my hands up to get Danielle to stop before she comes any closer.

I peer slowly around the bumper and watch the shadow on the ground and wait for it to move. It remains perfectly still. That's when I realize that it's a living person, and they are hiding. Whoever is back there could be afraid of us, or this could be a trap. I look back over to Danielle, and I point to my eyes, then to the front of the truck to let her know I spotted something there. I try to think of some hand gesture to explain that they seem to be alive, but it seems too complicated. She steps back towards the rear of the tanker and I wait a moment and consider my options.

"Hey there," I call out. When I don't get an answer, a bad feeling begins to set in. "I know you're behind the truck. I can see your shadow on the ground."

At first, there is still no response, so I cautiously peer around the edge hoping I don't get my head blown off. I can see the shadow has shifted and is now pressed up against the truck and looks to be holding a weapon. This situation isn't going to end well.

"You alone out here?" I probe again and wait for a response. I look around to the tree line across the road for signs of anyone else, but it seems quiet. The person behind the truck likely saw us coming and knows I have company. I can understand being afraid because you're alone and outnumbered, but I can't understand why I am getting no response.

"We're not getting off to a real good start here, man." I try a little laugh, but it sounds as forced as it is. "This doesn't have to end badly. I'll come out, and we'll just talk this out." I peer around the corner again, but the shadow at the back of the truck remains motionless. At least, I haven't been shot at so far. I take that as a pretty good sign.

"I'm going to come out now, okay?" I call out. I wait for a few seconds then shoulder my rifle.

"Okay, friend," the man says. His voice sounds too calm, measured. And he called me friend, which assures me the guy is totally psychotic. I immediately have second thoughts about trusting someone that isn't as anxious as me.

I raise my hands up to my shoulders with my palms spread and step slowly out around the vehicle and keep my eyes glued to the shadow. The shadow suddenly shifts when the guy pivots around the corner of the truck pointing some kind of submachine gun right at me. He hesitates when he looks at my surprised expression. Then something off to the right catches his attention, and he turns and raises the gun. I look on as several bullets burst into his upper body, jerking his shoulders and causing him to stumble backward. He stands there for a moment stunned, then lets out a yell and makes a desperate move to fire his weapon. Before he can get a shot off his head jerks back and his dead body falls back to the pavement.

Another shadow appears and approaches casually. Danielle emerges with the assault rifle in her hand and stands over the body looking down at the young man that she just killed. I walk over to her and watch her expression change from fearful to angry. Fletcher walks up alongside us and looks down at the body on the ground a moment, then pats Danielle on the shoulder. "Nice shot," he says and walks away.

Quentin pauses and glances down as well before he puts an arm around Danielle and leads her away. Natalie and Kyle emerge from the rear of the truck. I watch as they walk past and Kyle turns pale at the sight of the body. I linger for a moment and look around as though I might find an explanation somewhere in the trees or the sky or the earth, but things like this just happen now. I pick up the gun next to the body on the ground and follow the others up the road.

"That guy was alive," Kyle says.

Quentin turns and throws an aggravated look in Kyle's direction but says nothing.

"I can't believe we just shot somebody and left them in the road back there," Kyle goes on. "Doesn't anyone see how wrong that is?"

The lack of a response from any of us only seems to infuriate him. Somehow he feels he shares the responsibility because he stood by and did nothing.

"I can't be a part of this," he insists.

Quentin swivels around, his face filled with rage. He seems like a different person altogether. He grabs Kyle by the front of his collar and pulls him close. "If you want to you can go back there and bury that fucker. I don't care. But that guy would have shot you down and left you in the road like it was nothing. You better learn that, college boy."

Kyle tries hard to swallow and nods his head anxiously until Quentin releases him. He gives Kyle a hard stare until I lightly push him on as I walk past. We continue down a slight decline in the road towards the endless line of cars.

"You see that?" Fletcher calls back.

He doesn't need to be more specific for me to understand. As we approach the cars, we see dozens of dead bodies on the pavement and in the grass. Fletcher stops at the first one of the corpses and bends down to examine it. He uses the barrel of his rifle to roll it over. The smell hits me, and I cover my mouth and nose with my forearm.

"Look at that," says Fletcher gesturing at an entry wound in the forehead. He stands up and moves on to the next one. It also has been shot in the head. "Somebody already did all the hard work for us."

Moving past the police cruisers blocking the road, I see hundreds of other bodies among the abandoned cars on the road.

"God damn," gasps Quentin.

"We missed one hell of a party," Fletcher notes as he nudges another corpse over with his boot and finds the same wound as the rest.

Something about the scene bothers me, but I can't figure out what it is yet. I look over at Fletcher and notice he seems perplexed as well.

"Who do you think this was?" I ask. "The cops?"

Fletcher shakes his head. "No, this happened recently. There isn't a walking corpse left anywhere around here. Somebody was cleaning up."

"That's good then, right? Someone is taking this place back," I say. The thought briefly fills me with the hope that maybe it won't be as awful here as it was everywhere else we've been. But when I look back at Fletcher, he cringes at my optimism.

"Somebody might be taking it back from the dead, but that don't mean they'll be interested in sharing it. Maybe your friend back there had a hand in all this, but he wasn't alone."

I scan the trees and the road again, but there isn't anything to see except the endless line of useless cars and the countless bodies of the dead. I can't shake the feeling someone is watching us, and I suddenly wonder if we should be out in the open.

"But what do I know," Fletcher smirks. He must sense my unease as he tries to lighten his tone to express less concern. "I been wrong plenty of times before."

I nod, and I look around the quiet road again, but I don't feel a sense of relief at all. A feeling of dread claws at me and won't let go. I can't even figure out what it is about walking down this road that is paralyzing me. I stop suddenly and turn around. I realize I walked right passed Amanda's car. The black BMW looks like every other high-end SUV, but I had spotted the parking tag from her school district hanging from the mirror as I walk past.

"What's up?" asks Fletcher.

"That's my car," I stammer.

My legs go numb when I stare at the shattered windows, the blood splatter on the rear panel and the open passenger door. I try to will myself to walk over to it and look inside. With each step I take towards the car, I recall my memories of Amanda more vividly. It's so intense I almost expect to see her sitting behind the wheel when I lean over and look inside. The sight of the empty seat and the dried blood on the leather is enough to suck the air out of my lungs. I have to turn my head away from it and then I spot her cell phone on the ground. I pick it up and stare at the bloody fingerprints on the cracked screen. The shock is too much for me after everything I've gone through to get here. My hand starts to shake, and I drop the phone. I can't seem to find the strength to stand any longer, so I sit down on the passenger seat of the car.

"Blake," a soft voice calls to me. "Blake."

I try to answer, but I can't find the words. The moment seems endless and surreal. Firm hands grab me by the shoulders, and suddenly Danielle's face snaps into focus. She pulls my head to her chest and hugs me, and I close my eyes and let myself imagine for one last moment that Amanda is alive and here and everything hadn't gone to hell.

I open my eyes and give Danielle a little nod to let her know I haven't totally lost it. It still seems difficult to draw air into my lungs, as if my body no longer has the will to function. I look back and take in the empty seat in the back of the car. A small pink jacket on the floor catches my eye, and I pick it up. I try to ignore the flecks of blood on the sleeve. Abby wasn't in the car when it happened, I tell myself. It's not her blood. Holding the jacket reminds me that I still have a reason to keep going.

I get out of the car and carefully fold the jacket and tuck it inside the top of my pack. I pull it onto my shoulders and adjust the straps for a couple of minutes. No matter how much I mess with it, the pack seems so much heavier than before. Stitch runs over to me, circles my legs panting excitedly. He turns and sprints back down the dark road to the rest of the group sitting on the bed of a pickup truck. They silently sip from their water bottles while they wait for me. No one says anything to me because there isn't anything to say about it. This is just the world we live in now, and we just keep finding ways to go on into the darkness.

CHAPTER TWENTY-FOUR

We check the bodies on the ground as we pass them, but Amanda isn't among them. I don't know if I could handle seeing her like that. Every time we turn over a body with long dark hair, I breathe a sigh of relief.

"She might still be alive," Danielle tells me.

"Maybe," I shrug. I try to sound optimistic, but after seeing the car, I can't convince myself that such a thing is possible.

As we continue our slow approach into town, we find the dark streets are all clear of the dead. There is a faint odor in the air of meat cooking that seems to come and go with the breeze. Just outside of downtown, a pickup is parked on the top of a hill, and there is a heaping pile of bodies in the truck bed.

"I'm getting a bad feeling about this place," Quentin says.

Fletcher takes a moment to pull out the binoculars and look down the long hill into town. "Looks clear," he reports.

The school is on the opposite side of the downtown district, which is really just a couple miles of Victorian-style houses and the small-town shops that look exactly as they did sixty years ago. Seeing the town deserted is unsettling. We reach the main intersection, and there is still no sign of anyone alive. I still can't shake the feeling someone is watching every move we make.

The train station where I got on the train just before this all started is across the street. When I see it, it makes me wish I could go back and do so many things differently that day and every day since. The thought makes me lose focus, and I'm the last to notice the bullet that cracks off the concrete.

Fletcher grabs my arm and drags me into a doorway just as another bullet shatters the window I was standing in front of a moment before. I have no idea where the shots are coming from. Fletcher slowly looks around the brick corner of the doorway and tries to establish the location of the shooter. He makes a gesture that I don't understand to Quentin, who ducks behind a parked car in the street.

Quentin nods and then jumps up firing wildly and dives back down just before a bullet pierces the hood of the car parked behind him.

"I see you," Fletcher growls. He points up to the roof of the movie theater at the next intersection. He swings around the corner and fires off a grenade round then jumps back behind the bricks as a bullet strikes the pavement beside me. A few seconds later there is an explosion on the top of the building and bricks rain down on the sidewalk below.

Fletcher pokes his head out cautiously, then steps back out onto the sidewalk. "You messed with the wrong fucking hombre," he boasts. He slides the action on the rifle loading another grenade in place.

Quentin gets up off the ground and scans up and down the road. He signals Danielle and she leads the others out of the alley.

"You think that's all of them?" I ask Fletcher. I still don't feel like leaving the cover of the doorway is a safe bet, but I step out onto the sidewalk anyway and look around.

"Don't know," says Fletcher. "But if there's more, that'll give them something to think about." The smirk on his face disappears when we hear the sound of a large engine turning over somewhere close. A second automobile starts, and then the engines rev as the vehicles begin to move.

The dark alley seems like the best option, so we run between the buildings. We cut over to the next street, and we take that in the direction of the school. By the time we cross over the train tracks at the next block, we can hear the trucks getting close and see the headlights sweeping across the building behind us. It's just a matter of time before they'll find us on the road. We cut through a church parking lot and make our way down a residential side street.

The thought crosses my mind that we could try to hide out in one of these houses until they give up looking for us, but it seems like our best bet is to get as far away from here as we can and fast. We have no idea what we're up against, but we do know that we don't have a whole lot of firepower left.

A pair of headlights turn a corner several blocks behind us. We head up the next driveway and duck around the back of the home and hope to God they didn't spot us. The truck slowly rolls down the street. I take a look around the corner of the house as they pass and see it is a large blue pickup with track lights on the roof and several guys with shotguns riding in the bed of the truck. I duck back as they sweep a spotlight across the houses and wait until I am sure they have turned at the end of the block.

"We got to get off the street," Fletcher seethes.

"It's just a half a mile," I tell him. "We can make it."

Since they just patrolled this street, I guess we will have a few minutes at the very least before the vehicles come back around. We run back out to the sidewalk and keep going down the street. Up ahead the lane ends at an old newspaper printing warehouse. We reach the end and cut back toward Main Street. There is no sign of the pickup, but I can still hear them driving somewhere close by. We get to Main Street and find a barricade with dumpsters lined across the intersection. That must be how they are keeping more corpses from coming into downtown. If we can get past those containers the only way they can come after us is on foot.

"We have to go over those dumpsters," I gasp. I take a couple of deep breaths to try and finish my thought. "It's the only way out of town."

The headlights appear again several blocks behind us. The only thing to do is make a run for it now.

"Go on then," Fletcher urges us. He takes up a position behind a parked car and takes aim at the pickup that is creeping down the block. We make it halfway to the barricade before the truck tires squeal and the engine roars. I guess they have spotted us. I glance back to see what Fletcher is doing. He fires a round through the windshield of the truck. The vehicle swerves wildly and Fletcher springs up and starts running towards us. He doesn't even wait to see what happens next. The pickup strikes a sports car on the side of the road and flips over, throwing the passengers from the truck bed. The truck slides along the street upside down for a couple of seconds then grinds to a stop and lays smoking in the night.

In the aftermath of the wreck, the night is suddenly quiet, and now I hear the corpses moaning beyond the dumpsters. Quentin climbs onto the container and crouches on top of the noisy bags of trash. I hear him curse and know that we have another problem to deal with now.

"How many?" I ask.

His head appears over the edge of the container, and he drops back down to the ground. "About twenty," he reports. "And they know we're here."

The headlights of the second truck appear up the road, but the wreck is now blocking it from coming further. Still, we don't have much time. I remember the grenade in my pack and how Fletcher got us across the highway earlier. Without time to think it through I climb onto the dumpster and dig through my supplies.

"Move back," I yell.

I find the heavy grenade and pull the pin out of it and toss it into the middle of a group of corpses then cover my head and wait. The explosion rattles the steel container and a split second later an arm rains down on me followed by a spray of black, coagulated blood. I lift my head up and peer over the edge and see the immediate area is clear, but the noise is attracting every walking corpse for miles.

"Hurry up," I call out. I swing over the other side of the dumpster and start shooting at the partially dismembered corpses on the ground that are dragging what remains of their bodies towards me. Quentin drops down next to me and helps me cover the area while the others get over the dumpster. I have no idea how much ammunition I have left, but I know it's not enough to stay here very long. Finally, Fletcher makes his way over the dumpsters, and we push forward down the road.

There are walking dead all over the road, and all we can do is make a run for the school straight through an oncoming current of them. I shoot as many as I can until the magazine is empty and then I just shove them aside and try to keep moving and avoid getting surrounded. I'm so close now. The school is just down the road. I can't believe I made it all the way back. It had to be for a reason. She must be alive. My thoughts give me a surge of adrenaline, and I run faster than I ever have in my life. I don't even look back to see if the rest of the group makes it. Nothing matters right now but finding the only part of my old life that remains.

At the top of the hill, the dark outline of the school comes into view and the sight of it almost makes me forget that I have to keep moving. There is a large playing field that sets the school back from the busy street, and we gain some ground on the corpses trailing us from the road. My heart is pounding in my chest from running and the fear of what lies ahead at the school. As we move closer, I can make out shapes of children shuffling around on the playground outside. Some of them spot us coming through the parking lot, and they begin to gather at the iron fence. Their tiny arms reach through the bars, and their mouths release rasping moans. It's the most horrible scene I've ever witnessed. I force myself to walk over to the fence and look at their ashen faces until I come to a sight that pushes me to my limit.

"No," I plead.

"Do you see her?" Danielle asks. "Blake."

My little girl. The side of her face is ripped away. Crusted blood and grime coats her hair. Her milky eyes no longer recognize me, but I have no doubt it's her. Though I knew the odds were that I'd find her like this, the sight is too much to bear. I forget to breathe and have to sit down in the grass while I take it in.

"Damn," sighs Quentin.

"Well, what'd you all expect?" complains Fletcher. "This ain't no goddamn fairytale. I told you this was a bad idea."

"Blake…" Danielle calls to me.

"What do we do?" Quentin asks.

"We need to go," Fletcher urges. "Two minutes those things are going to be all over us."

In the back of my mind, I know there isn't time to stop, even for this, but I can't find the will to stand back up. I look up into her face again as she reaches out to grab me. I stare at her hand, trying to hold me, and I can't resist the urge to touch her one more time. I extend my arm, and she wraps her cold little fingers around mine. She opens her mouth and presses her face against the bars of the fence as she tries to pull me towards her. I pry my fingers loose, and then I reach into my pack, and I take out the stuffed animal I brought for her. I put it into her hands, and she closes her fingers around it and stares at it blankly. Then her dead eyes find me, and the monkey falls from her fingers as they reach out for me once again.

"Blake," Danielle pleads. Her hands grip my shoulders. "I'm sorry. I'm so sorry, but we have to go." Danielle helps me to my feet, and I step back.

"Wait," I insist. I pull my arm free and remove the last magazine from my pocket and load the handgun. I try to look at Abby's face once more, try to see her as she used to be. I search my mind for some good memory from before all this, but it's too hard to block out what's right in front of me. I raise the gun, but I can't handle seeing what I am about to do. I look down, and my eyes settle on the stuffed animal that she had no reaction to at all. It all means nothing now. I'm all out of time, so, I pull the trigger.

I lower the gun and stagger backward. Danielle puts an arm around me to help keep me on my feet. I just want her to leave me here. Let me sit down in the soft, cool grass and be done with everything.

"Don't you give up on me now, Blake," Danielle whispers. "I need you."

Stitch appears beside me too, wagging his tail and licking my hand. He barks and picks up the stuffed animal off the ground and runs off, oblivious. "Stupid dog," I mutter, but he doesn't know how much I envy him.

"Give me a hand," Danielle says.

A moment later, Quentin appears on the other side of me. "C'mon, boss," he says. He puts an arm on my shoulder and turns me away from the fence. My legs still tremble, but I know it's time to go. I turn my back on the last connection to my life and walk with them into the darkness.

EPILOGUE

I awake to the smell of fresh dew on the grass and lay beneath a blanket listening to the morning chatter of birds. The spring is almost over now and the farther we travel, the warmer the days get. I hear a faint rumble of thunder in the distance and decide to get up and get some chow ready in case it rains. I sit up and the nylon fabric of the tent rustles. Danielle murmurs softly beside me, but I pull the blanket up to cover her bare shoulder and she falls back asleep. I locate my shirt and pants and quietly unzip the tent and step out. Stitch emerges behind me, yawning and stretching his legs.

Fletcher sits watch at the base of an oak tree and nods to say good morning. I smile, then walk off to find a spot in the woods to take a piss and gather some kindling to start a fire. This has become my new morning routine.

I thought about ending everything the night I found Abby. No one would have blamed me, probably. In a sense, the person I was died that night anyway. I'm not that person anymore. None of us are. There's no point living in the past when that life doesn't exist anymore.

So we don't talk about it. We give ourselves nicknames to help us forget who we were. It just makes things easier when you compartmentalize everything. That's how you survive when you keep on losing people around you every day. Nothing is certain anymore, you just have to take your chances. And even then, it might not work out the way you thought it would.

The one thing I know how to do now that I never figured out before is to wake up each day and fight to hold on to what you've got. It might not be there tomorrow, and once it's gone, you might never have it again.

I zip my pants up and wander through the trees. We stopped last night at this rundown campground across the road from an abandoned airfield in the middle of nowhere, Iowa. I pick up a couple of twigs for the fire, then I notice the campground office building and decide to check it out. There might be something useful, maybe some old instant coffee if I'm lucky.

"C'mon boy," I call Stitch. He leaves a rock he was inspecting and runs to follow me through the woods.

A brass bell jingles over my head when I open the door, and I wait for any sounds or movement. Stitch sniffs at the air before he wanders into the store. I step inside behind him and stare at the empty shelves. Somebody cleaned this place out already. I check each aisle but whoever was here before was pretty thorough. I'm about to leave when I notice a couple of skinny cigarette butts on the floor. I squat down and get a closer look at the slim filters that are squished and flattened.

"It can't be," I shake my head. "What are the odds?" It has to be a coincidence. I can't believe Dom might have actually made it out of the city alive. If she did, I'm not sure how I feel about that, or what I'd do if our paths cross again.

I step back outside and turn to walk back to our camp, but pause when I notice a couple of posts in the ground surrounded by beds of sand. I walk over to one of the posts and step on something hard buried just beneath the surface. I bend down and uncover a metal horseshoe. I pick it up and brush away the grains of sand. Maybe I will take it back to give to Danielle. It might bring us some luck.

Stitch whimpers behind me. He must be getting impatient for his breakfast.

"Alright, I'm coming, you stupid dog," I mutter. I stand up and turn around to find Stitch staring in the direction of the airfield. He sniffs the air. The scruff bristles below his collar. He growls, low and steady, at the danger beyond the trees.

ACKNOWLEDGMENTS

This book would not have been possible without the help, encouragement, and support of these amazing people. Thanks to all of you for your contributions.

Thom Shartle

Heiko Syska

Fawn Colombatto

Vesa Hatinen

Angel Gonzal

James Moss

Steve J

Ben Wasserstein

Terese Thompson

Adam Erickson

Post-Apocalyptic.com

Marci Albrecht

Jorge

Anthony Tunis

Michael Baumeister

Valaen Clapsaddle

Gail Wasserstein

Spencer Wickerson

Brian Horstmann

Professor Stephen Candy

Terrin

Lisa Kruse

Cristin Hipke

Robin Allen

Katy Burnside

Angela Burkhead

Danielle Hall

Danielle Deal

Scout Johnson

Midhun Mathew

Brian Antonelli

Chris Davis

Xiomara Morris

Sean Berleman

Patricia Todd

Tara O'Malley

David Larson

Nicole Mohr

Kenneth Hayes

Steve Duncan

Kitty Milar

S. Mentzal

Valerie Campbell

Swordfire

A special thank you to my wife, Sarah, who makes my stories possible.

ABOUT THE AUTHOR

Jeremy Dyson is a fiction author, and Rise of the Dead is his first novel. He has worked for several years as a freelance copywriter, as well as a number of odd jobs that have helped him get by and have motivated him to focus on his fiction.

He attended the University of Iowa where he majored in English and owes many thanks to the many talented writers around Iowa City. He currently resides in Chicago, Illinois with his two adorable daughters and his loving, supportive wife. His family is what inspires him to write and motivate him to work harder each day.

Rise of the Dead was inspired by his love for the zombie genre. His writing influences are J.D. Salinger, Cormac McCarthy, Ernest Hemingway, Raymond Carver and George Romero. He is currently at work on a sequel to Rise of the Dead, a book of short stories, and a work of literary fiction.

For more information visit: www.jeremydyson.com